The Old Quarry

THE OLD QUARRY

A MYSTERY NOVEL

by

Anne Gumley

Order this book online at www.trafford.com
or email orders@trafford.com

Most Trafford titles are also available at major online book retailers.

Printed in the United States of America.

ISBN: 978-1-4269-5438-2 (sc)
ISBN: 978-1-4269-5439-9 (hc)
ISBN: 978-1-4269-5440-5 (e)

Library of Congress Control Number: 2011900181

Trafford rev. 01/25/2011

www.trafford.com

North America & international
toll-free: 1 888 232 4444 (USA & Canada)
phone: 250 383 6864 • fax: 812 355 4082

By the same author

Mystery Series

The Old Quarry

Thou Shalt Not

The Toadstone

Children's Stories

Woden's Day

Hayley's Apprenticeship

Tales of Harriet

To Phillip,

who gave me the precious gift of time.

Part 1

Canada 1996

Chapter 1

Rita stood by her apartment window, the fingers of her hand spread over the cold pane. From the top of the building she could look down and see the last of the ice flows being washed against the stony shoreline of Lake Ontario. The long strip of riprap was already losing the icy sculptures that had formed by the spray upon the rocks over the long winter months of freezing cold. It had been one of the coldest of winters for years, and any sign of spring was eagerly looked forward to.

Rita's eyes scanned the horizon of the great lake, then with a slight tilt of her head searched higher across the vast expanse of blue sky above. She never tired of looking at the vastness of the Canadian sky. It hung motionless like a huge quiet void where her often-turbulent mind would merge and find some resemblance of peace.

Rita's love for the Canadian sky began the moment her feet had first touched the ground of her adopted country. She remembered the moment of release from inner confinement, a feeling so intense it had stayed with her like an old friend through all the years ever since.

A shaft of light found a place on the side of Rita's face making her close her eyes against its brightness, but she didn't turn away her head, the warmth too great a thing to lose. So quick did spring come and go in this part of Canada, that it wasn't hard for her to imagine going to bed with the winter snow all around and awaking to a landscape of greenery and warmth. A few days of rain and the ground would erupt into life, buds popping out on the branches of the maples and the tender shoots of daffodils claiming their territory. No wonder the great poets immortalized spring in England with its months of blossom, fields of golden daffodils and carpets of bluebells.

'Oh to be in England, now that April's here.' Rita couldn't help recalling Wordsworth. It seemed so apt at that moment, but then sentiment quickly passed.

Leaving the sunlight and her contemplation, Rita shuffled into her small kitchenette. Her overly large slippers, each fashioned like the head of a bear, brushed against the hem of her long candlewick dressing gown. Both items of clothing she wore were new, a gift from her colleagues at the Toronto City Hospital. Although neither were the most comfortable or practical, Rita felt they were tied to her past friendships, something she could now wrap around herself on lonely days like today.

Retirement she knew would take some getting used to. It had been suggested that she and her work mates get together once a month so as to not to lose touch, but Rita knew in her heart she wouldn't. Putting the past behind her was something Rita did well. Now there were things she wanted to enjoy; like travelling or playing golf if she could find somewhere with reasonable fees that suited her pension. The thought of all these exciting possibilities kept her cheerful, although to-date none had been seriously pursued.

Life since her retirement was just the routine of everyday chores; a trip to the mall and the occasional natter with a neighbour in her apartment building, followed usually by a quiet evening watching TV. Not very exciting, but the unfolding new season to come began to affect her with a sense of restlessness.

Rita reached for the coffee jar. Circling the seal of the new jar with a knife, she smelt the fresh aroma of coffee and, with the seal still in her hand; she pushed out her foot from under her dressing gown and pressed down on the pedal that opened the top of the trash bucket.

Immediately her eye caught a glimpse of the envelope she had torn in half the day before and discarded. The tear across the envelope showed the still-unread letter inside. One half was stuffed beside an old coffee filter, its brown granules partly staining the vellum. The postage stamp was unmarked by the soggy contents of the filter but it clearly showed itself to be English. Rita didn't feel any regret for not reading the letter for she received one about the same time every year. The first one she received had been read but all the rest since were just torn in two and thrown away.

'Damn Elaine,' she muttered to herself. She had hoped this year she would have been free of this annual ritual. Elaine must have given her cousin John her new address. Rita sighed with hopelessness; it was so hard to get angry with Elaine.

The kettle began to boil. This morning she settled for instant coffee, having run out of the perked. She went over to the kitchen table, careful not to spill any of the dark liquid, sat down and stirred it slowly with a teaspoon.

Memories of Elaine brought a fond smile to her face. How proud her friend had been when she moved into her specially designed flat all those years ago in England. Rita remembered her manoeuvring her wheelchair into her custom built kitchen and her asking what she wanted to drink, to which Rita had replied,

'Coffee, but only if it's Instant.'

Elaine, quick as usual and a mind as sharp as a knife, had shouted back,

'Instant indeed, trouble with you Rita you can't ever wait for anything.'

Funny how she always thought of Elaine as she'd last seen her, looking young and waif-like rather than a person now in her late fifties. She remembered how her hair always looked half damp and lifeless around her long pale face. Part of Elaine's body was lifeless too; her legs had been dreadfully mangled in a road accident that had almost left her for dead. Rita was a second year nurse when Elaine was brought into the hospital. Their friendship had begun with compassion, and ended with respect. It had developed into a long-term correspondence that broached two continents. Letters and cards were exchanged regularly; neither had married and both were fiercely independent. Sometimes there was a mention of Rita's family in her friend's letters or some nurse they both had known, but generally the information was about Elaine's life and the things she was doing and what was going on in the town they'd both grown up in.

Rita wrinkled her nose, a habit she'd acquired when deep in thought.

'How long had she been in Canada?' she mused. She was twenty-two when she arrived in 1954, and now it was 1996. She counted the years on her fingers.

'Forty-two years,' she sighed, realising how much she must have changed herself since she last saw Elaine.

Rita glanced in the mirror that hung slightly askew by the ivy plant. It was almost impossible to recall what she looked like at twenty-two now that she was face-to-face with her familiar but older one. The bone structure hadn't changed; it just seemed her skin didn't fit quite the same, despite the miraculous claims of the advertised hormone creams she was using. Rita turned slightly and ran her finger down the ridge of her nose. It still resembled a ski run. She guessed noses don't change unless broken, recalling how Elaine had a permanent little bump on hers from her accident. Rita pursed her lips pushing out their fullness. They had definitely gone thinner with her partial denture. Had the crow's feet at the edges of her eyes lengthened, or it could be just a trick of the light? The eyes themselves, her best feature by far, remained vivid blue with a dark circle around them. She touched her hair, freshly coloured only last week, the natural curl returning after the last cut.

Abruptly startled out of her day-dreaming by the ringing of her apartment intercom; spilling her coffee as she suddenly jumped up. Pulling her dressing gown across her chest and nearly falling over the monsters on her feet, she managed to get to the wall and press the button.

'Rita Goodwin speaking,' she said in the tone that the receptionists use at the hospital's enquiry desk. She had always hated phoning and hearing someone answering with a solitary 'Yes,' then being left to guess who was on the other end of the line.

'Bell Express-Vu Service,' a young voice was heard on the line. Rita groaned to herself. How could she have forgotten?

She calmly answered, 'Yes. Sixth floor, number six-ten.' and then hung up.

Suddenly realising how she was dressed, she rushed into the bathroom, and began rummaging among a pile of clothes thrown over a wicker chair. Spying a piece of bright pink clothing she pulled it out, thankful the second piece of the tracksuit was with it. Hastily she donned it, turning the sweater twice before finding the front.

The doorbell rang and then again, without hardly a pause. Lipstick, almost ready to be applied was quickly forsaken for a comb, which she dragged through her hair whilst making for the door.

'Nice colour.' A tall gangly youth nodded to the bright pink and grinned.

'I like it,' snapped Rita, wondering why everyone thought it her colour. The tracksuit had been just another leaving present.

'TV fuzzy is it?' asked the service man, stepping past her and finding his way to the television like a homing pigeon.

'Only since they raised the orbit of the satellite.' Rita wasn't one to take the blame.

She gritted her teeth as the man dumped his repair bag down on her wooden floor. He poked around the back of the TV, checked wires then picked up her remote and settled himself down in her special relaxing chair.

Then 'click.' The noise was deafening and the screen dissolved into a mass of white dots. Rita was about to say something when he clicked the remote again. This time the screen was filled with legible print displaying the available programs and times.

'You had turned off the satellite signal.'

The youth sounded as if it was a common practice of the over-sixty year olds and went on to go over the functions on the remote extremely slowly with her, each time looking at her face to see if she clearly understood. She didn't mind that as much as him raising his voice as if she was deaf, as well as making out she was too old to understand this new technology.

Having done his job, Rita paid him the exact money, counting out the payment slowly into his hand and showing him to the door when he looked at her as if deserving a tip.

Needing a little fortification she padded into the kitchen and helped herself to a handful of cookies, then settled herself into her chair. She wriggled a little to re-establish her ownership, and then pulled the handle at the side of her chair and lifting her feet to engage the rising leg rest. Making sure the satellite signal was on, she clicked her remote.

'Not that difficult, when these things are explained up front instead of having to call someone in special,' she mused. Settling back, her mind boggled at the number and variety of the programmes offered. She might as well check all of them before the free viewing ended and she would have to choose only those channels to suit her budget.

The CTV news was almost ending. Something about the government taking the heat for cancelling the helicopter replacement programme which Rita wasn't really interested in. She clicked onto the BBC World News channel and listened to a young man with a very English accent giving a news flash. It was refreshing to hear her native tongue. Truth to tell, she'd had trouble with the Canadian pronunciation of medical terms forty odd years earlier, but now couldn't remember whether cerebellum was pronounced 'seri-bel-luhm or 'cer-e-bel-lum' and in which country. Time warps one's memory, although she still shuddered at the Canadian pronunciation of vase and tomatoes.

The newscaster was commenting on a skeleton that had been found, and forensics had said the death must have occurred in the 1940's resulting from a severe head injury. Traces of clothing had been found preserved by the sand and it was thought likely to belong to an American soldier.

Rita stared at the screen as if in a trance; clutching tightly the arms of her chair until her knuckles whitened. She felt the blood drain from her head and could feel herself starting to hyperventilate. Her heart raced as adrenaline was pumped throughout her body, and for a second she was convinced she was about to die, then gradually her vision cleared and she became aware of the commentator still talking.

The picture from the newsroom had now changed to the scene of the crime. .Rita recognised it at once as the old sand quarry she used to play in, although the site was now vastly overgrown and vegetation had taken over in the shape of bushes and trees. But the landmarks she'd grown up with were still there; the long low hill rising in the background as a familiar landmark.

Suddenly Rita gave a hysterical laugh. Here she was three thousand miles away and, with the click of a switch her worst fears were facing her. It all seemed so unreal that she asked herself if it could all be just a sick coincidence. If her apartment block hadn't changed to satellite signals, and if she hadn't tuned into the BBC news at that precise moment, she would never have known of the horror that was now facing her. She felt sick. Is this what retirement had got in store for her? Endless nights of recalling something she'd thought had been laid to rest many years ago.

The news ended and was followed by a debating panel, but Rita sat quite still, her eyes glued to the TV set. It took a while for the thumping to ease in her chest and the breathing to become more rhythmic.

Then she did something she only did in emergencies. She got out of her chair, walked like a zombie to the kitchen, pulled a full bottle of rum out of a cupboard and poured herself out a good measure, then straight away lifted it to her lips and drank it down in one gulp. Steadying herself by holding on to the kitchen table, she waited for the strange effect to move throughout her body bringing its pleasant warmth in its wake.

What made her do what she did next she'd never understand, or could have seen the consequences of her subsequent actions.

Rita lifted the lid of the trash bucket and pulled out the torn envelope, holding it between her finger and thumb she shook off the coffee grounds and laid it on the table. Having retrieved all the pieces, Rita went about separating the letter from the envelope, trying not to tear the soggy paper further. After carefully arranging the letter 'til the edges matched, she bent over to read; inwardly knowing it was the same as all the other letters that had found their way into the trash bin over the years.

Dear Rita,

The Family Reunion this year will be at the Green Man Hotel in Leek on the 2nd June.

Yours Sincerely
Cousin John.

The letter was brief and to the point. Rita noted the phone number written at the top of the page. Further down was a postscript obviously added as an afterthought.

'By the way, Elaine Bennett died; seems her heart gave out.'

Rita re-read the last lines with trembling hands holding down the paper that was now beginning to curl as it was drying. She felt as if she was in some awful dream state, all this couldn't possibly be happening to her. Elaine had never once mentioned any cardio problems. In fact, apart from her disability, she was in pretty good health.

The rum bottle looked tempting again, but the kettle began to whistle, which brought Rita out of further shock. She almost envied people with partners. They could at least feel a pair of comforting arms around them and share their woes. However Rita knew that was something she could never do. It was impossible for her to share her past with anyone. She must however, for the state of her mental health, cope with it like she'd always done before. 'Block it out and put one's energies into something positive,' she reminded herself. But it wasn't that easy now. Elaine's death was not to be pushed away so casually. She had been her friend.

Rita managed in the end to get through the day by cleaning her apartment, a thing she normally hated but it was good therapy. Yet sleep that night didn't come any easier with all the hard work and she found herself lying in the darkness with her eyes wide open and a hundred thoughts swirling around in her head, with images of Elaine and that BBC newscaster. Now in the dark void of her bedroom, her mind relived the words of the commentator: 'found and probably died around 1940.'

'1943,' Rita stated to herself, then realised it was the first time she'd let herself recall anything about that dreadful day. But now that her mentally locked door had been unlocked; it needed to be opened a little more for her peace of mind. Something had been nagging her since the news report. Then she had it. It came to her out of the darkness that now surrounded her. The cause of death didn't fit. Was it a different person after all? These questions were coming fast and more clearly now. Of course it was the same place, Rita had no doubt about that. 'Could there be two people who had been buried under the sand all these years?' she thought.

As Rita lay there untouched by any possibility of sleep, a new feeling began to stir within her. By the time it had taken over her complete thinking process, Rita had found herself sitting on the edge of a tremendous decision. 'Could she? Dare she go back and face her past?' although the thought was allowed to form within the neurons of her brain, the emotional part of her had already told her the answer.

She didn't sleep. There was too much to think about, parts of the past merging with plans for the things she would have to do, until nature, the healer of many trials, brought a short oblivion. These short dream states were mostly ones of confusion and Rita would often refer to them as 'out-of-control dreams' usually precipitated by overwork or anxiety.

Next morning, tired as she was, she struggled out of bed. The capacity of being able to block out things had been long mastered and it came to her rescue in the form of placing her mind on what needed doing here and now.

The torn letter still remained where she had left it, so it didn't take long to copy her cousin's telephone number onto a new slip of paper. Rita counted five hours forward. It would be 12.00 noon in the UK and even if John wasn't at home, which was unlikely since he ran the mill, at least she would be able to leave a message. It never crossed her mind that he may not have an answering machine; he being a businessman. Rita dialled the number, only to be told by an automated voice it wasn't complete. After some trial and error and a certain amount of stress building up in her already tense muscles, she managed to get through and was almost taken aback at the human voice that came down the line.

'Yes,' was all it said.

Rita stiffened even more, then, sharply with prolonged practice asked,

'Who's speaking?'

There was a moment's silence; then followed by an English accent once so familiar to the listener.

'John Taylor, who's that?'

Whether or not Rita expected something more when she identified herself, she didn't know, but was left feeling like a stranger instead of a family member that had re-surfaced after years of non-correspondence. The conversation was brief and to the point. Yes it would be nice to see her at the reunion, and to let him know when she would be arriving in the UK.

She began to think herself fortunate that John Taylor had also recalled that Elaine was to be buried at St. Stephens Church on the Friday before the reunion. Then he mentioned these long distance calls were costly. Rita said goodbye as politely as she could and wondered what the phone bill had to do with him anyway, as she was paying.

'Why were the British so paranoid about long distance phone calls?' she thought. She remembered Elaine never phoned but if she did, and that was only once on her birthday and it had lasted all of two minutes.

The next day Rita checked the flights from Toronto to Manchester. She as yet hadn't a clue where she was going to stay, as John Taylor hadn't offered any help on that score. But there were enough small hotels in her old home town, and these she could find on the Internet no doubt. Money wasn't a problem as Rita had earned a good salary and still had investments from her savings and which had grown in value considerably. Rita had thought at one time of buying a place in Florida for her retirement, but knew she wouldn't. Being alone was being alone wherever you were, and at least she was familiar with Toronto and knew people even if they were only acquaintances.

By that evening everything had fallen into place. She'd managed to get a ticket for three days hence from a late cancellation and had booked for a month's stay hoping the investigation would not come to anything. Rita knew she would have to face whatever came out of it; she was ready to deal with it in her own way. She hadn't got the years left to worry anymore. The price had already been paid. Rita almost felt a sense of relief. At last she was facing herself and was amazed to find an inner strength and purpose to her retirement years.

The following days were too busy packing and making arrangements to have any more sleepless nights. She made a quick visit to her doctor for pills to relieve her anxiety of flying and what she was about to face. Somewhere in the back of her mind she promised herself she would go over every bit of those blanked out years. It was important to try to remember every detail. Something didn't fit and she needed to know why. Yet delving into that deep space always brought up too much anxiety and up to the time she boarded the plane her mental block was still securely in place.

Rita had taken the pill prescribed by her doctor to be taken half an hour before she boarded, and so when she found herself squeezed by the window by a rather overweight man next to her, she'd already began to relax and was later marvelling at the great ocean of sky unfolding before her after take-off. Before long she was lost in its golden and orange tipped hills and the waste plains of white candyfloss clouds. Relaxation began to seep through her, lulled deep by the continuous drone of the jet's engines. Her eyes closed.

* * *

Now the sky was no longer blue, but pitch-black. A wailing sound, warning of an impending air-raid had sounded, and occasional bursts of searchlight beams were sweeping the skies, searching for the source of the low drone of approaching enemy aircraft engines

She was once again a child in wartime England.

PART 2

England 1942

Chapter 2

I awoke with something hard and uncomfortable pressing against my back. I tried stretching out my legs only to find them blocked. Turning cautiously and tucking my arms around my bent knees, I found myself gazing at the underside of the dining room table.

Last night the sirens had lasted a long time. For one brief moment I almost forgot my discomfort and seriously considered the possibility of recycling some old chewing gum that was stuck under the table above me. I wrinkled up the corners of my mouth in slight disgust at the random thought of its taste entering my taste buds. However it did give me the resolve to maybe hang around the building where the American soldiers were billeted. In addition to being given the odd packet of fresh chewing gum, there was always the possibility of a bar of chocolate coming my way from the same source. This thought encouraged my taste buds to change course rapidly as I imagined that rich creamy sensation melting on my tongue.

Mam said the yanks were being generous as they probably missed their own families back home. A lot of them had kids of their own. I was too young to be interested in nylons and even if I had been, I doubt whether I'd want to go around to the back of that building for them. I'd seen girls, older than myself, coming back giggling with a yank's arm around their shoulders and clutching a few packets of those much prized nylon stockings. Most of the older girls in the town had no stockings and had to make do by drawing a straight line in eyebrow pencil down the back of each leg to represent a fake seam. I had practiced this art in the secrecy of my own bedroom with bad results. Drawing a perfectly straight line down the back of my leg was still an ambition of mine though, but so far it had always turned out wavy and my mam's eyebrow pencil quickly became very small from my sharpening it so much.

I had never once visualized a future where no ration books were needed for food, or coupons for clothes or that those disused and rusting chocolate machines standing on railway stations would actually dispense a Cadburys chocolate bar whenever a coin was slipped into its slot.

My world was only what I was physically and mentally aware of. I didn't expect the streets to be lit or even a fraction of light to be showing from any window at night. Even knowing the right direction to go half the time was quite alien to me since most of the local road signs had been removed, just in case the enemy ever landed. If someone had ever asked me if I was afraid when the sirens blared out; I would have honestly answered the question with a firm 'No'.

Those loud wailing sirens were as much a part of my day as the school bell, and as natural as the carrying of a small canvass covered box that in turn carried my gas-mask. I'd never seen any houses destroyed in the town, although a number had had their windows shattered by a stray bomb landing in nearby fields. Nothing to compare with the daily news reports from Liverpool or Coventry. The countryside around my hometown in Cheshire was generally rural and set on the outskirts of the moors. The town hadn't got much to offer by way of national strategic importance, apart from the mainline railway and the Rolls-Royce factory in nearby Crewe, some twenty miles away. There were a handful of cotton and silk factories in our town and a whole lot of farmers. Like our teacher had said many times before, our town has been around since Doomsday, and Hitler and his cronies were not going to intimidate and subdue any of us that quick.

Sand was plentiful around the town, and quarries that were still working before the war had already been pressed into service to fill sandbags that were stacked around the entrance to the local police station and the ARP warden's positions dotted around the town. Even our back garden was really sandy with perhaps only a foot and a half of topsoil available, which was good for growing carrots if nothing else.

The hedge at the bottom of our garden divided us from an old disused sand quarry that was now generally overgrown with grass and bushes. A grand place to play war games, although we could never find anyone to be the Jerries; so we were always on the same side and the enemy was left to our imagination. There was another newer sand quarry a little way off, although it too was now little used, its silky sand slipping down the steep sides with no one around to dig it away.

Most of the men of our town, including my dad, had now gone off to fight or work in more essential jobs to support the war effort. Sometimes I missed my dad being around and wondered what it would be like to have him home all the time. I often surprised myself how used I'd got just having mam and I in the house. It was a bad thought not wanting to share her, so I always pushed the thought away and promised I would write him a long letter when I had the time.

The sound of the kettle whistling in the kitchen and the rattle of teacups stirred me out of my daydreaming. It was a secure sound. Everything was normal as long as my mam was there. Occasionally I would experience an awful fluttering feeling in my stomach if I allowed myself to ponder on mam dying, like Janet Johnson's mam did last month. The thought was too terrifying to let linger. Janet had to be sent away as her dad was at sea. She cried and cried and said she was now all alone. She's doing all right now though, as her latest letter to me told she was enjoying living with her grandmother on a Scottish farm with cows that had horns spread six feet across.

'I'll never go to Scotland, 'I said to myself. Not that I'd ever been away too far. In truth, Crewe was the furthest I had been from home and that wasn't for any sort of holiday, as my dad at that time was going off to war to fight for his country.

I managed to position my arms behind my head and see the lines under the table where the table insert slotted in. It reminded me of all those railway lines at Crewe station when we said goodbye to the man that didn't really look like my dad at all with his hair shaved around his ears and up the back of his head. The uniform was quite dashing or would have been if his hair had been a different colour. I didn't think that khaki suited red heads at all. There had been so many people around that day; soldiers, sailors, air-force men and wrens, weeping women with families, all jostling for position as the large black engines belched forth their smoke and steam in bringing the long trains into the different platforms. I remembered clinging to my mam's coat in case I got swept away into the crowds. Whistles blew and doors slammed shut. People were shouting, crying and children screaming as their fathers hugged them with often a little too much force.

I needed to use the lavatory so when my dad squeezed me tight I almost wet my knickers, in fact I did notice a very small puddle as we left for the nearest waiting room. The queue by this time was so long I couldn't wait and mam took me around the back and stood in front of me whilst I emptied my bladder right there.

Wet knickers are so awful to sit in on the 'bus and I was glad to get home.

'Do you want some dripping on your toast?'

Mam's voice quickly brought me out of my daydreaming. Mam always got up first from her place under the table whenever the danger had passed and the 'All-Clear' sirens sounded. I had slept on one side of the wooden central bar that held the table legs together, with mam on the other side. This was always the safest place to be when the sirens went. Like my mam said, it would only take one bomb, so it's best to take precautions. So, as we didn't have an Anderson shelter in the garden, it was either under the big oak table or down the pantry steps under the stairs. The latter was freezing cold and I think we had mice there, although they were always too clever for the trap and our supply of cheese was strictly rationed and not for use as bait.

The thought of toast and dripping got me from under the table so quick I bumped my head. Pushing the prongs of the brass toasting fork with its 'galleon-head' handle into the thick white bread and toasting it over the hot glowing coals was always comforting and secure.

Mam spread the beef dripping carefully over each piece of toast 'til it melted, then she sprinkled one pinch of salt over the tempting meal while another pinch of salt was cast over her left shoulder just in case she had spilt a grain or two. It was better to be safe than sorry she would say, and nobody wanted bad luck. It filled my empty hole of my stomach nicely and I washed it down with a weak cup of tea laced with evaporated milk. I didn't mind this sweet milk on a dish of prunes, but disliked it in tea.

A knock sounded on the back door, followed by the squeaking of hinges being forced open.

'It's only me,' a voice shouted. It was Vera, our next-door neighbour on the left side of our house. Like mam, her husband was away and was left with two young children.

'Just in time,' mam shouted back and set another cup on the table.

'Bad night?' mam asked; taking off the tea cosy and filling the teapot with boiling water, before setting the black iron kettle on the equally black iron stand by the hearth.

'Slept right through it.' Vera laughed; the Jerries were not going to stop her sleeping in her own bed she often said.

In contrast to my mam's fairness and delicate features, Vera bloomed in all quarters and was dark in hair and eyes. Although the top half of her body strained to fall out of everything, she wore; she had magnificent long shapely legs that displayed themselves wonderfully as she crossed them. I think it must have taken a lot of practice to manoeuvre the way she did. I noticed she practiced a lot every time my Uncle Joseph called around.

'Read my cup, love.'

Vera called everyone love or duck. Never once had she called me Rita. At one time I thought she didn't like my name 'til I realized she called everyone in the same way. I watched fascinated as Vera swallowed her tea down in one long swig and pushed the cup and saucer towards mam.

The cup was taken up and the dregs swilled around in a clockwise direction then abruptly turned over and placed upside down on the saucer. Vera and I waited with bated breath as mam lifted the cup and peered inside it.

'I see a tall man,' said mam, now tipping the cup on its side so the wet leaves re-arranged themselves slightly.

'Is he dark?' breathed Vera, trying to look over the rim of the article of fortune.

'Dark and well built,' mam answered. Vera sighed happily and I wondered if she'd forgotten her husband was blond.

'And,' mam continued, totally committed to her gift of fortune telling, 'there's money coming, not a lot but enough to be very welcome.'

'I could do with that, every little helps these days love.'

Vera leaned back on her chair, satisfied that her reading was worth coming around for. But mam hadn't finished, her forehead creased into fine lines and she pursed her mouth so that her lips went very thin. I knew there was something she was seeing she didn't like.

'I see people quarrelling,' she then added. 'There's a pram here, as plain as can be.' Mam pushed the cup towards Vera, urging her to take a look. Vera laughed and pretended she saw what mam saw.

'That will be our Doris, and I reckon her Fred will not be at all pleased. It's their sixth you know and he puts the blame for it squarely on her.'

Mam sympathized and I lost interest at that stage and went into the kitchen. Pulling the net curtain back, I could just see Vera's children sitting in a corner of their garden digging with a couple of spoons in the sand that lay beneath their feet. They were not old enough to take off through the hedge and into the overgrown disused quarry, but when they were, I promised to take them to the other quarry further on where you could slide all the way down from the top to the bottom. Oh I knew it was dangerous, for parents often warned their children about the possibility of slippages, but my friends and I had done it for years

Lifting up our skirts, we would slide down again and again, 'til our navy blue knickers were quite stained. The girls were lucky. We could wash the stains out, but often the boys displayed their staining adventures for all the world to see and, more often than not got a whopping into the bargain. Sand staining and grey flannel trousers were hard to part. I wandered back into the dining room just in time to catch Vera say,

'She's pregnant.'

Silence prevailed when my mam indicated with a nod of her head that I was back in the room.

'Who's pregnant?' I asked, not wanting to be invisible and knowing that it must be someone other than Vera's sister for that was in the teacup and had not yet happened.

'Oh no one, my dear.' My mam is very bad at lying so I didn't let it rest there.

'Someone is and I'm old enough to know.' I insisted and pulled myself up to my full height. Mam put her hands around the teapot that had been filled for the third time. I knew she was warming her hands, which were always cold when it was damp outside.

'Dolly Yates, she's gone and got herself knocked up,' muttered Vera.

The statement was to the point and it didn't take much reasoning or intelligence to know the meaning of 'being knocked up' that the yanks often referred to, but it came as a shock all the same.

'Oh you must be wrong Vera,' I said simply giving the reason as to why I knew so. 'She's not married.'

Mam shifted a little uneasily and looked over at Vera.

'That's the reason you mustn't say anything. She should have had more sense than get herself in that way.' Mam had an explanation for everything.

Now the penny dropped into my thick skull. Dolly Yates was going to be one of those bad girls who would be having this child before she was married. I'd heard people sometimes snigger and point at a young woman pushing a pram. It brought to mind the girl Uncle Joseph used to walk out with before the American service men arrived in town. After which I saw her a lot outside the U.S Army billet talking to a big yank with a cigar hanging from his lips. She had a baby later that year and she was only sixteen and Uncle Joseph said she was a slut. I wasn't sure what that meant, I wasn't sure about a lot of things that made grown ups look 'Holier Than Thou'.

Take the time when I told Mr Murray his son must be very fond of his friend as I saw them hugging each other. Mr Murray turned bright red and started to stutter. Later I heard his son had left home and gone away with his male friend.

Then there was that nice family that lived in our road. They left quite suddenly because the man was too friendly with the boys he taught. I felt it quite wicked for people to say he was too friendly, for the boys at the Reform School didn't get much love from anyone.

They were always nice to me and smiled and winked when I passed them walking two-by-two in a long line, usually each Sunday as they attended our church. They were very clean in their white shirts, blazers and grey pants, and never looked as bad as people made out. Their school was hidden behind a high brick wall that ran along the pavement beside the main road and ended with tall pillars that once supported big iron gates, but like all the iron railings in front of the houses they had been taken off and used to supply the much needed metal for the war effort.

My gran was very old fashioned and often told my mam.

'Keep an eye on that that girl of yours, you never can be careful enough what with that Reform School and the Americans in the town.'

Mam would give her the same answer each time with, 'Oh mother,' to which there was no real reply.

I guess it all boiled down to the fact that some people disliked anything different whilst people like Vera were far more liberal. She made friends easily and I know she had invited an American once or twice back to her house. Late at night maybe, but then he had to work during the day. Our landing window looked over Vera's drive and having a need to get up to use the toilet downstairs when it was often quite late, I had seen him leave as the moonlight broke the darkness.

I also know for sure my Aunt Ada isn't prejudiced in any way, for she always has plenty of nylons in her dressing room table. It's not that I make a habit of looking into other people's dressing table drawers, but sometimes I stay over at Gran's and sleep with my Aunt Ada. Once her dressing table drawer had been left open a little and I just thought I'd tidy it up so it would close better. Oh she had some lovely things. French cammy knickers in real silk and, embroidered on the leg, was a lovely butterfly. What I'd give to be old enough to exchange my thick navy blue knickers for the feel of real silk.

My thinking took another turn and brought me back to the present moment. I'd almost forgotten I needed some rhubarb for my domestic science class the following day.

The object was to make a rhubarb pie and after last week's pathetic attempt at custard I'd really made it my goal to do better this time. It always caused a bit of panic wondering where some of the ingredients would come from, especially when so much was rationed. The shop on the corner didn't have any and the woman there had suggested I found someone that grew it and my gran came quickly to mind.

In a corner of Gran's garden next to the rubbish pile was an old bucket with a large rusted out hole in the bottom. Inside the upturned bucket was a root of rhubarb. Uncle Joseph had told her the bucket forces the rhubarb up, and then added with that silly grin of his.

'Some people put manure on their rhubarb, but I like custard on mine.'

I'd now stopped telling my friends that joke 'because they always looked at me afterwards as if I was half-a-penny short.

'I'm going down to gran's,' I stated, licking some of the dripping off my fingers.

It was Sunday but we didn't go to church that much, apart from christenings and funerals. I had instruction enough at school which being Church of England meant we had the Rev. Swindells every Thursday morning to learn our Catechism and recite the Magnificat, and on Friday mornings we all had to troop dutifully to the church that was next to our school.

'Bye love,' shouted Vera as I left, leaving her urging my mam to take a second reading in case anything had changed within the hour.

I half-ran, half-skipped down the drive, hopping down the step onto our road then slowed down my pace in reverence as I passed Number 15 whose curtains were drawn across. Mrs Roberts' husband had been killed, shot down they say and only married the year before.

Turning the corner at the bottom of our road, I ran along the pavement flanked by the reform school's high wall, past the Victorian terraced houses with their tiny front gardens and small grey stone walls trimmed with the remains of the stumps of the once iron railings running uniformly along the top.

It was Sunday morning and the main road was never busy as not much went out of the town or came in. An occasional double-decker bus stopped and started as it rumbled along from one bus stop to the next. There were always a number of bikes around, mostly sit-up-and-beg, and generally with brackets behind their seats that held small packages. A jeep flew past honking its horn. I waved and the driver waved back. The place where the yanks were billeted was quiet for once. The jeeps and tanks stood silent, although their big flag with the stars and stripes flopped and fluttered with the breeze that had built up.

The churches were full at this time. There were always a lot of yanks filling the pews as well as girls from the factories. The Rev. Swindells told us the war made people think more about God, but I think the factory girls were thinking more about the yanks around them, for there was more attention given over to them than prayer I was told.

The local newsagent was open, its rack that leaned against the wall outside looked unsafe as it was stuffed with copies of the News of the World newspaper and John Bull magazines.

Tommy King came out laden down with his canvas bag loaded with newspapers. I glared at him 'til he blushed and made off down the street. He'd tried to kiss me in the schoolyard following a dare. I warned him to just try anything like that again and had backed up this threat with a very hard punch from me where it especially hurt.

My gran's house stood back beside a row of terraced houses. It wasn't certain whether gran's house had been built first or a number of the terraced houses had been knocked down for gran's drive to be put through. It seemed that both types of homes were at least a couple of centuries old.

Gran's house was known as a 'gentleman's house.' Its large grey stone walls had leaded windows and a huge old door rising above the front steps that had been worn with time. To one side was a coach house that had been converted into a car-less garage and now filled with junk. A brick wall surrounded the back and sides with a door that led into an alley. The door was permanently locked and I don't think anyone knew where the key was.

As I neared the opening to gran's drive I saw Frank Cole. He's the chap that fancies my Aunt Ada. He straightened up as I got closer and he grinned back at me showing his front tooth that slightly overlapped the one beside it.

'Waiting for Aunt Ada?' I asked innocently, whilst fully knowing he was.

'Be a love and tell her I've been waiting here for ages,' Frank pleaded, throwing away his cigarette stub and rubbing his hands against the chill air.

'OK.' I smiled, because he was quite nice even though little thick as far as Aunt Ada was concerned. I bet she well knew just how long he'd been waiting and how much longer he would have to. The net curtain slipped back into place as I looked up at Aunt Ada's bedroom window before reaching the front door.

Chapter 3

I had my own key to the front door of gran's house in case of emergencies. Mam was always thinking the worst could happen and wasn't having me left out on the street. The four occupants of the house, namely my Gran, Aunt Ivy, Aunt Ada and Uncle Joseph had no enthusiasm for housekeeping, which made me wonder if my mam was adopted. There was always some article or other lying around and the only time shoes came in pairs was when they were on someone's feet.

Stepping through the front door I nearly fell over a Wellington boot. Mam told me the house hadn't been so disorganised when she was a girl and grandpa was alive. In fact in those days before the war there was always a cleaning lady and a gardener around. When I asked why they couldn't have someone to clean now, I was informed that women could earn twice as much in the factories and a lot of the younger women had joined up or were working on the farms. I didn't blame them for joining up for I thought I might become a Wren myself when I was old enough, as I didn't like housework either and the uniform was smashing. Neither did I fancy working in any of the town's mills.

I'd often seen the factory gates open and scores of girls surging forward, mostly wearing head-squares and some even with curlers protruding from them at the front. I told myself I must be a bit of a snob but actually they frightened me to death with their loud laughter and the linking arms, walking three abreast through the town. Funny how I could never imagine our two princesses in curlers. They were my idols and I often cut their photos out of the papers. My friend, Eunice Platt and I often pretended that we were the princesses, and would walk through the town nodding our heads at the surprised passers-by with a fixed smile on our lips.

The familiar tick-tock of the grandfather clock welcomed me into the hallway of gran's house. It has never failed to strike the hour with its loud clanging as long as I could remember. The hall coat stand opposite it was a magnificently carved piece of furniture, sporting a bevelled mirror and brass hooks and, in the centre, a place for walking sticks. Apart from the odd visitor's coat adorning it occasionally, the acorn-topped post at the bottom of the stair rail became far more convenient for the rest of the household members.

The marvellous thing about the hallway was the huge stag head with large antlers that hung over the doorway at the end of the hall. It was somewhat moth eaten and had only one glass eye, yet nevertheless was something to behold. Uncle Joseph was extremely clever at standing well back and throwing his cap at it where it landed most times squarely on one of the protruding parts.

There were three other doors down the passage where the stag's head hovered, not counting the kitchen door. One door was permanently locked, one was permanently closed and the other was permanently open. That doesn't mean to say I didn't know what was behind the locked door. There's a window to this room at the back of the house. Under this window stands a dustbin, and balancing on it gives anyone a perfect view of the interior of the room. There's a roll-topped desk and on it sits a framed photo of a rather old-fashioned man with whiskers growing down the side of his cheeks. I think it must be of my grandpa. Grandpa once owned a furniture business; the business gran said Uncle Joseph hadn't the nouce to run, not that I know what 'nouce' means, but hope to get some for myself one-day.

There was also a glass-fronted bookcase with a spider's web clinging between its corner and the ceiling. I hadn't bothered to look through the window lately, following the time the dustbin tipped over and I ended up with a very a sore knee.

The room with the closed door proved no a problem as I only had to follow closely behind in my gran's footsteps whenever she went into the room. I think it was the most beautiful room in the house with its big bay window overlooking the lawn outside. There was a real carpet on the floor with patterns of roses on it, not at all like the rugs pegged with cloth strips and backed with sackcloth now so often seen. There was a china cabinet filled with gold edged dishes, little figurines and two big brown carthorses, delicately adorned with gold painted horse brasses. Silver and glassware was all pushed up together as there was too much to be displayed properly.

In the centre of the room stood a three-piece suite in brown leather studded with brass studs. But the object that caught my eye was the tiled fireplace with a wood surround. I'd never seen a fire in it, but it looked far too elegant to be messed up with the smoky coal or coke. What really amazed me was that the room was tidy and there wasn't an article out of place. However there was a film of dust everywhere and the windows looked a little neglected, but then the room was never used.

The third door was never closed; in fact it was wedged permanently open by an iron doorstop in the shape of a dog. Today I peeped around in case gran was asleep in her rocking chair as she was quite often these days. But the rocker was empty with a crocheted blanket thrown over the back of it. I suppose you would call this room a drawing, cum dining, cum everything else room. Two things dominated the room, the extra large table with its linen cloth embroidered around the edges with pink flowers and other various colours not sewn on but more consistent with jam stains. The other was the black iron grate with its two ovens and brass fender.

It was what was on the table that caught my eye's interest. Passing over tea stained cups and the knitted teapot cosy, my gaze rested on the opened can of condensed milk. To my utter joy, a loaf and the crust lay waiting to be picked up and sampled. Nothing was as good as a thick new crust of bread spread lavishly with condensed milk. As I licked around the edges, a bluebottle buzzed around my nose, then headed straight for the yellow sticky fly-paper that hung over the table. The fly stuck and struggled amid the mass of other dead flies. For a second I thought of helping to release it, but then remembered the time when one fly left its legs behind as I attempted to pull it off.

From upstairs came the refrain of Vera Lynn's 'White Cliffs of Dover' badly rendered by my Aunt Ada in her usually off-key Danesburyian accent. It was no use my thinking of using the toilet for the next hour, Aunt Ada was well known for commandeering the bathroom. Of course I could always use the toilet outside if things got desperate enough but the spiders in there often made me hold myself to bursting point. I considered knocking on the bathroom door and telling her that Frank Cole was waiting outside, but then remembered his lovesick face and carried on eating.

The sound of water boiling broke my musings and I stared awhile at the black iron kettle hissing over the fire on its stand. I did something I knew was wrong but as there was no one else around so there was very little choice. Taking the poker I slipped it into the iron stand the kettle was standing on over the fire and swung both towards me. Mam would never have let me do that in case the kettle fell off, but it felt good to do such a grown-up job. The smell of a rice pudding cooking wafted from the fire heated oven, enticing me to stay around 'til it was ready. I loved the brown skin that formed on the top.

A shuffle behind me broke into my vision of the rice pudding. The silly black cat from next door had jumped on the table and was about to tip the tin of condensed milk over. I whacked the cat and it flew behind the blackout curtain, which was the best hiding place it could hope to find, it being all black too.

'Cat got in again?' Uncle Joseph had come into the room. He was laughing.

He did a lot of laughing did Uncle Joseph. He had mam's bright blue eyes, but his eyes twinkled, whilst mam's were sort of dull and sad. I liked his hair. It was quite blond, combed right back and all plastered down with Brylcream.

'Gran's gone shopping,' he stated, without expecting any query of her whereabouts from me. He walked straight over to the radio that stood square on the sideboard and turned it on. Lighting a Woodbine cigarette, he pulled up a high-backed chair and leaned over, his ear by the radio. I knew I was not to make a sound during this time. If I did, grown-ups always glared at me and put their fingers to their mouths; so I stood like a statue, eyes glued on my uncle's face. I could tell by his facial expressions whether the news was good or bad. First came the familiar sound of Big Ben striking the hour that always preceded the national newscast, then the droning voice with a London accent.

'Axis forces capture North African port of Tobruk, thirty-five thousand allied troops feared taken prisoner and seventy tanks destroyed.' My uncle put his hands over his face. It was indeed bad news. The news continued…

'General Rommel's Africa Corps today surprised the Allies by turning back towards Tobruk. Securing this port now places the Desert Fox in a position to move on towards Cairo and the Suez Canal.' Another Woodbine was lit.

'My dad's in Cairo.' I ventured remembering the name from one of my mam's letters. My uncle took a deep drag on his cigarette and blew four perfect smoke rings. Oh how I wished I could do that.

'Blast the Jerries,' was all he said and switched off the radio.

'Why do we call our chamber pots jerries?' I thought it safe to talk now. He took another drag of his cigarette and crossed his long legs, looking at me for a moment as if considering whether to answer or not, then he laughed

'We Brits call our chamber pots jerries so we can piss on them.' He waited for me to say something, and chuckled as my eyes grew round and a grin began to gather on my lips.

'Now don't you go telling our Rose I told you,' he said, knowing full well I probably would. Rose is my mam's name and as she's Uncle Joseph's eldest sister, she tells him off now and then. We sat there for a moment both comfortable in each other's company.

'Have you got yourself a girlfriend,' I asked out of the blue, not really knowing why I'd asked it.

He blushed just a little, before adding; 'Sort of.'

'Mam says if you are old enough to fight for your country, you are old enough to be married.' I'm sure she wasn't referring to Uncle Joseph when she said that but I knew he would be called up very soon as he was nearly eighteen.

'One thing at a time girl,' he raised his hand up as if trying to stop me, then took another drag and had a faraway look in his eyes. I decided to change the subject.

'I need some rhubarb,' I stated straight to the point. For a moment my uncle looked bewildered, but I persevered and explained about my domestic science class needs.

'Good heavens,' he breathed out, I wasn't quite certain whether he was impressed at the possibility of me making a rhubarb pie or just where I was getting the ingredients from, so I had to remind him.

'There's some under a bucket in the garden.'

'Well, don't let's tell your gran you snitched her two precious stalks, maybe she'll think the rabbits ate them.'

He got up and I followed him to the kitchen where he picked up a long knife and a piece of newspaper. In the garden two rather anaemic stalks of rhubarb were poking out of the holes in the bucket. Uncle Joseph sliced them both off neatly at their base and laid them on the newspaper.

'It will have to be a small pie,' he remarked looking at the sad offering.

I really didn't care as long as I got the necessary ingredients, big or small didn't matter anyway.

We returned to the house. Aunt Ada was in the kitchen pulling a pair of stockings off the airing maid that hung on pulleys from the ceiling. My mam is the oldest in the family and after she was born there was a ten-year gap before Aunt Ivy arrived, then two years later Aunt Ada; followed by Uncle Joseph.

Both my aunts worked at the factory; although not on the machines. Aunt Ivy had done well for herself and is the secretary for the boss's son. She's a hard worker and has to stay late a lot in the office helping him, but he always brings her home in his car, which is thoughtful.

Aunt Ada proceeded to pull on her stockings and I watched fascinated as a small ladder began to creep up her leg.

'Damn' she said, obviously irritated at the speed of the forming ladder. She looked up at me.

'Fetch my nail varnish; there's a luv.'

She's another one that forgets people's names so they all come under the umbrella as 'luv'. Placing the precious newspaper-wrapped packet down, I flew upstairs to bring her nail varnish, which she then proceeded to place dab of the bright stuff at the top and bottom of the ladder... I thought it brought more attention to it, but what did I know about nylon stockings anyway as I still wore either ankle socks or long brown woollen winter ones that were held up with elastic.

Leaving my gran's, I passed Frank Cole looking very miserable and surrounded by cigarette buts. I bet he'd smoked the whole of his ration. He looked up hopefully at me but I just shrugged my shoulders; not giving him the satisfaction of any more information as to how long his waiting would be.

Crossing the road proved difficult for once as a whole convoy of jeeps and trucks were passing and I was happy to see movement outside the American's billet. As I neared it, I resolved to walk slowly past, looking as if I was half-starved and just maybe I would be called over and handed a bar of chocolate. My plan failed as someone on a cycle passed them at the same time. Its rider was a pretty blond whose skirt had ridden up over her knees with the pedalling. A series of whistles and catcalls from the soldiers were heard and the bike wobbled as she attempted to pull down her skirt. I noticed she didn't seem too put-out at all the attention she was receiving.

Moving off disappointed, the self-induced thought of chocolate had activated my taste buds and, without thinking I began to unwrap my precious parcel and chew on one of the sticks of rhubarb. Surprisingly it was quite sweet compared to some other I'd had. Then the elastic garter that held my brown stocking broke and I could feel the gradual wrinkling begin and knew the whole of my stocking could fall around my ankle at any moment. I wished I had that safety pin my mam always had pinned to her knickers in case her elastic ever went. It was a safeguard most adults thought almost as necessary as having clean underwear on all the time just in case one got involved in an accident. 'Better to be safe than sorry' was an old motto in our house and, at that moment I wished I'd taken more notice of it.

There was only one thing to do, so I sat on a low wall outside a row of houses and twisted the top of the stocking tucking it under itself. It would hold up 'til I got home. After which I ate the other stick of rhubarb. Placing the newspaper and broken garter in my pocket I made for home, hoping my blood supply in my leg would not be cut off.

Mam looked tired and a little pale, but she'd made a plate of marmite sandwiches and some stewed damsons with a little bit of cream from the top of the milk covering them. I do wish damsons grew without stones as I always managed to swallow one. Later we decided to sleep in our own beds and hope the sirens wouldn't go off.

I knelt on the cold lino with my hands together at the side of my bed and said my prayers. My prayers were fairly routine and I always asked God to look after my dad and bring him home safely. Next I would ask God to make Hitler a good man, which didn't seem so out-of-line, as the Rev. Swindells told us God often performed miracles. I prayed for all the children whose father's had been killed in the war and lastly that all my classmates wouldn't have any rhubarb tomorrow.

Chapter 4

As my tiny round night candle flickered in its saucer of water and dark shadows crept around the white walls of my bedroom, I would lie awake. Mostly my thoughts would centre on the street lamp outside my home.

Beside our broken gate which the coal cart had backed into, stood a lamp standard. It was tall, thicker at the bottom and tapering to two cross bars at the top. The ironwork of the lamp standard was fluted and was painted a dark green. The iron lantern itself atop the standard used to support four panes of glass on the sides, one of which could be opened, allowing the gas mantle inside to be lit. Sadly the lamp standard was now very neglected as most of the functioning parts of the light had been removed deliberately as part of the blackout restrictions.

Mam told me a man, called a lamp lighter, used to come around every evening before the war started and light the street lamps. I've climbed the iron post many times, swung on its bars and even used it as a maypole at times but never ever remember it being lit.

My memory is not so good before I was six, apart from going to Belle Vue in Manchester and seeing my first and only elephant. So as I lay in bed I visualized the curtains drawn all the way back and the light from the gas-lamp outside shining into my room. Once I peeped from behind our black out curtains at the night sky with its thousands of stars. That wasn't a good thing to do for on that occasion I'd forgotten to blow out my candle and the air raid warden rapped loudly on our front door.

During the night I had been warm and cosy in bed, the thought of getting out of it and feeling the cold seep into my bones was quite loathsome; plus the fact I didn't have any idea what I was going to put inside my pie at school later that morning. I shivered in the bathroom, as there didn't appear to be any hot water and, after dressing, was eager to warm up by the fire.

It came as a bit of a shock not only to find no early morning fire, but the room smelling of chimney soot. The hearth was covered in the black dust and a film of soot lay everywhere. Mam stood by the hearth, hands thrust stiffly into her pinafore pockets and a tear ran down one cheek, whilst the other cheek was smudged with black soot.

I stood in the doorway like a statue not daring to move. When soot came down the chimney it covered everything and although it looked light and fluffy, it quickly became sticky and messy once touched. It would take all day and maybe the next to clean it all up. Newspaper would have to be taped around the fireplace opening. Then Uncle Joseph would have to climb up onto the roof. He would get a piece of holly from the holly tree in the back garden and tie a long piece of string on it that held a brick.

The whole apparatus would then be put down the chimney 'til the brick fell into the fireplace with a loud clunk, bringing the holly and the remaining soot with it. After which the whole room would have to be cleaned, curtains washed and most probably the pegged rugs as well. No wonder mam looked fit to cry. At least it wasn't raining outside. I did try to look on the bright side, although at that moment it was extremely difficult.

'Make a cuppa pet,' Mam said with that resigned voice she used a lot these days.

Things always go wrong in threes, so when the gas dwindled to nothing as I put a match to it I wasn't surprised. The shilling jar on the pantry shelf was empty; the idea was to always to have a shilling handy when the meter ran out. The meter was at the bottom of the pantry steps, another reason I hated sleeping down there during an air raid as the metal with its knobs and dials was cold and hard to be pressed against.

'Mam, the gas as gone and we've no shilling,' I yelled.

'Look in my purse,' mam yelled back. There was frustration in her voice. Fortunately her handbag was on the hall table and so free from soot. I took two sixpences out, as there were no shillings.

'Got to change sixpences,' I called again, keeping right away from any contamination.

To get change meant going next door. Actually it was really one building built as two houses called semis, so our inner wall was the only thing that separated the Graces from us. Mam often asked Aunt Ada to keep her voice down when she was talking, as mam often said, the walls have ears.

I like the Grace family. Old Mr. Grace didn't work anymore. His hair was quite white apart from on top where there was none at all. He coughed a lot, but still maintained a garden from which he produced all different kinds of vegetables. Mrs Grace was a tiny woman who wore a wrap-around paisley apron all the time. I'd never seen her without it. She and their two daughters were always cleaning. The clothes-line was forever filled with washing and the woollens spread out on towels over the top of the hedge. We often wondered where they got their soap ration from. It must have been a different place from ours.

As always the Grace's kitchen smelt of disinfectant and soapsuds as the washing boiler was bubbling away. Doreen, one of the daughters, was cleaning her shoes over the sink. The back door was open as I stepped inside holding out my two sixpences.

'Can you change these for a shilling?' I asked first, before relating how our whole house was filled with soot. She gave me a pitying look and took down a big jam jar filled to the brim with shillings. Taking one, we did the exchange.

Doreen was the better looking of the two sisters; in fact her hair was something that most women envied. No need for the big curling pins. Doreen's hair was thick and beautiful, naturally curled with a deep auburn colour, although the face that peeped from under it was unusually pale and had succumbed to large spots mam called acne.

Ethel on the other hand was fresh-faced. Small like her mam, she tended to hold her head like a tortoise, which gave the impression she was always about to make a move forward and, as her movements were quick and jerky, it was sometimes quite unsettling. Both worked on the factory floor and where one was, so was the other. As they walked along the road to work, all four feet were always in step. Their cardigans always hand knit and matching.

Uncle Joseph used to wink at Ethel and would often ask if he could take her out to the pictures. Ethel would always go bright red; her neck extending and would just giggle and giggle. Mam tried to warn Uncle Joseph that Ethel might say yes one day and then where would he be. Uncle Joseph just winked at me and we both went into fits of laughter.

On coming home, I slipped the shilling into the meter and turned the handle, then had to make haste to light the stove as the gas came out for I'd forgotten to turn the gas tap off. I made tea with just one teaspoonful as I noticed our ration was getting very low.

Making a jam butty and leaving mam to her cleaning, I raced to school clutching the bag with some weighed out ingredients, although I was short on the margarine and had forgot the sugar. One of the yanks cheered as I raced past a work party, my gas mask case swinging up and down behind me. I don't mind school apart from Fridays. There are two Church of England schools and one Roman Catholic school in our town. I had no friends that were Catholic. In fact I'd never spoken to any of the Catholic children. It's not that we went out of our way to ignore them or anything. It is just that we are us and they are them, which seems rather silly considering I pass their school everyday, but that's the way it is.

On Friday afternoons our vicar always swept into our classroom, his long black cassock flowing behind him. By habit he would take off his strange three-cornered hat, called a biretta, and place it on our teacher's desk by the cane that was always within easy reach in case it was needed. Sadly that need was not always to just point with at the blackboard.

Ernest Heath was almost certain to become a victim of the Rev. Swindells and the cane was quite a familiar companion to Ernest Heath's buttocks. Often a book, usually the Book of Common Prayer that the Reverend was reading from, would come flying across the room generally in Ernest's direction. Not that it truly bothered Ernest. He said he had better bruises from his own dad. We all reckoned it was his penance for being the toughest and best fighter in the school. I liked Ernest but wished he wouldn't wipe his nose along the arm of his jumper that left his sleeve permanently shiny.

This morning, being the beginning of the week, we had longer to stand in assembly and more prayers were uttered for our deliverance from the bombs, which seemed a waste of time 'cause all the air raids had been on Liverpool.

Five fainted today. There was always one or two that slipped to the floor in a heap. Mam said it was the lack of good food that all growing children needed. I wanted desperately to faint and have all eyes on me with the accompanying chorus of 'aaah' from the others all around me, but I never did. Even holding my breath never worked. I invariably just got a frown from one of the teachers as I was forced to noisily gulp air in afterwards.

In class we always sat in the row according to our test marks of the week before. Because we were in our last class before the sort out of the eleven-plus exam, we had a test every week. This morning I was sitting in the second row, having found it hard the week before to sneak a quick look at some of Eunice's test paper answers. Just seeing one or two of her answers always helped a lot with the marking.

Sometimes the sirens would go off during the day. We didn't mind in the least having to troop, class-by-class, into the shelter next to the school. It was always preferred to doing fractions and other sums in pounds, shillings and pence. But today proved as much a normal day as could be, after drinking down our milk ration that was really enjoyed. It was always cold from the dairy and was left stacked outside in metal crates. When Jack Frost arrived, the cream froze at the top of the bottle and we would scoop the icy mush out with our fingers and lick off the creamy substance. Mam said it was the nearest thing we could get to getting real ice cream, now only seen on old shop signs since the day war broke out. Then as today, the boys kicked a ball around in the school yard having made a goal with their jackets, whilst the girls generally played games like Twosy against the school wall singing

'One alara, two alara,
I saw my sister Sarah,
Sitting on her bumtiarah,
Eating ripe tomatoes.'

I preferred skipping and joined a group of girls. Two held the rope, one at each end whilst a line was formed. Each one in the line taking turns to skip as the rope whirled around and everyone chanted:

'Long nose, skinny face,
Put her in a glass case,
And if you want to know her name,
Her name is ....'

as the next girl's name in the line was called out. Barbara Potts and I stood at the end of the line.

'Saw your Aunt Ada with a yank in the top field,' she stated, and then waited for my reaction.

'Wasn't my Aunt Ada you saw. She goes out with Frank Cole.'

'Was so then. Saw her I did,' she insisted, then just to make the point she added, 'they were kissing I tell you.'

I was about to tell her she needed glasses when someone pushed me forward and Barbara Potts was not going to be quietened.

'My mam says that girls that do rude things with the Americans are hussies,' she was now warming up for the final dig. 'So your Aunt Ada is a hussy, and no-one will speak to her anymore.'

Neither Barbara Potts nor I truly knew what a hussy was; apart from it wasn't nice to be one. I hated Barbara Potts from that very minute on and shouted:

'Long nose skinny face,' with real meaning when it was her turn to skip.

I wasn't in a very good mood during school dinner and for once didn't go up for a second helping. Often a table would be set out to finish off any of the day's leftovers. Anyway today it was semolina pudding, which I thought was like frogspawn. After dinner the boys and girls in our class separated, the boys doing PT and us onto the domestic science class. I was feeling pretty miserable. I was the only one without rhubarb.

I wouldn't have minded too much but because Barbara Potts had produced a nice big bunch from their garden, our teacher suggested she share half with me. I rolled my pastry with vengeance 'til it felt like a piece of cardboard and it even cut like cardboard as I ran the knife around the circle. Barbara made a rose and two leaves which she placed to one side of her light creation, whilst I just dug in the knife and made two slits in the middle of the pie. Of course she got good marks when all the pies were laid out for inspection. Mine was stared at in disbelief that the texture of the pastry was so hard and crisp and was told maybe I'd do better next time. 'Not with Barbara Pott's rhubarb,' I wanted to say and nearly said, but just kept my eyes down and tried to ignore the giggling going on around me.

I gave my pie to Ernest after school and he sat on the school wall and ate every crumb. He was about to lick the dish before I snatched it away. His nose looked as if it needed wiping again at any minute. But it was because of what Barbara Potts had said that put me in the mood to walk home across the top field that day. It was known as the top field because the field entrance was at the top of a narrow lane that began close to the school grounds.

I'd only once gone home that way before and it was with a girl that lived in the next road to ours. She left last year after her mam decided to go back to Ireland. We had crossed the field which was overgrown and covered in blackberry bushes, skirted a hayfield, crawled under a fence to where the sand quarries were and made our way home. We had thought it quicker and probably adventurous but it actually took longer.

Once I'd made my decision I was too angry with Barbara Potts to feel afraid of doing it on my own. I was mad, and being mad made me decisive. Somewhere in my angry state I thought that not seeing any sign of my Aunt Ada made Barbara Potts a great liar. I didn't reason that if I saw no one, it wouldn't mean anything at all. I admit I tried to persuade Eunice to come with me, but she looked at me daft like and ran off the other way.

I ran as I mostly do up the lane, trying to ignore the bushes on either side, and stopped for breath at the top before pushing open the swing bar that separated the lane from the field. It was still light and the sky was as blue as it could be for this time of year. Everywhere looked comforting like an English Constable painting, although there were no sheep around. Clusters of blackberries hung from the brambles and tasted wonderful. My gas mask canvas case came to mind as a holder of the fruit, but then perished the thought after seeing the juice stains on my white blouse.

I kept to the worn path at the edge of the field thinking of ways of getting even with Barbara Potts and her evil tongue, when I saw them. I knew beyond a shadow of doubt that it was my Aunt Ada entwined around the figure of an American serviceman. She was wearing the very same dress that had been hanging on the airing rack in gran's kitchen. I stopped in my tracks and side stepped into the bushes along the perimeter of the field. Carefully parting the branches of a hawthorn bush, I had a good view of my aunt.

She was being pressed up against a tree trunk that grew along side the hedge. Her dress was pulled up showing black suspenders emerging from under her french knickers. The American that was doing the pressing had his hands up and down her thighs, his head deep in the nape of her neck. I actually heard Aunt Ada give a little moan and half wondered if he was hurting her, but after what Barbara Potts had said I knew this was an arranged meeting to the benefit of both persons.

Yes, it was Aunt Ada and a yank. I hated my informant twice as much for being right. My second thought was for poor old Frank who worshipped the very ground she walked on, and I for one wasn't going to be the one to tell him he was being two-timed. Part of me was horrified but another part of me was fascinated and, if it wasn't for the thought of getting caught, I might have been tempted to stay longer. As it was, because I couldn't continue walking the way I'd intended I had no choice but to retreat. So I carefully retraced my steps keeping well out of sight; then once reaching the lane, flew as fast as my legs would carry me past the school's high stone walls.

Nearing the main road I spotted a group of old men. Now, I've nothing against old men as a rule and truly liked old Mr Grace. But I can't stand the way some of them cough up their guts then spit a gob of green phlegm onto the pavement.

I was more than thankful to get home. It had been a terrible day and I needed some normality and calm. Mam looked just as drained and tired as I felt, but the house looked clean, although old sheets had been placed over the furniture and the net curtains were gone.

'Any post?' I asked, I always asked that when there had been a long gap between my dad's letters coming.

'No post,' came back the answer. 'There's always tomorrow,' she added and placed some Marmite sandwiches on the table in the kitchen. I say table, but it was really a very large mangle that served a number of purposes. Its main function being of course was wringing excess water out of clothes after being washed and flattening sheets after they had been folded. The second function lay in the fact the wooden rollers could be swung over and a hinged wooden top lowered to cover the whole machinery. Ours was a small kitchen, only large enough to hold the gas stove, a stone sink and a wooden draining board one side with a clothes boiler pushed underneath and the mangle on the other side. The table cum mangle then was extremely important. A meat grinder could be screwed on one side to mince meat, when we had meat that was.

Occasionally some one would give us a rabbit and I used to watch in awe as the animal was laid down on the table, head and legs sliced off cut down the centre and its skin pulled off like an old coat. Carrots, cabbage and anything chopable was chopped up on the white scrubbed wooden mangle top and, once in a blue moon, piecrust pastry would be rolled out. Put a piece of linoleum cloth on top of it and presto, it became a table to dine upon again. Even Marmite sandwiches looked good on it when you were hungry.

I must admit we were never short of milk. The milk woman arrived every morning leaving two bottles for us on our step with the horse from the milk cart regularly leaving his large round droppings on the road outside. The latter didn't stay on the road long as someone always managed to scoop it up for it to end up on someone's rhubarb or vegetable patch. The thought of which often made me want to gag. I ate my sandwiches in silence, aware that mam had glanced at me a couple of times, probably to see if I was sickening for something, as I wasn't usually that quiet. But I was thinking of Aunt Ada and whether she was now a hussy, and would she offer mam some of the nylons she was bound to be getting. Maybe I could ask Aunt Ada to mention chocolate if she ever got the opportunity.

The sound of the sirens shattered my contemplation and I grabbed the remaining sandwiches and headed for the pantry door. Three steps down and mam and I huddled together on the floor at the bottom of the pantry that was actually located under the stairs. There was no light and, with the door closed, we were in total darkness, which didn't stop the Marmite sandwiches from finding my mouth. Then there was that frightening drone of aircraft overhead. Not long afterwards, the all clear sounded.

'Uncle Joseph is coming tomorrow to do the chimney,' volunteered mam when we entered the light. I was glad she'd forgot to ask where my pie was.

Chapter 5

We received no post for a whole week and just as I was about to question the postwoman about it, I found two letters pushed half way through the letter slot in the front door. I gave them a slight tug and watched as they dropped to the floor before bending down and picking them up. Our postwoman started last month and everyone was talking about how strange it seemed not to have a postman for the job, but I guess there were changes with men away.

Ignoring the envelope edged in black, my attention was focussed on the one I knew came from my dad. I recognised the writing and the Egyptian stamp, which I knew I would get after mam read the letter.

I spotted the secret code on the envelope flap with the letters SWALK written with a big X underneath. I looked over the rest of the envelope in case the letters BOLTOP or BURMA were written there too, but to my disappointment they couldn't be found. Eunice and I kept a secret record of most of these codes words

SWALK meant – 'Sealed With A Loving Kiss'
BOLTOP meant - 'Better On Lips Than On Paper.'

We hadn't yet cracked the one written on most of Aunt Ada's letters she kept under her undies in her dressing room table drawer. It said BURMA, but everyone's lips in the family were sealed when we enquired. Even Uncle Joseph, who was generally a good source of knowledge, just stuttered, turned bright red and changed the subject when we asked him. Aunt Ada had other things written on notes to her, which were also hidden under clothes in her dressing table. One note was a poem that I remembered by heart, it went:

In the parlour there were three,
Ada, the table lamp and me,
Now two is company without a doubt,
And so the table lamp went out.

I used it at school when we had to write a poem for our homework, writing my own name at the bottom of course. I don't think it was a very good poem because it was handed back with a thick red line across it and 'Poor taste' written underneath.

Mam had a little cry when she opened the black edged letter. One of my dad's uncles had died, but mam cheered up quite a lot when she read he'd left us £30. I told Eunice about the £30 and how my mam was going to buy me a new outfit, but I knew at the time I was lying and wished I hadn't showed off like that.

We had to suffer through a one-and-a-half hour church service once a week. Starting after assembly we marched, crocodile fashion from our school and through a gate in the stone wall that led into the church's graveyard. We followed the ancient path past very old and worn gravestones. Some of them were leaning over at quite awkward angles and looked unsafe.

On entering the church we all obediently dipped our fingers into the holy water before crossing ourselves. No matter how warm it was outside the church was always cold and damp inside. We pushed and nudged each other with our elbows to find the most favoured part of the pews where the Rev. Swindell's gaze was least likely to settle. The vicar did go on a bit that day, it being a special one in the church's calendar we were told.

The choirboys took their places behind the carved screen in the sanctuary. One of the choirboys, who lived down the road from us, was standing and looking 'like butter wouldn't melt in his mouth'.

This was another of mam's sayings and I stuck my tongue out at him and crossed my eyes whenever he looked my way.

The Reverend Swindells said we were all going to be burnt in hell fire if we didn't attend church more. I gazed at the stained glass windows. I always liked the one of St. Barbara with the sheep but wished her name had been different. Gladys would have been much better as no one seemed to know who St. Barbara was, not even Rev. Swindells.

A thump interrupted my thoughts. Ernest had been piling up the hymn books in our pew and they had suddenly collapsed in a great heap. That was sure to mean the cane for him again when we got back to school. I sighed and took a deep breath. That started off a bout of coughing, as I hadn't noticed the incense burner being swung around. The blue haze had drifted in the general direction of our pew and hung over us. It must have been the cheapest scent the Wise Men brought to baby Jesus. It was really awful.

I had been christened at St Alkmund's and did have a feeling of belonging to the church. But then, as the church was very old and the sandstone font looked quite worn, hundreds of people before me must have felt the same. One thing for sure I didn't ever want to be in the choir for I had the same flaw when singing as the rest of my family, and that was being completely off-key.

The last hymn began. 'Onward Christian Soldiers.' I loved to sing this one and let all the air out of my lungs as I echoed 'So-wo-wol-odiers.' Our teacher frowned at me and Eunice quickly smothered her chuckle. At long last the service was over and the cross was taken out followed by those sanctimonious looking choirboys walking in pairs.

As we pushed our way towards the world waiting outside, I caught a glance of Ernest being led off by his ear towards the school by the vicar. The rest of the day passed pleasantly as we were read to by our teacher from 'Prester John'. He liked to hear his voice and we liked to listen. The trouble came when we had to write about it afterwards.

A yank called to me from their billet as I passed by on my way home from school. Not only did I get a bar of chocolate but also a small metal model of an aeroplane. The yank said I reminded him so much of is daughter back home, so I thought I'd keep my eyes open for him again.

Today had certainly made up for the bad day I had yesterday and I was feeling quite good with myself. I hadn't been home long, before Vera came around from next-door; opening the back door and yelling,

'Are you there, Rose?'

'Mam's upstairs,' I called back and that seemed to be an invite for her to come in.

I only partly remembered Vera's husband. He was a real blond not like Aunt Ada. Their family name is Van Doorninck but Vera always calls him Wilhelm. He is a Dutch soldier, now away fighting like the rest. Their two little girls are very nice and I look after them for Vera when she needs to do errands and occasionally to baby sit at night. I quite liked baby-sitting and have, on occasions, been given a whole a shilling and the run of their pantry. Vera's parents are farmers and she is able to get stuff that we can't. Often, like today, she'll bring mam some fresh laid eggs.

'There you are ducks,' and she handed me a brown bag with eggs in and a small jam jar with some red jelly in it.

Mam came downstairs. She'd recently had her hair trimmed and styled and she looked very young and pretty. I wanted very much to have ringlets. Eunice's mother curled Eunice's hair with the iron curlers that have to be heated in the fire, but I'd rather have rags twisted in mine to make the curls, even if the rags looked awful in the process.

I glanced in the mirror that hung over the mantle piece. I cannot say I was any great beauty; my hair thick and a little wavy but the colour was what's termed as mousy. I had nice blue eyes and the dark ring around the blue made them especially interesting as my lashes and eyebrows were also dark. I thought my mouth was a bit big and spent much time pursing my lips together; but often forgot to keep up that exercise. My teeth were even and straight and not one had been filled to date, which was just as well, after the stories I'd heard from my friends about their visits to the dentist.

I turned back to Vera as I thought she'd asked me a question. She looked excited and flushed.

'Rita, be an angel and baby-sit my girls tomorrow night.'

I must have taken too long to reply as she was fidgeting with the egg bag on the table before saying:

'How's two shillings for baby-sitting. Will that do?'

Mam tried to protest that it was far too much, but I accepted without a qualm and answered simply

'Okay, what time?'

'Say 8.0 pm,' Vera was beginning to relax once that was settled and even suggested a teacup reading. I was surprised when she dug into her apron pocket and produced a little waxed paper packet with some tea leaves in it.

'Oh no I couldn't,' insisted mam, although we both knew she would as our tea caddy was practically empty.

The kettle went on the stove instead of the fire as Uncle Joseph couldn't clean the chimney 'til the weekend and mam didn't want to risk yet another fall of soot. We all sat in the kitchen and the cups were duly turned over and read. There would be news from a tall blond man and a good time was forecast soon.

'Are you going anywhere nice tomorrow night?' I asked wondering if the good time would be something to do with it. Vera looked at me smiling. She certainly looked very happy.

'Your Aunt Ivy and I are going to a dance at the Town Hall,' she volunteered.

'Is Ethel going too? I asked innocently wishing something nice would happen for her, but Vera and mam just started to laugh.

'She's a right one is your Rita,' Vera chuckled. Vera had brought a bag with her curlers in it and, almost as if it was forethought, mam began to roll lengths of Vera's dark hair 'til her head looked quite big. Then a length of scarf was fastened around the curlers and wound into a turban. I was hoping to see mam drawing a line down Vera's legs but after the hair-do, but Vera was ready for off.

'Must feed my brood,' she sighed as if it was a great chore.

'Aren't broods chickens?' I asked seriously. Mam and Vera stared at me then Vera picked up her bag.

'You're such a card.' She ruffled my head, which I immediately straightened. I hated people doing that.

I was quite excited at the prospect of seeing Vera and Aunt Ivy dressing up for the dance, for as they were going together Aunt Ivy would be getting ready at our house.

In due course, Aunt Ivy arrived with a large bag and pulled out the dress she'd made. It was the prettiest dress I'd ever seen, not that I'd seen many dance dresses. It was bright yellow with black spots with little puff sleeves and a broad black belt.

'William got me the material without coupons,' I heard Aunt Ivy tell mam in a confidential tone.

William Taylor was her boss's son, the same one she does a lot of overtime for.

'Does William Taylor mind you going dancing?' mam asked her sister.

I thought it a queer question to ask as it had nothing to do with him, but Aunt Ivy didn't seem to mind and said he was away in London for the week. Aunt Ivy tried the dress on, with mam and I as approving spectators. Well almost, because mam remarked,

'It's rather short, our Ivy.'

'No it's not; this is the new fashion these days.' Her sister twirled around and I admit with legs like hers it looked wonderful.

'What about stockings?' asked mam.

'You'll have to do my legs Rose; I've gone and laddered my last pair.'

This was just what I was waiting for. I fetched a chair from the kitchen and placed it among the covered up furniture because the light in the living room was better in there. My aunt had taken off the dress and was ready to get her line drawn. I watched fascinated as mam started near the buttock and drew a perfectly straight line down Aunt Ivy's left leg and, all in one go, she did the other just as perfectly after telling her sister to stop twisting around to see what she was doing.

'Pity we don't have any coffee' my aunt remarked, now sitting and admiring her legs.

'If I did, it wouldn't go on tanning your legs, that's for sure.' Mam punched her sister's shoulder in a friendly gesture.

There was a lot of resemblance between my two aunts and mam; although Aunt Ivy was taller by a good six inches and more rounded. It was difficult to make a judgement on hair colour. I'd never seen Aunt Ada's hair any other colour but blond. Aunt Ivy's varied between black and brown, whereas my mam's was always mousy like mine. But there was something about the shapes of their faces and all three had the same blue eyes.

The following evening, I looked at the clock and thought I'd better get round next door. I was greeted by a dazzling Vera in a bright red dress that enhanced her dark hair. The two girls were already in bed and Vera said if she was late, I could sleep on the couch. It was a done deal that if the sirens sounded my mam would come around right away, but fortunately that had never happened whenever I baby-sat. Baby sitting was a welcome change especially as our dining room was presently unusable.

I made some sandwiches. I always checked out the food in the pantry and nibbled on a little piece of this and that. There was half a Queen's Pudding. The bread and egg in it was cold, but the jam made it quite appetizing. I tried a pickled onion, but had to have a little more pudding to get rid of the taste. The coal in the fire glowed warm and the coal bucket was still half full. I found a few American magazines under the cushions of the couch and got totally absorbed in the photos of film stars and the way they dressed. I would have liked to cut out the one of Ray Milland, but thought better of it.

The girls upstairs never woke up. I peeped in to see their blond heads peeping above their blankets. I checked their toys, stepping over their books which were too young for me, visited the bathroom, looked in the cabinet, we hadn't got one and I wondered what was kept in it, but it was only the stuff we kept on our pantry's top shelf like cough medicine and aspirins. I put little dab of scent on my wrist, and then washed my hands three times to get rid of the smell. The desk in the living room was locked so I sat and gazed into the fire through the mesh of the fireguard feeling very sleepy. The next thing I remembered was the front door opening. I was most likely dreaming because I thought I heard the voice of an American.

When I awoke I found someone had put a coat over me and I was lying in pitch darkness as the fire was out. I lay there for a long time before I lifted a corner of the blackout curtain. It was dawn outside. I drew back the curtains and snuggled under the coat again and half slept 'til Vera came down to light the fire. True to her word, she handed me the coveted two shillings, and she looked as if her evening out was worth every penny of it.

Chapter 6

My right eye was itching something terrible all morning and rubbing it only made it worse. I thought it may-be due to staying up late and reading all those American magazines in the poor light. One of the mantles of the gaslight was broken so I did have to squint a bit to read. I made a mental note to ask Vera where she got the magazines from, and then thought better of it because they had been well hidden under the sofa.

Mam had the eye of an eagle when it came to health and I soon found myself sitting upright on a chair with my head tilted back. Mam's face didn't half look queer as she bent down beside me to investigate my problem. It was like looking through a magnifying glass. After lifting my eyelid and having a good examination she'd found my problem.

'You've got a sty coming.' She went over to the sink to wash off any germs.

I felt as if I had to wait to welcome my visitor and saw a big fat pig in my imagination. What daft names those medical people use, most of them are so foreign I can't pronounce them or just plain silly like sty – boil – shingles. I felt my head being pulled back again and cold metal was being rubbed along my eyelid, together with hard knuckles. Mam was rubbing my sore eye with her wedding ring still attached to her finger.

'How can that help cure a sty?' I managed to ask under her restraining arm.

'It's gold,' she said simply as if it was a barmy question. 'Your gran always rubbed her wedding ring on us when we got eye trouble,' she continued, before taking a final look at her handiwork.

My sty proved too powerful for mam's wedding ring and we ended up at the doctor's surgery. The wooden forms, placed against the walls, were hard and the stone-flagged floor cold. Every one sat bolt upright staring at the pathetic flickerings of an old gas fire set into one wall. The bottom half of the walls were painted dark brown with the embossment of old wallpaper showing through, then topped with an equally brown chair-rail, whilst the top half was painted cream. English people are very conservative, for I reckon most of the kitchens were either brown and cream or green and cream.

Over on the far wall was a step up to the doctor's door and when you weren't staring at the fire your eyes were generally centred on the opening of this door. By the side of it was a small square hole that framed the top of a receptionist's head that continually bobbed up and down as she took down patients' names or called out when their turn had come. Not that she needed to remind us, and I was sure everyone in there knew exactly who was before each one of them and who the next in line were. There was always a lot of coughing, but I was glad to say nobody ever spat on the waiting room floor.

The entrance door opened and Ernest Heath came in sporting a swollen black and blue eye. He glanced at me once then dropped his head to hide his chin under his jumper and sat slumped in the corner. I wondered if he had won his fight and I hoped very much that he had.

'Rita Goodwin.' It was my name being called as an old lady was being helped down the step from the doctor's office.

I'm not at all afraid of going to our doctor, because he is so nice and he always makes a lot of fuss of mam and me. Once when I had measles, he came to visit and was wearing big fur gloves. He pretended he was a bear and made me laugh so much, mam said it made my spots run away. He likes talking to mam too and often pops in our house when he's out doing his rounds, just to see how we are doing. He's quite good-looking with his fair curly hair, and slim moustache.

Dr. McKenzie sat in a leather chair with his stethoscope around his neck, neatly dressed in a shirt and tie and a patterned pullover. He swivelled his chair around and motioned mam to sit down on the one in front of him. I was left wondering what I should do. Mam was flushed but looked quite nice as she crossed her legs and posed on the chair with her hand crossed delicately over her handbag.

'You look well Rose.' He smiled at mam who smiled back and, for a second, I thought I might have to remind him I was the patient.

'It's her age,' he revealed to mam after peering around my eye with a magnifying glass. 'It's not uncommon for a lass of her age to come out in boils and sties: Lack of fruit that's the trouble.'

Mam agreed with him and I was forgotten once again as they bantered with each other, although I did get a prescription written out eventually: Cream to put on my eye at night, and some tonic for good measure.

I mentioned school and he thought about it, winked at mam, and said a couple of days off wouldn't do me any harm. I walked past Ernest with a brand new patch covering my eye, which left him staring at me in admiration.

Mam and I strolled through the town to the chemist. She seemed in an excellent mood and suggested we call in the café and have a bun after picking up my prescription. I perched myself on top of the tall three legged stool at Johnson's chemist shop and gazed in wonder at the huge glass ornamental jars that contained different coloured liquids. They were like something out of the Arabian Nights. They were only for show, but they looked very mysterious. The chemist shop was very old and had a lot of the original glass-fronted cupboards with stacks of small drawers beneath them. The counter was of thick solid wood and polished with age. I think it would have withstood a German bomb. A round jar of rosehips standing at one end of the counter reminded me I should start picking them. We got sixpence a jar full, as long as they were orange and not green. Rosehip syrup was full of vitamins that were missing from our diet. It was probably what my tonic was made of.

I watched the exchange of money, the chemist's podgy fingers trying to extract a three-penny bit from the drawers in the ornate gilded till. Our chemist was the roundest man I'd ever seen. His head was like a round Christmas pudding plopped on a bigger round ball and even his glasses were two perfectly round frames.

Later, as we neared the small black and white café situated at the corner of a cobbled street, three yanks were just coming out.

'Got any gum chum?' It was out before I could stop myself and in return I got a sharp clip across the back of my head.

Mam pulled me into the café. I hoped the yanks thought the English could be very cruel to their children, especially when a child only had one eye. I might get a bar or two of chocolate in the future. Holding that thought I followed mam like an abused orphan to a table by the window. It was a very old place, one of the oldest remaining Elizabethan buildings in our town. Over the door outside was carved on the black wood '1600' and under it the word 'WOM'. That day I discovered what the word WOM meant. I had found my heritage and a new understanding of my town's dialect.

'Got go wom' translated itself as 'Got to go home.' In the past I thought it common to call children – childra, or cows – kine. I disliked people saying they were feeling bad instead of poorly. But now being aware of my part in the distant past and having generations before me living in the same county, I was proud to be Cheshire through and through and, as I sat there at the table in the cafe, took to uttering out aloud

'Ha-doo, duz thee wona cuppa tae? Well cum on in an' sat thee sen doon.' This provoked yet another slap from my mam.

The ceiling of the café was low, with large black beams that were displaying hanging pewter mugs. I was always surprised the war effort didn't claim them. The tables were old and wobbly with chequered lino cloth covering the tops. The stone fireplace was never lit, but a gas fire stood over in one corner. The yanks seemed to like this place and so did the mill girls, but as it was well before dinnertime, there were only a few people in there. We got a cup of really weak tea. Mam called it shamrock tea, implying it only had three leaves in the pot and quite a challenge for tea cup reading no doubt.

All at once mam started to rap on the small leaded windows and was pressing her face against the thick glass. I caught a blurred vision of Uncle Joseph's face staring back. A moment later he pulled up a chair to our table and mam beckoned the girl for another cup. She came back bringing a small plate of tarts that looked so flat they shouldn't have been called tarts at all. My Uncle Joseph looked very smart today. He had a stiff collar and tie on and was wearing his one and only suit. His hair was brushed back, sleek with Brylcream and quite short around the ears.

'So,' said mam, waiting for whatever her brother had to tell her.

'Done it.' Uncle Joseph sat looking like the cat that had just got a mouse.

'Done what?' I asked pushing my teeth into the hard piece of pastry topped with equally hard jam.

'He's gone and joined up,' mam said looking very proud and a little tearful at the same time.

'In the Navy?' I hoped he had, for I loved the sailor's uniforms. They were so romantic with their square collars and round hats.

'Nar, it's the army for Frank and me,' he answered very seriously. 'We leave this coming Friday.'

Mam put her hand over his and began patting it, while routing for her hanky with her other hand. I helped myself to another tart thing, and then put it back feeling ashamed, as there were three of us but only one tart remained. Before Uncle Joseph left us, he gave me a two-shilling piece. Mam said no he shouldn't, but I was glad he got his way,.

Friday that week was an important one in our family. First my patch came off and the sty had gone. Of course it was the wedding ring that did it according to gran. Secondly Uncle Joseph was going to fight the Jerries and I again found myself on Crewe station.

The place was alive with movement, apart from the ones sleeping on the forms or sitting up asleep next to the waiting room looking like rag dolls. We'd all come to see Uncle Joseph and Frank Cole off. Gran wore her black hat with its floppy feather. Aunt Ivy came in her work clothes because she'd had to take time off. Aunt Ada wore a scarf because her roots were showing and hadn't had time to fix it. Frank's old mother had arthritis and his father, it seems, had a continual thirst problem and always had to have a pint of beer close-by. He did say however he'd see to it to drink Frank's health. There was a lot of hugging and kissing and all that stuff. Gran cried and mam and Aunt Ivy bought her a cup of tea to calm her nerves after waiting in a long queue for it.

The bus ride back presented a problem as the bus was packed. But a kind gentleman let Aunt Ada and I squeeze in on the front row seat upstairs, whilst he stood and balanced himself by putting a hand on Aunt Ada's shoulder now and then. We didn't talk much. I thought Aunt Ada would be upset at Frank's going. She took out her compact and lined her lips up with a bright red lipstick. It had smudged when Frank kissed her goodbye.

She fiddled with her hair that peeped from under her scarf, and then began looking through the front window of the bus as we neared our town. For some reason she got off the bus before we did and I watched her trotting across the road in her high heels towards an American standing around the corner of the chip-shop. Because I was on the front row and upstairs I got a very good view.

We all, apart from Aunt Ada, had tea at gran's with sardine sandwiches and stewed apples with evaporated milk. William Taylor came around in his car. He has more coupons for petrol because of the factory and always spent time explaining the difficulties he was having in changing over from making dresses to parachutes. Then he told us he'd give anything to be called up and join the lads but the government thought his work far too important. Gran nodded, but her lips were held together in a thin tight line that made me think she was having other thoughts on the matter.

William Taylor asked Aunt Ivy to accompany him on his trip to Manchester as he would need her to type up some orders and just maybe they would have time for a meal before they returned. Gran sniffed, but didn't comment and the conversation turned to the possibility of me passing the up-coming eleven-plus exam at school. If I did pass, I would be the only one in the family and great store was put by it. Gran promised to help out with clothing coupons and said I was quite bright. The only trouble was I didn't want to pass as I dreamed of going to the art school instead.

We all took our entrance exams to the grammar school, but only a gifted few could also take the exam to the art school. I knew I had a fairly good chance of making one or the other, even though never more than six ever passed from our school each year. However I wanted so badly to be an artist and one day live in a flat in London when I was grown up.

I'd read a book about a famous artist that had done just that. Drawing was something that came naturally, although I could get carried away with creativity like the time I drew a life sized figure of Jesus raising Lazarus up from the dead on the whitewashed wall of my bedroom. I was experimenting with charcoal until I realised the charcoal from charred sticks of firewood was far too primitive. So like always I promised God I'd do many good things if only he'd let me pass the art school exam.

I did have a great deal of faith that God could do any-thing. God did work miracles, especially when, shortly afterwards, after two letters dropped on our hall doormat.

The trouble was I'd passed both exams and I knew which one mam would be insisting I accepted. It was a terrible thing I did that day and I hope one day I will be forgiven, but sometimes temptation is too much to let go. I handed the letter from the art school to my mam and later dropped the one from the grammar school accidentally on the fire. William Taylor asked my mam what good an art school education would be to me. As a result mam's back went up and she signed the art school acceptance papers there and then. Barbara Potts had passed for grammar.

It was because of the art school that I found myself witnessing something I wasn't prepared for. I needed some paper to draw on and mam said she'd ask gran because there was a stack of it in the front room desk where she used to do the accounts when grandpa was alive. But gran had gone to Chester to see her sister whose son had been killed, and the thought of waiting a whole week was testing my patience to its limit. I convinced myself gran wouldn't mind if I helped myself and I would be very careful not to touch anything else. I opened the door of gran's house with my key and tiptoed to the closed door. I'm not sure why I tiptoed, probably because I really knew I shouldn't be there.

I was surprised to see the door cracked open for it was always closed. I squinted through the crack concerned there may be a burglar in the room. But burglars didn't lie on the sofa and have four feet. Two bare medium size and two large with socks on. It was a frightening shock and my heart thumped like crazy in my chest. I turned and crept out of the house, leaving the front door off the lock in case it made a sound.

Curiosity has always been my downfall and my feet, rather than heading down the drive, seemed to turn on their own towards the rear of the house. The curtains were still drawn, but not quite altogether in that room. The slight crack in the curtains at one side offered the opportunity to look right into it. I got a rock and stood on it and peeped through the window. Aunt Ada was in her all together with her arms wrapped around a man who was stripped down to his underpants. His broad back was facing me, but I saw his American uniform lying on the floor in a crumpled pile. I gaped at the scene for a full minute or two, watching the wriggling and hand exploring, when I felt the rock I was standing on start wobbling under my feet and thought it a good indication to leave. I was all for telling Eunice about what I'd seen, but then realised she might just tell Barbara Potts.

Chapter 7

I suppose it was unrealistic of me to expect a brand new uniform, as clothing coupons went nowhere. Gran did offer some but mam was always independent, worst luck. I ended up with a second hand blazer that I needed to grow into. We took up the sleeves but the width was too daunting a task. My gymslip was finally recognised as having no more seam to let down, and I did get a new one and without pleats, which cheered me up no end. Then mam managed to get hold of an old art school badge, as the school hadn't supplied them since the war started. It was the very best of badges; a large boar's head threaded in gold, with big bold red letters 'B.S.A' beneath it. The B stood for Burslem, the town in the Potteries where the school was situated. I was very proud of showing the badge off 'til Ernest asked if the red letters stood for 'Bloody Silly Ass'. It was going to take me a long time to forgive him for that.

Gran gave me grandpa's old briefcase; it was old and heavy, even without my art supplies but satchels were hard to come by, and mam promised if she saw one she'd take the money out of her 'rainy day jar' of coins. I'd long ago learned not to complain because I was always told the same thing. "Don't you know there's a war on?" It was a daft thing to say. Every time I ate Marmite sandwiches, had milk poured over pieces of bread, wiped my bum on squares of old newspaper that hung on a piece of string in the lavvy, I was reminded about the war. If I ever forgot for a moment, the 'Air Raid Warning' sirens followed by the 'All Clear' signals' were so very inescapable.

The knocker on the front door sounded, and I jumped up in haste to see who it was, for nearly everyone else used our back door. Gran stood there, in her black coat and felt hat that fitted so well that the waves of her hair looked almost part of it, until you saw the big hairclips separating the waves. I was surprised to see her as I can only ever remember her visiting once before and that was when mam caught the 'flu. She pushed passed me and, as it wasn't raining, she hung her long still folded umbrella on the back of the hall chair and relieved herself of her coat. The hat stayed on and so did her pinafore.

'Rose, are you there?' she bellowed. She had a good set of lungs. Mam popped her head over the banister upstairs, looking a little bewildered.

'What's wrong?' She sounded a little worried; no doubt it was a shock seeing gran in our house.

'I'll put the kettle on.' Gran's answer obviously indicating she needed time to sit and talk. I followed her into the kitchen, and handed her a match and the box of Swan Vestas matches to strike it on. I was trying to be helpful, but it didn't light and she struck the box another three times before getting a flame. Tea, it seems, cures all worries for the English. Mam came in rubbing her hands and looking agitated. Taking control, she got gran to sit down whilst she took over.

'What is it Mam?' she said pushing her face up close to gran's.

I think they had forgotten me, and I am very quiet indeed on these occasions, just in case I get sent out of the room and miss something really important.

'She's been sick again Rose,' gran confided to my mam. I could tell she was having trouble getting her words out, but once it had started she was unable to stop.

'Now Mam, we all get sick sometimes,' said my mam consoling her. 'She could have caught a germ or something. I remember only last week Mrs Collins couldn't keep anything down.'

'No it's.....' Gran gave that funny look of wisdom. 'You know, you've had one.'

I hadn't a clue what they were talking about but I hovered around just in case it was interesting.

'Give us a biscuit love.' Gran indicated to the biscuit tin, which to my surprise produced a biscuit. Only one though, and it went to gran who dipped it in her tea. I hated that for bits always floated in the teacup.

'I think she is….' Gran looked at my mam long and hard, until she had made her point. Mam shook her head and her lips thinned. Whatever they were talking about my mam obviously disapproved. Gran bent her head closer to mam and I just managed to make out her words.

'Can't be Frank's. He's been gone too long.'

Mam nodded, then sat back and thought, sipping her tea very slowly 'til she was ready to say her piece.

'Frank's due to come on leave soon before he goes to France, isn't he?'

Gran nodded.

I was so very glad to hear that Frank would be home soon then Aunt Ada wouldn't be so lovesick without him. Mam always had the answer. Then all at once the two women realised I was standing there and gran closed her lips, indicating my presence with a slight twist of her head towards me.

'Children should be seen and not heard.' Gran said. I think she had got that one quite wrong as mam directed me towards the outside door.

I passed old Mr Grace, our next-door neighbour as I walked up the road. He was leaning over his front gate, a Woodbine packet clutched tightly in one hand and a bucket in the other. The fag drooped from somewhere under his large brown stained moustache.

'Rita Goodwin,' he said, nodding his head in a way that I knew he hadn't said my name to ask or tell me anything. It was just his way of acknowledging me. Why do old people always call you by your full name? I hated the name Rita and really wanted to be called Elizabeth like the princess. Parents have no sense at times.

'Mr Grace.' I nodded and left him to his coughing and wheezing and I'm glad I ran because he was making sounds as though he was about to spit.

The rag and bone man had just turned into our road. I always felt sorry for the old horse pulling the overloaded cart. Not only did it have much to pull, but its head and neck were also weighed down with so many horse brasses. The horse's mane was the only thing about him that looked as if it had any attention, for it was plaited and tied up with red ribbons. The horse stopped and strained and I saw Mr Grace with his bucket coming down the road.

I ran 'til a yank called me over as I passed the garage, but I didn't quite like the look of him so I carried on running pretending I was a deaf child. I pretended so good I nearly got knocked down by a bike, which brought me back to my mission. I had been feeling very guilty about my promises of good deeds in my bargain with God.

The main object of my mission that day was leaning over the kitchen sink, and when my Aunt Ada lifted her head it came as quite a shock. It was only her voice that saved me from thinking Aunt Ada must have a plain pasty-faced twin. She looked awful; the once blond shining hair was quite black two inches from her scalp and the face devoid of any make-up didn't look like my Aunt Ada at all.

She must be really worried about Frank. It was amazing how she had concealed it so well, as she had always played hard to get. I felt a warm fussy glow inside for Frank, away in the dreadful war and here was some-one making herself sick with worry for the love of him. I just couldn't contain myself any longer. I blurted it out; my face must have been like a shining penny with all my enthusiasm.

'Frank's coming home on leave then.'

Aunt Ada fainted. She slid onto the floor like a rag doll. I was horrified and blamed myself for allowing her so much happiness and causing her to faint with joy.

I flew to Gran's medicine cupboard and hunted around for the small bottle she always stuffed under somebody's nose if they were feeling fainty. The bottle did the trick and my Aunt Ada came to, only to sit up and be sick again.

'What did you say about Frank?' She managed to utter between her heaving and holding her stomach.

'I heard Frank was coming home on leave.' This time I spaced out the words and had the bottle ready in case it was needed again.

The smelling salts must have been very good, for a colour crept into Aunt Ada's face and she asked me to hand her the calendar from the wall. Still sitting on the floor, she started counting days, and then she gave a great sigh.

'I must do my hair,' her hands reached up and touched her parting, and then she examined her cracked nails. Then all at once she seemed to acknowledge I was really there, and she smiled weakly.

'Make us a cuppa dear,' she said and began to get up, staring at me for a moment as if wondering what else to say.

'I've got gastric flu,' she ventured as if that settled the whole issue.

Now I'm not a great friend of germs of any sort so I backed away and made an excuse I had an errand to run, leaving Aunt Ada to make her own tea. I was now walking on cloud nine. I reckoned that one good deed was rated very high in God's record book, together with another good omen when Father Swindells gave me a smile as I passed the church. I had momentarily considered giving Father Swindells my two-shilling piece that I still had, but decided God would surely show me a more noble cause to support. And I was right, for by the time I had reached the chip-shop I knew what I should do with my money.

Ernest was sitting on the pavement, feet stuck out in the gutter poking at the bubbles the sun had made in the tarmac. I knew Ernest had a lot of brothers and sisters, well one of each actually but that was a lot to an only child like me. His dad had been missing for a few months now and mam had told my gran, the children looked as if a good meal wouldn't do them any harm. I couldn't see it really, for Ernest was taller than me, and not terribly thin, as thin goes. In fact if it wasn't for his cuts and bruises from fighting, I thought him rather nice, but of course I would never let him know or I would get laughed at.

'Hello Ernest.'

'Hi,' he called back.

Hi seemed to have appeared in the English language ever since the yanks arrived. Before that he used to say 'watcha-cock'. I think I now much preferred 'hi.'

I've always had trouble doing things without thinking and buying Ernest some chips seemed the right thing to do, but I had a major problem. My mam hated the smell of chips on my clothes and would know at once where I had been. I considered the situation for a while and eventually found a solution. Yes I would take off my jacket coat and eat the chips outside, sitting next to Ernest on the curb edge with our feet in the gutter.

'Ernest,' I said, squatting down beside him.

'What d'yer want?' He started to look at me as if I was an alien.

'I want some chips but my mother doesn't allow me to go into the chip shop.' He grunted something; about if he had some money he wouldn't care if he got a hiding.

'You go in Ernest, and buy for the two of us.'

'Honest?' He had already leapt up. I was getting quite animated now. Here I was holding a conversation with the class's hero and, before I could control my tongue, I'd already told him to get two very large packets of chips with salt and vinegar with two tubs of mushy peas and, just to top it off, two teas made with dried milk. Ernest forgot that mussy peas need something to eat them with, but we were not deterred and ended up making a fold in the newspaper they were wrapped in and letting them slide down our throats.

'You live near the sand quarries?' Ernest asked wiping his greasy mouth on his sleeve, and I just kept licking my fingers hoping to neutralize the smell somewhat.

'Yes our house is built on the edge of an old one that's now overgrown. It's like a valley with bushes and some trees, but there is a newer one further on.' I went on to describe the area.

'Have you ever slid down one?' he asked. Ernest glanced at me hardly turning his head, while licking the chip paper before screwing it up.

'Yes, thousands of times,' I lied.

'Come on then, let's go slide down the quarry.' He'd already quickened his step heading in the general direction of the quarry. I don't know why I followed. I don't even know why I didn't tell him I'd been warned never to go near the open one. This warning was always embellished by the story of a quarry man who had been killed after the sand had suddenly slid down over him, but we'd done it anyway.

I took off my coat, pulled up my skirt and slid all the way down the quarry that day, not only once but three times, and we loved every minute of it. The sand was soft and light after the warm summer, and it was only after I realised my navy knickers were covered with brown at the back and somehow the sand had filtered under the elastic and was making my skin itch. Afterwards, Ernest and I lay on the green grass at the top of the quarry. I stared at the fluffy white clouds and imagined small islands in a blue sea to swim in with just Ernest and I around. I didn't know what Ernest was thinking about, probably more chips. However later he twisted some long stems of grass into the shape of a ring and shyly handed it to me.

All good things must be paid for I guess, and I willingly accepted the hard hand-smacks across my buttocks and legs for going near the quarry and eating chips, but I resented the whacks for upsetting Aunt Ada. I didn't often get smacked. It had to be something truly bad, and mam's hand could be extremely hard. I wondered if something else was worrying her, as she was quite quick to yell at me even for the smallest of things, and try as I might to not to place my foot on her freshly stoned step or bring mud onto the kitchen floor, she still snapped at me.

Aunt Ada seemed to be around a good deal after that and she and mam would often stop talking whenever I entered the room. I think Vera next door came down with the germ too, and because mam probably didn't want me to catch it, she wouldn't let me baby sit or even pop around to see her.

Chapter 8

A series of loud knocks shattered my dream and I sprang out of bed. Mam was already in the hallway trying to comfort sobbing Ethel. I sat on the top of the stairs wondering if a bomb had hit next door, before I realised it was a daft thought as our house was alright and the only noise I'd heard was the thumping on the front door.

Apparently old Mr Grace had suddenly died after a coughing attack and no one knew what to do. After calming Ethel down a degree or two, mam slipped on a coat from the hallstand over her nightie and led Ethel back next door. I too followed also donning a coat over my night attire and, as Wellington boots seemed to be the only footwear close by, I put these on as well. Nobody appeared aware of my presence as they hovered around Mrs Grace.

The first thing my mam did was to get Ethel to put the kettle on; adding, 'and if you have a wee bit of sugar put away, I think this is the time to use it,' noticing Ethel's hands shaking. In fact they were shaking so much that I feared for the cups staying on their saucers. Then Doreen was sent to call the doctor from Mr Clayton's house at number six. Mr Clayton, being a policeman had a telephone in his own house, so it saved Doreen the walk to the nearest public phone box.

I had taken off my Wellingtons by the front door and padded upstairs after mam in my bare feet that were by now freezing cold. I didn't get far up the stairs before mam turned and saw me.

'Go outside see if the doctor's coming,' she said sternly.

I knew it was to get rid of me for a while, so I sighed and turned around. I had to pull the now cold boots over my feet again and as I stepped outside, I noticed the curtains on the other side of the road moving and faces peering around them. Doreen came back shortly after with P.C Clayton, and I followed them back inside.

P.C. Clayton asked questions like 'When he'd dropped down dead what was he doing?' and, 'is he still lying on the floor?'

My ears pricked up at that. I'd imagined him lying peacefully in bed, not stretched out on the floor, stiff and very dead in the room above. P.C. Clayton was certainly a good man to have around. He walked about, his black notebook and pencil in hand and in full uniform too, keeping his hat and shoes on all the time.

We heard the doctor's car, and our police constable nearly knocked my mam over to get to the door. I think he was a bit put out when the doctor remarked he needed no help with Mr Grace, as the old gentleman was light enough for him to lift onto the bed. That started old Mrs Grace crying again and more tea was called for.

'It seems Mr Grace died of a heart attack,' said Dr McKenzie in very official voice. He then wrote out a prescription for a tonic for Mrs Grace before deciding maybe Ethel needed one too.

'Have you got anyone?' he asked my mam as if it were her responsibility.

Mam nodded.

It was quite a while before I found out the 'anyone' was Mrs Winterbottom who looked after those that entered the world and those that departed it.

A few days later I was allowed to say my last goodbyes to old Mr Grace. He lay on the dining room table, in a coffin of course. P.C. Clayton had helped carry the table into the front room or parlour as we called it. I wasn't at all frightened because he, Mr Grace that is or was as the occasion warrants, looked very nice. He lay stiff-like in a nice wooden coffin. He had his best suit on and a clean shirt with a black tie, his moustache looked as if it had been neatly trimmed and he had a lovely straight parting in his hair. His hands were crossed beautifully across his chest and I noticed his non-smoking hand covered the nicotine stains on his other fingers. Mam actually kissed his forehead but I couldn't manage to do more than place a small bunch of Michaelmass daises by his hands.

Every one was in black. It's surprising what the blackout material can be shaped into when the need arises. I was allowed to see old Mr Grace in his coffin but not allowed to see him buried. Mam said it wasn't fitting for a child, so I spent the day of the funeral holding wool for grandma to wind into a large ball. My knitting lesson later didn't get anywhere. I have enough trouble doing knit-one purl-one on two needles, but grandma had grand ideas of me knitting socks on four needles for 'our lads away in the war'. She gave up on me and made a cup of tea with that awful sterilised milk. It always made me feel quite sick.

Frank Cole came home on leave before joining another unit. He looked very grand and grown up in his uniform, although his haircut did nothing for his large ears. Aunt Ada was over the moon to see him and his face was quickly covered in lipstick, which nearly matched his red face that flushed so much with pleasure.

I must admit Aunt Ada had gone to town on the way she looked, her blond hair was now blond all the way down to the roots with her hair cut in a pageboy style. She had a lovely loose top over a short black skirt with a little slit down the side. I loved the high platform shoes that did justice to her legs. Her extra weight suited her; she told me she couldn't stop eating when she knew Frank was coming home. I think myself that Frank thought his uniform had something to do with this newfound attraction of Aunt Ada's and couldn't believe his great fortune when Aunt Ada said she just couldn't bare the thought of his leaving unless they were married. And that was that.

Aunt Ada and Frank were married by special license. Grandma and my mam did justice to the happy event by laying out a wedding breakfast. Everyone it seems had given a little bit of this and that, so on the day the table looked like a feast fit for a king. Someone had made butter by spending hours shaking cream in bottle, at least that was part of a conversation I'd overheard. Eggs had been obtained from someone's cousin who owned a farm, probably Vera's relatives. Mrs Grace had sent around some sugar and fresh vegetables from the garden, which I didn't eat because I remembered the rag and bone man's horse and Mr Grace's bucket.

The wedding cake was just beautiful with pink and white icing and the ingredients inside made as much of a fruitcake as there could be in the wartime. Although I found a plum taste was quite strong in my mouth afterwards. William Taylor brought in some champagne and I caught Aunt Ivy and him drinking from the same glass and looking deep into each other's eyes. I suspected it wouldn't belong before I was blessed with yet another uncle. Frank's father got drunk and his mam cried and said he was too young to marry, until gran pointed out if he was old enough to die for his country, then he was old enough to be married. With that and a lot of nodding heads, a line was formed across the floor for the hokey-cokey.

William had managed to get a roll of cotton material. It was green with white spots and with Aunt Ivy's skill at the sewing machine I now wore a rather pretty dress. Standing there in my new apparel with ringlets tied in bows and sipping champagne I really wished Ernest Heath could see me. Everything was going well until the sirens started up. The droning sound of distant planes could be heard with the accompanying thunder of anti aircraft fire. For a moment there was complete silence as if all ears were tuning into that of the single rushing sound that was quickly followed by an explosion that shook the whole house. I heard someone shout 'air raid shelter,' and the next moment I was being dragged along, still holding my glass. The whole wedding party spent the night crammed into a rather small shelter next door to gran's. I managed to fall asleep and someone covered me with a hairy coat that made me itch for days after.

By dawn, a bedraggled wedding party crept out into the daylight. The big Catholic Church down the road had been hit and all that was left standing was the wall that held the rose window with the sun shining through it and the blue haze from the still smoking ruins. Frank left two days later. We didn't go to Crewe station as

Aunt Ada's germ had come back again. Mam's mood had improved since the wedding and she even went on to hint at the possibilities of another one in the near future. We even got a long letter from dad with lots of kisses for me.

I was by now enjoying the art school and quickly made new friends, although unfortunately none of us lived near to each other. William Taylor actually pinned one of my drawings in his office. It was of a glamour girl sitting on a high stool with her legs crossed and I'd written Ivy underneath.

One day, as I was coming home from school I passed the little café in the town and idly looked in through the window. I was surprised to see my mam sitting very close to Ada's yank, and both were immersed in deep conversation. My mam's hand was covering his and he was listening to her intently. My heart nearly stopped beating. I was growing older now and knew about women getting lonely when their men folk were away, but surely not my own mam and Aunt Ada too. I was stunned. This was all too much on my home turf.

I took off and walked along the riverside that ran through the town with a face like thunder. A walk totally forbidden to me because of the loneliness of the path that was flanked on the one side by a very dense wood and by the winding deep river on the other side. If you looked across the often-flooded river, there was nothing to see but soggy fields with a few cows wading there. It was a lonely place to be. Sometimes a friend and I would take a dare and, starting at the bridge, would run along that forbidden pathway, but generally saw nobody but courting couples who always looked startled as we ran past.

Today I walked slowly, head down and numbed in every way. Part of me wanted to deny what I'd seen and tried to blot out the image of mam's hand clutching his with tears in her eyes. I felt sick and cold as I walked up the stone steps at the end of the lane. I even passed a group of old men sitting outside the Crown and Anchor.

Ernest Heath called out to me from the other side of the road but I just kept going, watching my feet as they moved one after the other. I don't know how I got home but I did and got the key from under the mat at the back door. It must have been two hours that I sat looking up at small crack that had started in the corner of the ceiling. When my mam eventually came home we didn't talk, she seemed preoccupied and sat drinking a cup of tea and looking out of the window. Once she turned and asked me;

'Everything alright Rita?' I didn't answer and she didn't even notice.

The only thing that saved me from losing my control and confronting her was Vera. Vera had become quite fat and didn't go out so much. Which began first I don't know, but my baby-sitting was non-existent and mam kept finding me jobs to do whenever Vera came around. Mam and Vera were on better terms now than earlier and they would sigh a lot. Sometimes mam's voice was a little accusing 'til Vera cried, then there were muffled tones of comfort.

A few days later, Vera's daughter Juanita came running into our house without even knocking which mam didn't like one bit.

'Quick Mrs Goodwin,' she screamed 'Something's happening to my mam.'

Mam jumped up and raced around next door. When I say around, it was more through a hole in the hedge that had been formed by many past visits. Of course I was hard on her heels and was second to witness just how ill Vera really was. She was sitting on the couch holding her stomach, her legs apart and it looked as if she had pissed herself. Juanita and Wilhelmina, Vera's children, just stood goggling, their faces white.

'Alright, it's going to be alright.' Mam was talking in a smoothing voice she puts on when she tries to be calm.

'Rita, go and fetch Mrs Winterbottom and tell her to be quick.' Then, noting the young children were also there, she added, 'and take them with you and ask Mrs Winterbottom if her Gladys can care for them until it's over.'

I took off like a bat out of hell, tugging the two little blonde girls along, their long pigtails flapping behind them. I thought Mrs

Winterbottom would never come; I banged and banged on her door 'til I heard the lock slide back. Gasping, I relayed the message.

'Vera's dying, she pissed herself and the kids have to come here.'

I knew I'd got it jumbled up but Mrs Winterbottom seemed to understand and shouted to their Gladys, whose ample arms quickly enfolded the kids to her huge frame.

Mrs Winterbottom's coat was on in a jiffy and, grabbing a leather bag, we walked briskly up the road. Usually she rides a bike with a basket on the front, but I noticed the bike was leaning against her garden fence with a flat tire. Mr Winterbottom was scratching his head, trying to find the best way to find the puncture and repair it. When we got back to Vera's, she was nowhere to be seen, but I didn't have time to panic before hearing mam's voice coming from the parlour.

'She's in here.'

Following behind Mrs Winterbottom so closely that I seemed almost attached to her, I was amazed at the changes that had taken place in the parlour since I last was there. Normally there was nothing in it apart from an old carpet and the girls' toys, and, oh yes I lie; there was an old wicker chair in the corner from which I often supervised the order of the girl's play.

Now, in addition to the wicker chair, it seems a bed had been brought down from the box room and a table that used to be in the dining room now stood beside the bed and a fire was actually lit in the fireplace, although an airing maid was hiding most if it. Towels were draped around airing and what appeared to be a little nightie.

Mrs Winterbottom suddenly realised I was behind her and quickly shooed me out; banging the door closed behind me. I sat on the kitchen step, watching the kettle and a saucepan with scissors in it, come to the boil. Mam came out, filling two bowls of hot water and carrying them in together with the scissors and some old newspapers.

I had no idea what was happening, I just kept praying that mam wouldn't catch the germ Vera had. I'd forgive her anything. I even daydreamed of ways of killing the yank like letting down his jeep tyres, but that didn't seem to be a good enough plot, as he'd know before he drove off. I got no further than scheming out a way to give him chocolate with rat poison in it, when I heard a faint cry. At first I thought a cat had got in, then it started again and I knew there was now a baby in the house. Mrs Winterbottom came out and put something wrapped in newspaper on the fire before turning to me.

'Would you like to see the new baby?'

'Baby! Whose is it?' I asked

'Vera's of course, she's had a little girl.' Mrs Winterbottom stared at me for a moment as if I was a little dim.

I followed her into the room where Vera was, and there it was, all wrapped up tightly in a linen cloth, its black hair standing up like a chimney sweep's brush.

'It doesn't look like the girls' I remarked staring at the black mop. Vera began to cry and mam gave me a little slap and ushered me out of the room. She grabbed me by the arm and gave me a shake.

'It's just like the girls' she said, 'Don't you go saying it isn't. Sometimes babies are born with black hair and it turns another colour later.' Then she relented and ruffled my hair.

'See what happened to yours and you came out with black hair.'

That was something I didn't know and spent the rest of the day looking at my mop of mousy hair and wondering what I would look like with straight black hair. We slept at Vera's for nearly two weeks whilst Vera lay in bed with the baby who they called Jessie. No neighbours came to visit the new baby, apart from Ethel who cooed and slobbered over it all the time; that is until my mam asked her to let it sleep.

The girls thought their baby sister was a real live doll and would spend ages rocking the pram, which now stood by the bed. Vera got stronger and got up, but returned back to bed for a few days not feeling well after a letter came to say Mr Van Dooninck was coming home on leave. He was in the army and had been away for a year. I guess it would be a wonderful homecoming what with the new baby and all.

Chapter 9

I was walking down our road one morning when Mr Van Doorninck was coming towards me. I knew it was he at once from his photograph that had suddenly appeared on Vera's desk. Long strides and a very straight back gave him a military look even if he hadn't been wearing his uniform. He marched rather than walked, and the heavy kit bag he was carrying swung in rhythm with his gait. He must have recognised me at once for the bag was put down as he came to a halt.

'Rita Goodwin?' It was more of a question than a statement and sounded unusually nice with his Dutch accent. We stood looking at each other for a second before I nodded my head. Now his feet were parted and he placed his hands on his hips.

'Well I'll be damned.' He looked me up and down. 'You've grown.'

Again his sentences were clipped and to the point, and I didn't really know how to answer, so I pulled at my tunic and hoped it covered my knees. I was only too aware of my growth and hoped it would stop or I'd end up a giant.

While this one-sided conversation was going on I was amazed how Vera's girls resembled him. The blond hair was a perfect match and so was the fresh pink complexion and pale blue eyes. He broke the spell by asking,

'How are things at your house?'

Well that opened a torrent of information and I found myself rambling on about Aunt Ada's marriage, Uncle Joseph being called up, my school and the bombing of St Mary's Church. He never moved a muscle of his face until I had finished then he laughed,

'Well now I know all this, I won't have to buy the local rag.'

The local rag was the town's newspaper and told of all the goings on, but wasn't likely to print my news, so I looked at him oddly before guessing he was joking. He picked up his bag and looked towards his house.

'Can't wait to see my two girls,' he said with a happy smile.

'Three,' I amended.

'You're right young lady, but I daren't call Vera a girl because she likes to be considered a woman,' he chuckled and made to walk off.

'I was meaning your Jessie.' I thought it very unfair he should leave her out just because she was a baby.

'Jessie?' he turned around with a quizzical look.

'Your new baby,' I answered surprised.

'Baby?' By now there was a real look of bewilderment on his face.

I was getting annoyed now and wondered if he understood English words at all; so I almost shouted back at him,

'Yes, your baby, the one Vera had three weeks ago.' Something made me want to make her more real to him so I added: 'She has lovely black hair and big brown eyes.'

Mam had once told me that men sometimes come home from the battlefield shell-shocked. I really believed Mr Van Doorninck had had a relapse at that very moment and I thought it wise not to hang around in case it got worse. As I rounded the corner, I looked back to see him quickening his step towards his house and I thought of how Vera would be so glad to see him.

I often did shopping for mam and knew which shops she liked best. Gran liked the Co-op for her groceries but my mam preferred Boyce Adams. Today the queue wasn't that long; I must have hit on a good time. I watched as the shop assistant weighed out our ration of cheese, and hoped the extra piece he usually placed on the top was a big one. I always considered that piece that made up the exact weight was my reward for doing the shopping. Unfortunately Mrs Grace didn't always agree with me when I did errands for her.

I called in the newsagent's to pick up my Beano and looked around to see if I could spy any of the magazines Vera had. Mr Wilson, who owned the shop, was sitting on a stool behind the counter reading a magazine that had brown paper folded over its cover. I plopped down my Beano and asked,

'Have you any of those magazines with pictures of pin-ups in?' Mr Wilson's head popped up and his reading material was quickly tucked under the counter.

'Cheeky thing.' He glared at me and looked to see if I'd anything else under the Beano and said 'That's tuppence.'

As I couldn't remember what Vera's magazines were called I decided to let it go. I ran home, the basket hooked over my arm, humming softly to myself:

'Run rabbit, run rabbit, run, run, run.' A tune which I had heard coming from the back of the newsagents shop. It was quite catchy.

Our path ran alongside the one to Vera's house and only a small hedge divided them. The kitchen window faced ours and Vera's window was open, allowing loud voices to be heard from inside. Juanita and Wilhelmina were sitting on their back door step playing with dolls. Jessie was screaming her tiny lungs out from her pram that stood near the hedge. I lingered by our back door and stood on our step leaning out to get a better view, but mam pulled me in and closed the door giving me a little shake.

'It's nowt to do with us,' she said sternly. But I noticed her eyes were focused on our kitchen window that gave a good view of next door.

Later I wanted to go next door, mainly to see those new dolls the two girls had, but mam told me to not dare leave the house. I understood really. It's only fair Mr Van Doorninck would want his family to himself for a while.

Our budgie died that night. He just fell off is perch and lay at the bottom of his cage with his feet in the air. I wanted to bury him in a box in the garden but mam just threw him on the fire. Poor Joey. I had christened him after Uncle Joseph. The feathers went first then he sizzled and turned black and smelled awful.

The next day I told my school friends about Joey and cried a little. It seemed appropriate as every one looked sad and gave mournful sounds. Beryl Perkins gave me some of her chewing gum. People are very kind so I walked home with her after school, although it meant getting off the bus one stop before mine. Trying to take a short cut home I decided to go down the lane that was known as the Cockshuts. It was a very narrow cobbled lane that ran between a high wall of the churchyard and some old buildings on the other side. The lane's name came from an old Saxon word meaning; where birds were trapped. The lane cut out a big piece from my walk home. It started between rows of terraced houses and came out by the church. Halfway along the lane I was stunned to see my Aunt Ada and that damned yank. They looked as is they were arguing and she was crying into his shoulder. I retraced my steps feeling very frustrated and my legs were tired. I sat on the church wall looking mournfully into the churchyard. I came to the conclusion he must have bewitched all the females of our family, apart from gran that is, who no one could bewitch. I spent quite a while contemplating ways of getting rid of the yank; once and for all. I gazed into the ancient graveyard that held the oldest of graves and tombs. Our ancestors had planted four yew trees in each corner hundreds of years ago and I knew the yew trees were there to keep evil spirits away. I thought of rushing down the lane waving a piece of yew at him, but I was just too tired.

I pulled my thoughts out of the realm of my imagination and tried to concentrate on a more practical solution. Going around and around the problem, I kept coming back to the simplest of solutions. Yes, I just had to confront him and tell him if he didn't leave my Aunt Ada and my mam alone, I'd just have to tell my dad or Frank and they would sort him out. I admit I had reservations about bringing my dad into it for he was not half as big as the yank and Frank Cole wasn't a fighter at all. Still once I'd cemented the idea together, my energy seemed to return to my legs and I set off home the long way around, getting in just before dusk came; which meant a telling-off and promise to always come straight home in future.

With the night-light beside me, I began to plan my way of meeting the yank and pleading with him, which would require me to write a note. Using my very best handwriting and mam's fountain pen, I composed my bait.

> *Could you meet me by the quarry*
> *gate tomorrow at 7-00 pm?*
> *Yours Sincerely,*
> *R.*

I had been clever enough to just sign R. I wanted him to think he was meeting my mam but didn't feel too good about being so deceptive. This way I wasn't telling a lie really. The place of meeting was another good idea of mine. The original road up to the quarry led past the side of the American's billet. It was just a dirt road overgrown and lumpy as two deep ridges had formed over the years from lorry wheels. It was a bit of a long walk but at the entrance to the sand quarry was the gate. Not really a gate in the ordinary sense, more a very long bar supported on poles at each end. A torn piece of cardboard bore the writing in red paint:

'DANGER – KEEP OUT'.

Not that it meant much to us kids and it didn't stop us ducking under it and climbing up the side of the quarry along the path that ran along to the highest point. It was always from this point where we would slide down. For me to get to the meeting place from home would be no problem. All I had to do was slip through the gap in our hedge at the bottom of our garden, walk through the old quarry, green with grass and up the path to come out from a small knoll of trees and brambles to the top of the second quarry, and then nip down the side edge to the gate.

I read and re-read the note, tucked it into my pocket and popped around next door. Ethel was scrubbing the kitchen floor. She did it every Saturday whether it was dirty or not. I think she took 'Cleanliness next to Godliness' far too much to heart Still I was glad it was her.

I asked if I could borrow Mr Grace's old bike, it was never used and was always propped up by the garden shed. Ethel nodded and scrubbed harder at a stubborn stain that had been there for years. I think it was the original colour of the tile but didn't want to confuse her.

The crossbar of the bike was a bit high but with careful balancing I managed to go in a straight line. God must have known what I was doing was truly right and had worked one of his miracles; for the yank was leaning against the back of a jeep smoking and there was no one else around. I promised God I'd be a missionary for doing this for me. I jumped off the bike, thrust my note into the yank's hand and pedalled off as though the devil was after me.

Mam was out when I got home. There was a note telling me to pay the window-cleaner with a shilling beside it. Our window cleaner was a bit of a nosey-parker and mam always closed the bedroom curtains when he was due, which was once a fortnight. He'd gone to school with mam in the olden days and I think he fancied her a bit. He's the only person I ever saw ride a bike with a long ladder strapped to it and a bucket dangling from the handlebars.

He eventually came; looking disappointed when I told him my mam was out. I filled his bucket and listened to the squeak of his shammy-leather on our windows. I emptied his bucket and handed him his shilling. Vera said he must be a millionaire, but didn't look very much like one to me, dressed in trousers that hung below his protruding stomach and his green cardigan buttoned across by its only remaining button.

Mam came home in style. Dr. McKenzie had given her a lift as he was going her way she said. It sounded a bit daft, as there was no road that continued past ours. Our road ended in a field. Still it was nice of him as she was wearing her tight skirt and high-heeled shoes and her feet must have been tired.

Sleep deluded me later as my mind was going over what I should say to the yank. Did I have to cry, plead or what. I was still thinking when sleep overtook me and I dreamt the yank was offering me chocolate.

Barlow's cock across the road woke me up and I started thinking again until I had rehearsed my speech to my satisfaction. The chill morning air made me shiver, so I lifted the bedding over my head and pretended I was dead and lying in a coffin, that is 'til I needed to breathe. I can never understand why my mam opens windows all the time and the bathroom was freezing. I leaned over the sink to pull the window catch towards me and heard cooing sounds. I leaned over further to see Mr Van Doorninck rocking young Jessie in her pram and making those silly noises at her. Vera was standing close by, grinning like a Cheshire cat.

Vera popped around later for a bit of sugar. She stayed an hour and of course mam got into the cup reading again. There was the usual good luck, extra money and a surprise in her readings. I wondered if mam had got the ending muddled up somehow with Vera's husband's good fortune. Mam popped off to the corner shop for her fags. Returning home again it looked as though she had forgotten something, because she kept looking down at a piece of paper in her hand and frowning.

Chapter 10

All afternoon my eyes kept flicking towards the clock on the mantelpiece. Time was passing slowly and the hands hardly appeared to move. To take my mind off my venture, I got out my old pleated tunic and began sewing long tacking stitches up the crumpled pleats. I also considered lowering the hem 'til I realized there was nothing to lower. Mam became cross, but gave up when I almost burst out crying. It became important for me to iron the tunic, although I knew I'd never wear it again. The iron went over the fire on its stand, and a blanket with a flannel sheet on top of it went on the dining room table. Mam wet a tea towel and I steamed the pleats so sharp they looked more like knife-edges. My school tie got pressed too, which would prove a good thing because it always looked like a piece of rag around my neck from my many attempts at trying to tie a Windsor knot.

We had lunch, tomatoes toasted on bread and two squashy black plums. Waiting for the right moment, I told her I was going to see Barbara Potts. Now where that came from I don't know, as Barbara Potts and I didn't even speak to each other. Mam said 'no staying out late', as she was going out too, but wouldn't be all that long away.

The sirens had been silent for a week after the bad bombing of the iron works at Shelton Bar. German planes frequently flew over the Potteries but because of the smoke haze from the pot banks, had trouble finding the railway lines and other targets in the district. St Mary's must have been a stray bomb because, apart from the cotton mills, our town didn't have anything worth destroying it seems; not like the Rolls Royce factory at Crewe or the city of Manchester.

I had been standing in a bread queue a week earlier with my mam, and Barbara Potts's mam was in front of us. She was very much interested in education ever since Barbara Potts started at the grammar school. She eyed mam up and down and said the Germans wouldn't bother with the Taylor's factory because it wasn't important to the war effort. It was obvious she was getting a dig in because Aunt Ivy was driven around town in William's car a lot. Mam didn't bat an eyelid. She just told Mrs Potts if the Jerries knew how well the factory was doing in the war effort, it would be first on their list.

The clock fingers had started to move much faster now and each time I looked over to it, I began to get a funny feeling in my stomach. At five o'clock I couldn't wait any longer and started to put on my gaberdine. I had intended pulling on my Wellington boots in case the ground got wet from the evening dew, but decided I couldn't run in them if I had to, so exchanged them for my black pair of shoes with a single strap that buttoned on the side.

I nipped through the hedge and walked quickly through the old quarry that resembled a natural valley more than what it really was. It was still quite light, chilly but fresh, and with the birds twittering in the bushes I didn't feel at all afraid, for it had always been my playground and I knew all the nooks and crannies around. The ground underfoot was soft under the long grass, which made me miss seeing the root of a bush that had surfaced before me. It caught the strap across my shoe and I felt it snap. The little round button had broken off and fell somewhere in the grass. It took me ages to find it, which was necessary, as we didn't have any more like it in our button box at home. The strap flapped wildly as I walked on and my heel kept popping out of my shoe. So much for thinking I could run in these shoes. They now made my walking slower than before. I knew it must be now near to seven o'clock but having no watch I was lost for time.

I thought of my grandpa's gold watch hanging from its chain with the gold sovereigns attached to it. Gran had showed it to me once, how I wished I had it with me now. My mind always wanders when I am anxious. A bramble branch caught my gaberdine and I struggled for its repossession. I began to climb a small rise on the path and had great difficulty holding on to the back of my shoe.

'This wasn't how it was supposed to be.' I muttered to myself. Instead of being calm and very controlled I was feeling like a total wreck and probably looked like one too.

I was coming up to the cluster of trees and could now just about see the gate down the hill of the second quarry.

There was the yank leaning against one of the posts. I was just about to hurry as much as I could; the trees still hiding his view of me. So I was surprised when he snubbed out his fag and began walking up the side of the quarry and was even more surprised when into my vision I spotted another figure walking towards him.

I lay down in the shadows and watched him. His hands were tucked into the pockets of his trousers now, and his shoulders moved forward as he climbed. He appeared so big I was almost relieved that someone had decided on taking a stroll. Then it became obvious that the other person wasn't there just by chance, but was expecting to meet him.

I crawled forward to get a better look and couldn't believe what I saw. There my mam was as large as life. She'd stopped, waiting for him to join her. I felt sick with apprehension and my mind raced with thoughts of what she was doing there. I know he would think she'd written the note. But how on earth did she know anything about it? The thing to do now was to keep well out of sight and I thanked God again for breaking the strap of my shoe. It's true; He does work in mysterious ways. I haven't as yet worked His plan out, but hoped I'd get plenty of brownie points for promising to be a nun if it all turned out right.

Instead of walking back to the gate after meeting her; mam and the yank continued to walk to the top of the quarry, both still within my sight and sometimes I was able to catch the odd word or two. I stayed as still as I could and watched as they stood talking very close to the edge of the quarry at its highest point.

Mam shouted something at him, and he stood still raising his arms in a gesture of denial. They stood arguing for ages and I noticed the evening was creeping in and a light mist was forming. Mam was now pleading, her hands banging against his chest.

A thorn dug into my leg and during that brief moment of taking my eyes off them both, something happened. Mam was now running off towards the gate and the yank had gone. I ran too, holding my shoe in one hand. I didn't follow her but made for the spot where they had been arguing. I looked over the side of the quarry and watched in horror as sand-slip after sand-slip covered the solitary figure that lay at the bottom. After a few moments there was not a sign of him left.

I cannot remember how long I stood there with mist beginning to surround me, but long enough to realize there was no movement below. This was the worst thing I could ever have imagined, a murder right there before my eyes. I had actually witnessed my own mam push the yank down over the edge of the quarry. It was no accident. I saw her with her hands against his chest and she hadn't made any attempt to help him once he'd fallen over the edge.

I ran away in shock. Somewhere on the way home I lost my shoe, my legs got scratched and I could feel trickles of blood running down. Once I stopped and ran my hand down my leg only to see the redness on my fingers. A branch hit my face and I pushed the offending obstacle away. I automatically retraced my steps home. Everything appeared at a distance as if I wasn't there, just seeing and feeling, but somehow only as a witness. It was someone else there; someone other than me.

I had a dim memory later of sitting under our hedge, wishing a bomb would drop right on that very spot, but the Jerries were too busy killing more innocent people than me, but I knew I was the very cause of what had taken place.

I must have looked a sight as I stumbled through the back door. Grass and twigs all over me, blood on my legs and face, scratches down my legs, to say nothing of having only one shoe on. Mam went frantic the moment she saw me and shouted by the back door at the top of her voice for Vera, then she ushered me into the dining room, firing questions of me as she gathered the rug off the sofa and pulled it around me.

'What in hell's name has happened to you?' she screamed at the same time as she was hugging me to her.

I didn't answer. I tried but couldn't, for no sound would come out. I felt dumbstruck, all emotion gone and there was nothing left of me but an empty shell. Vera came charging in. She had a dressing gown on and curlers in her hair. She took one look at me and said,

'Bloody hell,' then just repeated it again. 'Bloody hell.'

Mam told Vera to make a cup of tea and not to be miserly with the sugar, while she went to fetch Constable Clayton. Vera nodded. She stared at me again and put the kettle on, then sat down in the opposite chair not knowing what to do but saying,

'Oh luv, it will be alright.'

Of course I knew nothing would ever be all right again so I didn't even nod. The next thing Constable Clayton was standing over me with his notebook and pencil. It's a funny thing how clear some things hit you when all the rest is a haze. I'd thought it was nice of him to put on his uniform and his hat, even though he was off duty. He stood over me looking very large and commanding.

'What did he do to you?' he asked pencil poised over his notebook.

'What sort of question is that?' Mam objected, 'can't you see the girl's in shock.'

I didn't want to look at the person that had just committed murder, so I pulled the blanket over my face.

'I'll kill him, I'll kill the bastard,' mam wailed.

Constable Clayton asked if she had some brandy in the house. It was good for shock he said, and when mam pulled a little bottle out of the cupboard, he said we all could do with some in our tea.

The front door knocker went and Vera came back with Dr. McKenzie who straightway ushered the constable and Vera out before setting his black bag on the table.

'I've got to examine her Rose,' he said, taking off his coat and bringing something out of his bag. He made me drink some medicine that made me feel like I was floating on water. My mind and body felt so relaxed, but I remember him saying

'Help me lay her on the sofa,' then I was in the clouds, with angel's fingers caressing parts of my body that mam calls private.

'No need to worry Rose, she's fine. The bugger must have got frightened and run away.' Then I felt his face near my ear.

'Rita, was it anyone you know?' he asked. I shook my head and rolled it from side to side, trying to get the face of the yank out of my mind.

'Oh God.' Mam started to cry and through a hazy veil, I saw her place her head on Dr. McKenzie's shoulder, as he stroked her hair. I must have drifted away into a deep sleep. When I eventually opened my eyes it was to see a tin bath on the pegged rug in front of the fire. Mam was adding steaming water from the kettle to it, and then testing it with her elbow. Not a word was spoken as she placed a bar of soap on a saucer beside it and a scrubbing brush was put on the hearth and a towel hung over the back of the chair. Mam made me undress right where I was sitting and hurried out with all my clothes as if they were contaminated. Not only did she wash me all over, but she also used the scrubbing brush on me as if she'd never get me clean.

After a cup of hot milk, I was put on the sofa with one of my bed pillows for my head to rest on. Constable Clayton came around three times that week as I lay there half sleeping and staring at the ceiling. His notebook was as blank at the end of the week as when he'd first came around. Every time he came I feared it was my mam he'd come for, but he never mentioned the yank or of mam's whereabouts on that fateful night. Aunt Ivy called for five minutes, but looked very ill at ease and suggested mam keep it in the family. Mam replied,

'Bugger the Taylors; I'd just like to get my hands on that bloke.'

Aunt Ivy went home and mam said she'd play cards with me like we used to in the long evenings. However, I just didn't want to talk to her yet. I couldn't forgive her for not showing any remorse for what she had done.

P.C. Clayton came around for the last time holding my shoe, and asking mam to identify it. She looked at me queerly for a moment, then her colour returned when he said it was found by farmer Jones, whose dog had brought it home. Two days later there was a pair of brand new patent leather black shoes waiting for me by the hearth.

I stayed at home from school for three weeks and during that time I prayed as I never have prayed before that the yank would never be found and mam would someday be forgiven. I then I prayed twice as hard for myself who was, after all, the cause of my mam committing the murder.

It must have paid off for as the weeks rolled by, nothing was discovered and life went on as normal. Mam must be incredibly strong at putting things out of her mind for she grew brighter and laughed more, whilst I suffered from black thoughts and became more insular. The only thing that changed noticeably in my life was that on no account was I allowed out after dusk, and for a whole month mam would meet me whenever I went to any of my friends. Dr. McKenzie was very kind and popped around to see mam even when I was at school. I knew that because once he'd left his gloves and mam had to put them on her dressing table so they wouldn't get misplaced.

It's difficult not to change when a dreadful secret lies buried in your heart and I began to see how it affected those around me. Gran and mam would share a reticent look and one or the other would make a remark like,

'It's her age.' or 'It's not a nice thing to happen to a young girl.'

People in town, some I didn't even know, would ask, 'How are you luv?' and gaze at me as if I was half-witted when I didn't answer.

Not talking very much didn't stop me noticing that Aunt Ada had grown fatter and Aunt Ivy was looking quite bonny too. No one was the least surprised when my Aunt Ivy announced she and William were getting married, although gran was far from pleased when Aunt Ivy told us they were getting wed at the Registry Office in Manchester and were not going to make a big fuss over it. Gran was real put out. I think she envisioned a better than most wedding meal, what with all the Taylor connections. Aunt Ada took the hump and said it was all right for some, then in the same breath said she would have Aunt Ivy's bedroom when she'd gone, because she'd need the extra space. She rubbed her tummy and glared at everyone to deny her the room. Gran snorted like she does when she's not pleased and asked me to pass her the whisky bottle as a wee dram always helped her arthritis.

Chapter 11

Aunt Ivy got married very quickly which wasn't too unusual during the wartime, although it was generally when the man had to leave for a long period. That wasn't the problem for William, but everyone seemed happy with the arrangement. Even gran was happy, after mam had had a quiet word with her.

It must have set Aunt Ada off for she began talking about when Frank was coming home again. She'd been writing to him a lot lately, and was marking off the days 'til he had a weekend pass before going to the real war. Both he and Uncle Joseph had finished their training in the South of England and hoped to get back home for a few days

I'd never seen Aunt Ada so thrilled when Frank knocked on gran's door. She couldn't do enough for him and kept placing his hand over her tummy. It was no secret anymore that she was pregnant and Frank was the father. He was like a kid with a new toy, all smiles and looked like the cat that had got the cheese. I suspect he couldn't believe that he and Aunt Ada were to be parents.

Frank left two days later nearly in tears at leaving, but Aunt Ada encouraged him to be brave and go and do his bit. She had a whisky with gran when he'd gone and sat looking at the ring on her finger and her hand on her tummy. No one went to see him off this time. Aunt Ada said it was too much with the baby coming and all, and gran didn't say anything.

When Uncle Joseph came home it wasn't the way any of us ever expected. There had been an accident where he was stationed. An ammunition dump had blown up. Uncle Joseph happened to be walking nearby and got badly wounded. He was lucky as the mate he was with was killed outright. Gran fretted and sent letter after letter to him in hospital, but never got a reply directly from him. Some nurse wrote back and said she was writing for him and just put down what he told her which wasn't very much. Gran thought there must be something wrong with his hands and got quite upset and suggested she ought to go to the hospital herself, which we knew she wouldn't as she'd never been out of our town in all her life.

Joseph did arrive back at gran's in due course in an army vehicle with a red cross on it. I was there the day he arrived home and a man walked him up the drive. It was very plain to see why he needed to have help. A thick white bandage was wrapped around his eyes. Gran was beside herself and didn't know what to do so she talked extra loud to him.

'Ah Mam, I'm blind not deaf,' he said in a monotonous voice, as if he'd repeated it many times before.

Aunt Ada actually relinquished her comfortable chair and patted a cushion behind his head before sitting on a stool and holding his hand. I do believe the tears in her eyes were quite genuine. Gran's certainly were for they rolled down her cheeks. Mam asked if Annie knew he was home.

'No, it's no use; she'll not want someone like me around now.' He turned his face and I caught a glimpse of an ugly scar protruding from under his bandage.

A week later his photo was splashed over the front page of our local paper. 'War Hero Blinded.' was the headline. It said nothing of it being an accident; just that he'd been blinded by an explosion and that others around him had been killed. No one in the family argued with the paper and Uncle Joseph couldn't read it. Dr. McKenzie took Uncle Joseph's bandage off and had a good look into his eyes with his torch. He told gran to sit down, and then told us all Uncle Joseph's eyes had been badly damaged and there was no chance he'd ever see again. It was an awful moment and everyone talked in hushed tones as if it wasn't right to talk normally. There was a lot of scarring about his eyes and on the upper part of his cheek. He looked different in one way but Uncle Joseph was still very much there, especially when he took off his uniform and replaced it with his own clothes.

Annie Cooke, his girlfriend, had seen his photo in the paper and came around right away, and although Uncle Joseph kept turning his head away, she insisted on holding his hand tightly. She was a quiet little thing, pale eyes and long thin mousy hair, a lot more mousy than mine. She wasn't pretty or yet plain; just somewhere in the middle. She wore no make-up and it wouldn't have looked right on her anyway. She always wore a twin set with a plain skirt and flat shoes, but Annie Cooke was kind. She was just about the sweetest and kindest person I ever knew.

'Annie will keep him going,' confided gran while I helped wash up a few teacups. There didn't seem to be any point of washing up things not immediately needed was gran's general philosophy, so the dirty plates and things often stayed where they were.

William Taylor came over often and walked Joseph round and around the room 'til he knew where everything was, then walked him down the drive and back 'til he felt comfortable doing it for himself. I'll always remember William for his kindness to Uncle Joseph. Aunt Ivy said William felt bad at not being in the war, especially when he looked at Joseph.

When anyone asked my gran how her Ivy was taking to living at the Big House, gran's voice became a little posh and she swanked about how nice it was. Gran even asked for her groceries to be put on tick at the Co-op, something she'd never done before but she's also smart and always made sure her dividend stamps were accounted for. When the Co-op man once asked mam if she wanted the stamps she said, 'Oh, give them to Russia,' which I understood many years later meant give then to the Russian War effort. Although at the time I doubted Russia really wanted a whole lot of stamps from our Co-op. They had terrible winters our teacher said so I think they'd have preferred some knitted socks.

The truth was however, that gran had never been up to the Big House. For that matter, William and Ivy had never invited any of us there. We called it "The Big House" for it was set high on a hill overlooking the river and built of the same brick and in the same square style as the cotton mill below it. Its real name was the Mill House. At least that's what was on the sign on the double gates that led up to it. But even to the townspeople around, it was always known as "The Big House". I called it that too. It sounded nice the way it rolled off one's lips, short and yet so expressive.

Over the next few months Annie Cooke had gone from being a shy timid person to one who knew what she was about. There was no messing with her when it came to Uncle Joseph. Getting hitched appeared to be catching and the Banns of Marriage for Uncle Joseph and Annie were now being read out in church each Sunday morning over the next three weeks.

'Joseph can do that for himself.' she said to anyone who tried to help him. In fact she became quite bossy. Yet during their time alone, I'd seen her kiss his scarred eyes and put his head into her chest just as a mother would do with a child. Annie really surprised everyone by insisting on a white wedding saying there wasn't anyone who could say they had no right to it. Aunt Ada left the room in a huff and Aunt Ivy went quite red. Mrs Cooke had saved her own wedding dress to be made into a christening dress she hoped to see on her first grandchild. Annie however had another use for it and insisted she get married in it herself. I thought the idea was quite mad as Mrs Cooke was very plump and I was quite amazed how well it fit Annie after a few nips and tucks in the right places. Annie looked beautiful standing there in gran's living room all dressed up. I wondered how she felt about her new husband not being able to see her and I know gran was thinking the same thing as she kept looking at him sitting quietly in a chair. They had one bridesmaid and that was me. Aunt Ivy made my dress, which to my mind didn't do me justice. The colour was all right and blue suited me, but the style could have been a little more grown up. As it was, the blue cotton was smocked just under the bust line, and the white lace collar with three pearl buttons down the front reminded me of the Van Doorninck girl's dresses. Fortunately my feet fitted into a pair of my aunt's white buckskin shoes that were fine 'til after the wedding when two big red blisters appeared on my heels.

Uncle Joseph wore his uniform and left his stick at home as Annie forbad him to use it on their special day. We all came down the isle after the service to smiles and tears, apart from that is, Annie's dad who was shaking his head, as if looking into the future.

All this time I was plagued by nightmares and would awake sometimes pouring with sweat. No one had discovered the yank's body and mam carried on as if nothing had ever happened apart from being very strict about the times I'd get home. Mam had taken to seeing some old friend each Thursday night, although she never mentioned whom it was. She made herself look extra nice on these evenings, which I think was a good sign that she was getting on with her own life.

We'd had three air raids in one week and the bedding was put under the table again. It was so bad one night and the 'warning' and the 'all clear' sirens seemed to go on repeatedly all night long. Vera brought the three girls around and we all sat in the dark apart from the glow of the coke fire. The radio was switched on and the volume turned up high so nothing was lost in the hearing. Liverpool had been hit bad. The Jerries were after the docks but streets of houses in Bootle had been flattened and there were many dead. Manchester was also targeted. It had been a night that would be remembered by those who had lost so much. Vera told us the Dutch were suffering much more but that piece of information didn't lift our spirits any. The only good piece of news was announced at the end. A special Dambuster Squadron of the RAF had successfully attacked and severely damaged three dams on the Ruhr with bouncing bombs. This we celebrated with a nice tot of Sanatogen tonic wine.

One Saturday I met Eunice in town and we strolled along the path that ran alongside the river with the flowerbeds of the park on the other. Flowerbeds were really a misnomer for no flowers existed, rather weeds with a few perennials that needed no special care.

A group of lads stood by one of the wooden benches that provided a resting place and at one time a place to view the scenery. They stood in a half circle. Some had their feet plonked on the bench, using their knees for rolling their fags. Peter Parker was handing out old cigarette stubs from a paper bag while Ernest handed each a thin piece of cigarette paper. Eunice and I sauntered past pretending they weren't there, but when Ernest called out my name I was quick to turn around.

'Fancy going to the pictures tonight?' he shouted, getting a chorus of hoots from his mates.

I knew Mrs Miniver was on at the Regal and was very tempted, but somehow I couldn't say yes. I didn't feel worthy of allowing myself any enjoyment. I shook my head and knew if I looked at him I'd see disappointment in his eyes, so I pulled Eunice along to quicken her step.

'But you used to like him.' Eunice shrugged my arm from hers and looked puzzled, for she was the only one that knew I'd had a crush on him for years. I wondered if I should have said yes and got on with my life like mam, but it was too late. Later that Saturday I saw Ernest standing in the picture queue with Barbara Potts. I suffered a deep depression for a whole week that worried mam so much, she got Dr. McKenzie to call and give me a tonic.

Chapter 12

Aunt Ada's baby son was born in the middle of the night at gran's. By the time mam and I arrived to welcome the new addition to our family, Aunt Ada was sitting up in bed drinking a glass of milk. Gran said everything was straightforward and Mrs Winterbottom had said Ada could produce a dozen like that with no trouble.

My aunt looked smug and asked for her baby to be handed to her. Gran fetched her grandson and spent a few moments holding him like a precious object before laying him in his mother's arms. I couldn't see much of him as the linen sheet enclosed him like a cocoon and all I saw was a wrinkled red face and a tuft of dark hair. New babies can be pretty ugly in my estimation, but nobody else agreed and it was all 'darling this' and 'darling that' until he got fed up himself and balled his eyes out.

Aunt Ada unbuttoned her nighty and flopped a large breast out that had the brownest nipple on it I'd ever seen. Not that I'd seen many for the sixth form girls I'd seen at the swimming baths had little or no breasts at all like me. She pushed the swollen nipple into the open mouth of her offspring and there was silence. Not even gran or mam said anything. We just all watched in wonder and Aunt Ada lay like a queen with her new heir. Everyone appeared content 'til the subject of the baby's name came up. Aunt Ada had already decided.

'Charles,' she stated defying any objection.

There was a lot of arguing from everyone in the family except me, for I thought Charles sounded quite royal. Gran said the boy should be called Frank as it was no use stirring the pot, and all the rest nodded in agreement. Even William who came later and had been quiet up to now, said it would be a good idea to call it Frank, as he was rather big for a prem. baby, what ever that meant. Aunt Ada gave him a look full of hatred and told him to mind his own business. Charles it was going to be and Charles he was eventually christened and Charlie was what the family called him.

Gran's house was always higgly-piddly, but Charlie's arrival had made it a total breakdown of any housekeeping rules. The place smelt of talcum powder cum gripe water, not to mention the unmentionables that got dropped into a bucket until someone decided to wash them. And when they did, nappies were everywhere, on the kitchen airing rack, on an airing maiden and on every corner of the fireguard that stood around the fireplace. The steam that arose on washdays cleared one's nose in a trice. But nobody could say Aunt Ada wasn't a good mother, for she clearly adored young Charles.

School began again and there was talk of the government putting up the school leaving age up to fifteen. All my class moaned and agreed it was just our luck to come under the proposed new law.

I cannot imagine how I missed the fact that Ivy had been pregnant. She'd got fat granted, but all the way around not like Aunt Ada who had carried all before her. Maybe it was because I didn't see much of Aunt Ivy and she usually wore a loose camel coat. So it was quite a surprise when I saw her in town pushing a pram. I admit I first thought Aunt Ivy had brought another pram for Charlie, but when I looked into it, the occupant was half Charlie's size and bald. Not knowing what to say, I said what I'd heard all adults say:

'Have you been churched?' It was the daftest thing to come out with but Aunt Ivy just answered as if it was a normal question.

'I don't believe in all that rubbish.'

I could believe her, because she never went to church unless it was for a christening, a wedding or a funeral, as gran would tell mam in a sarcastic tone.

I couldn't help admiring Aunt Ivy though. She wasn't bothered by what people said and looked very posh in her tweed suit and a fox-fur that wrapped around her shoulders with the fox's mouth set biting at its own tail. The Rev. Swindells didn't seem to mind she hadn't been churched, for three weeks later he almost tripped over his cassock while thanking William for the most generous donation after the baby's christening. The baby was called John William Taylor. John after William's father and it was fairly clear where the William came from. We had a grand do at The Big House and one wouldn't have known there was a war on. Gran said it was time we went but insisted on being given the grand tour before she left.

Mam was starting to behave differently. She stopped going to her friend's on a Thursday night and I caught her crying a time or two. It must be delayed shock I reasoned, and hoped she didn't go and confess everything to P.C. Clayton. I vowed to tell untruths about that night if I had to.

I began to get panic attacks and had to go outside a couple of times to get some air. Each time gran put it down to my age and asked me once if I had any signs. I hadn't a clue what she was talking about and wondered if she was getting some religious mania until mam said she meant my period.

Eventually the Americans left, and their billet was boarded up. The place stood empty and silent and grass had already begun to grow between the cracks in the broken concrete. There didn't appear to be any of our lads around in uniform either. In June, the whole of the population of the British Isles seemed to have their ears trained to their radio sets. The BBC had informed us that thousands of British and American troops had landed in Normandy. The broadcaster went on to say hundreds of vessels could be seen rolling and pitching in the heavy seas, from warships and merchant ships to the barges and landing crafts ferrying the soldiers and their equipment to the beaches. It sent mam into a nervous state and she began to talk of dad more than she had for ages. I also noticed a picture of him had appeared on our dresser, the one of he and mam together just after they were married. I suggested she get a tonic from Dr. McKenzie but she just turned away and didn't answer. Worry is a strange bedfellow.

As for the men that were still around town like William, they were more reserved than usual, as if weighing up their own worth when so many men were at the front line. Every one had Normandy on their lips; although I did hear that Mr Rankin was had up for killing a pig without a license and the window cleaner had fallen off his ladder and broke his leg. I did wonder whose window he was cleaning at the time.

That summer was the coldest I could remember. The constant rain chilled you through to your bones. We were low on coal and had to burn some old garden fence wood to keep warm until our next coal ration became due and then, to cap it all, the coal man arrived when we were out and dumped it by the back door. Mam and I filled bucket after bucket to pile it in the coalhouse, which was adjacent to our lavatory as you came in through the back door with yet another half glazed door leading off to the kitchen. Not a good architectural feature of the house, but better than having the lavatory and coal shed at the bottom of the garden like Eunice's.

As the days passed the rain helped nature along and the weeds sprouted quickly. Given time the quarry would look like the old one at the bottom of our garden.

Chapter 13

Life appeared to stop whenever the news came on, as everybody's ears were trained to catching every word spoken. There was a measure of nervousness as memories of Dunkirk and the dreadful waste of life there was still fresh in people's minds. The churches were full. Gran thought it fitting I accompany her each Sunday. As we walked there, I noticed people were flocking into the Methodist and Congregational churches also.

The Rev. Swindells insisted 'Onward Christian Soldiers' was sung at each service, excepting of course the 8.00 am service at which no hymns were ever sung. However, the church swelled with vibrant voices at the 10.00 am and 6.30 pm services.

The sermons of the Rev. Swindells were full of arm shaking and fist banging on the pulpit rail. I wondered if Hitler had ever wanted to be a priest but when I mentioned it, gran clouted me and forbade me ever let such evil thoughts into my head again. After that I saturated my forehead with holy water on leaving the church just in case.

I was now allowed to baby sit once again, although Vera only went out by herself if she had to go to the dentist or somewhere she couldn't take her kids. The magazines were gone and there was never any lovely underwear drying on the airing maid. Mr Van

Doorninck's photo was perched up on the mantelpiece and a smaller one of the family with Mr Van Doorninck holding the baby.

I held little Jessie to me. She had such beautiful large brown eyes, which made a nice change in a family that had all got blue.

Mam had developed a silly secret smile and sang songs like 'When we get too old to dream' and 'A nightingale sang in Berkeley Square'. I preferred a good old rendering of Nellie Dean or Sergeant Major myself, but at least she wasn't dwelling on that awful evening. I'd now accepted it was not her fault the yank died, and that I was fully to blame for sending that note, even though I still couldn't explain what had brought my mam to the scene that night.

The Grace's pig bin began to stink something awful next door. Ethel had put it around the back by their shed so when the pig truck came to collect it they couldn't find it. She's different is Ethel, that's for sure. Mam had to tell her more than once her cardigan was on the wrong way around, and it's only eggshells that are put on the garden and not the pieces of chalk she often picked up at school where she cleans in the evenings.

Doreen, her sister, had a young man. He's as shy as she is and they both walk along looking for every crack in the pavement, but always two feet away from each other. He worked for his dad on the farm and always smelled of cow muck. But Doreen was quite taken with him and cooked huge stews when he came around. Mam said the Graces were well set up with the little packages he brought in newspaper that ended up in the stew.

I couldn't have ever visualised how much my life was going to change that summer as I leapt from one life experience to others so quickly. I was just beginning to think it time to get on with my life when the front door bell rang. Mam was opening the door; as I popped my head around the kitchen door that led into the hallway. It was the telegram boy, the only time I'd seen him at our house before was when a relative in Scotland had died and we got an envelope edged with black.

Mam was standing very still staring down at the envelope. I heard the telegram boy say:

'Hope it's not bad news Mrs.' as he sauntered away after she'd signed for it.

Closing the door with her empty hand, she went straight into the parlour, something she rarely does because there's only an old piano and an armchair of grandpa's in there.

She half closed the door behind her. I slowly pushed the door open again and stood in the doorway not sure what was going on; but instinctively knowing it was a time to keep quiet. Mam put the telegram down on her knee after she had sat down.

She stared at it for what seemed like ages, then deliberately took a hairpin from her hair and slid it under the flap. I think she already knew what was in the letter. She raised her head slowly after reading it and looked at me standing by the door. It was a strange look as if her gaze was unfocussed and it went straight through me.

'Your father's dead,' she said simply and waved the letter for me to read. Taking it off her, I noticed first the very official letterhead.

Army Records Office of Ashford

Madam,

I am directed to inform you, with regret, that a report has been received from the War Office stating that Corporal Sidney Goodwin of the Cheshire Regiment has been killed in action. Please accept my sympathy.

I am Madam,

Your obedient servant,
Major Guy Dawson.
Infantry Records.

My dad dead.... It took some time for the full impact to hit me. I'd never ever see him again. I sobbed and sobbed. I'm not sure whether I felt sorry for my dad or for myself. All I felt was a great loss of the past and a future now filled with uncertainty. I dropped on my knees and buried my head in mam's knees and cried 'til I couldn't anymore. I felt her hand stroking my head and crooning softly to me. Thinking back it was the only time I really felt a deep intimacy between us.

There couldn't be any funeral although our curtains were closed and we wore black, or rather I wore a black band around my arm. Lots of people visited and brought whatever they could spare from their small enough rations. Dad's photo was draped in a black ribbon with a bunch of lilies beside it.

There was a service in church in which the Rev. Swindells gave an impressive sermon about our brave soldiers. The hymns we sang were 'Abide with Me' and 'Onward Christian Soldiers' again, but this time sung in a far more sombre tone. Mam told me he would be buried somewhere in France along with thousands of others that had been killed over there. Barbara Potts came up to me and said she was very sorry I hadn't got a father any more and all the church ladies told me I had to be a brave girl for my mam's sake. There was a write-up in the paper.

I did really try very hard to be brave the day a parcel was delivered at our house. It contained some of my father's effects. I wasn't very brave when I saw the tatty rust coloured and stained photo of me he'd carried onto the battlefield. There was a silver lighter his own mam had brought him at sometime, because it had "To My Dear Son" engraved on it. There was a piece of lined writing paper with writing on it. It was folded up but had no envelope. My mam didn't even open it but just tucked it into her pinafore pocket.

The curtains were eventually opened and the black ribbon taken off the photo; the latter, mam asked if I'd like it in my bedroom. I guessed it was too sad for my mam to have to gaze at everyday. So I put it on my dressing table, and whenever I remembered; put a few flowers beside it in a glass vase. I was always extremely careful to never pick 'Mother's Die' which some people call Queen Anne's lace or even the lilacs that grew wild at the bottom of our garden; for gran had said if you brought them into the house someone would die. I couldn't afford to be careless with any superstitions now, so I never walked under a ladder or let a black cat cross my path and I always threw salt over my right shoulder, whenever I used it. Gran took it a little further by not ever wearing green, but I have to wear my green jumper or I'd freeze. I vowed I would never break a mirror, for seven years of bad luck would just be too much to live with.

Vera was very good to us and spent a great deal of time drinking tea. One day after swilling her cup around, mam had mentioned a fat lady and did she know anyone with dark hair. Vera thought for a moment then laughed and leaned over the table to say confidentially to mam

'It must be Mrs McKenzie,' and she laughed again. I was sewing by the window at the time and glanced up, thinking the same thing as mam.

'But Amy Mackenzie is quite thin,' she said surprised. Why was it that slim became thin for some people? I always thought of Mrs McKenzie as having a rather nice figure.

'She's pregnant.' Vera went on adding, 'didn't you know?' When there was no answer Vera continued her now interesting topic. 'Mrs Winterbottom told me when she came around to see Jessie.'

Mam's cup crashed to the floor, spilling its contents and rolling under the table. I got up to help but mam had already snatched the tea towel that was draped over the teapot to keep it warm. The tea cosy was drying with the rest of the washing on the line outside. The spill was running over the lino and mam was on her hands and knees. When she surfaced her face was flushed and she looked quite upset. Vera studied her for a moment, concern written on her face.

'Are you okay Rose?' she asked.

'Yes, yes.' Mam fidgeted with the other teacups. 'It's just I've a lot to do today and feel a little tense.' At that Vera took the hint and got up abruptly.

'I'd better go anyway, didn't mean to hold you up.' She left a little put out.

Whatever mam had planned to do never got done for she developed a bad headache and lay on her bed all day face down and sobbing, sometimes into her pillow. I made her a cup of tea and a slice of toast with Marmite spread on it. But later, when I went to collect the plate she hadn't eaten it. I thought my dad's picture would comfort her so I took it into her bedroom and quietly placed it by her bed. It must have done the trick for when I took her a cup of tea in the morning she had it in her hands together with the letter that had been in his personal effects. She looked at me sadly and said the strangest thing

'I've been such a fool, but I do love you.' At that I sat on the bed and wrapped my arms around her.

I really wanted to tell her I'd never say anything and her secret would die with me, but nothing came out.

The sirens came and went that day but we didn't even get up to go under the stairs. We just lay quietly together. I knew that moment was too precious to pass.

Chapter 14

1944 was the worst year of my whole life; although I'm certain many humans had suffered a great deal more than I had. But I didn't know much of the rest of the world, for mine revolved totally around my mam and her family. They were now the only security that I'd got left to hang on to.

Our local newspaper had always got a photo or two of someone who had been killed or missing in action and every one was wondering who would be next. For the first time during the war, the full force of it began to hit me. My security had been shattered and the world took on a terrifying vision of what could happen.

I envied my friends with their dads at home more than I ever did before. Envy so close to hate had only a thin line of separation at this time for me. Irene Leckie's dad worked at the Foden's factory that produced lorries for the war, but it didn't stop her dad from making her stilts and a cot for her doll. Mrs Leckie always had nice things in her kitchen from the greenhouse; bowls of fresh tomatoes and crisp lettuce. But most of all I saw a family all together.

Mam really worried me. She'd sit in her chair gazing into the fire for hours, occasionally I caught her looking at dad's picture, then she'd wipe the glass with the corner of her pinnie and put it back on the dresser. She ate very little and did the household chores automatically.

Mrs Grace beckoned me to her gate once as she was leaning over it, obviously waiting to catch me.

'Is your mam alright love?' she asked, with real concern on her wrinkled face.

I answered, 'She's fine, just misses my dad that's all.' But Mrs Grace was not giving up so easily

'Maybe that nice Dr. McKenzie should come and take a look at her; he's not been around for some time.'

Because I agreed with her, I promised her I would talk mam into seeing him; but mam said he wouldn't come, which was a strange thing to say.

Aunt Ivy drove up to see us. She could drive now and used it as much as the petrol coupons for the business would allow her to. Little William sat in the front in a small wooden chair strapped to the seat. He had a good view of where they were going and banged his fists on the tray in front of it. Like always, the curtains from across the road moved whenever the Taylor's car parked in front of our house, or someone would take a stroll down their path and lean over their gate to greet Aunt Ivy and, I guess, hope for some idle gossip about the mill. Aunt Ivy never accommodated them. She always lifted young William out of his seat and would march straight to our front door. She was the only visitor, apart from gran, who never used our back door.

'You've got to get a hold of yourself Rose.' She would advise mam whilst she sat upright on one of our dining room chairs holding young William on the side of her knee so he didn't crumple her skirt too much.

'Oh leave me alone Ivy.' Mam said, slumping further into her chair. 'What do you know, you've got it all,' and to that her sister didn't have any reply.

That was the end of her visit. I guess she thought she'd done her job and there were now other things to do like shopping. Gran was no help. She was now getting a little wobbly on her feet. Her arthritic knee pained her a lot and her customary tot of whisky was having less and less an effect, so she needed more now that only increased her wobbliness. I tried to tell her about mam but gran only complained her daughter never came to see her.

Aunt Ada was no help either. She just sneered and said.

'She's made her bed, now she has to lie on it.'

I thought it was a dreadful thing to say about a woman who had lost her husband, but Aunt Ada and mam had been on bad terms ever since the yank episode. I didn't want to burden Uncle Joseph or Annie with my problems and Vera wasn't any use as she had made friends with P.C. Clayton's daughter, who had now come to live with him. Vera hardly came around at all anymore and I can't say I blame her for there was no way now she'd get her fortune told. So I'd go back to gran's again and hope someone would be of help, but Aunt Ada was as bitchy as ever.

'Heard from Frank?' I'd ask, trying to make conversation, but I'd just get a shrug of her shoulders and she'd find something else to do, which was usually reading a magazine.

'Miserable, that's what she is,' gran would grumble when we were alone. 'Never used to be like that. The war does funny things and it isn't natural for a young girl to have her man away.'

Ethel, bless her, would pop around to our house and ask if I needed anything doing. I think she'd seen my pathetic attempts at washing on our line. Last week I'd hung out the towels and it was so frosty that they became stiff as boards. When mam stopped washing herself and wouldn't get dressed I realised I had to do something.

I took a day off school, which mam never noticed and went to the doctor's surgery to see our doctor. I knew Dr. Mackenzie would fix mam up again. When the receptionist told me Dr. McKenzie had left to take up a practice up North, I was on the verge of crying.-

I met Dr. Proctor who had taken his place but it wasn't the same. Dr. McKenzie was broad shouldered with a sunny smile and pleasant to look at. Dr. Proctor was just the opposite in all ways; slight, with powerful glasses that enlarged his eyes. Everything about him was neat; to the way he dressed, to the way he jotted down his notes as I told him about my mam. He said he'd pop up tomorrow and he'd get my mam back up and running. With that, I felt a whole weight lift off my shoulders.

I managed after much persuasion to get mam into a bath and I washed her hair, although she refused to let me put any curlers in it. I stoked up the fire and made her a hot cup of milk. She seemed much more at peace and she said she hoped I'd meet the right man one day. I pampered her by saying I certainly would and tried to get her to talk about when she was young. Being thirty to me was quite old and especially when she was the eldest in the family. For the first time in months she gave a little smile.

'I thought I knew everything,' she said. 'Your dad and I were courting since we were at school. I knew nothing about real emotions.'

How strange it was listening to her ramble but I thought it better out than in. I, in turn, told her I'd been down to see the doctor. She immediately became very angry knocking over her glasses and shouting in a dreadful voice:

'You saw Dr. McKenzie?'

'No, no mam.' I tried to calm her growing agitation down. It was a Dr. Proctor I saw. Dr. McKenzie's left the surgery and gone off to Scotland.' Mam's mouth hung open, and then she went very pale.

'Gone,' she stated weakly. I nodded giving her my half drunk glass of milk, which she pushed away. Then leaning back in her chair, she closed her eyes. I sat 'til one o'clock in the morning just watching her but when she didn't move, I thought it best to let her sleep and crawled upstairs to my bed praying Dr. Proctor would be as true as his word.

Nothing can prepare you for finding your mam dead. I knew she was dead the moment I came down into the living room. She had slumped to one side; her head hanging in an awkward position, one arm was flung out, the hand opened in the final moment of dropping the bottle of aspirins on the floor. My cup with the remainder of my milk was turned over in her lap.

I screamed and screamed and banged on the wall with my fists. First Doreen came around, then Ethel. Mrs Grace was sent out to fetch P.C Clayton, who appeared still having his pyjamas on under his trench coat.

Dr. Proctor arrived, flinging the door open and pushing his way through the gathering neighbours. Nobody tried to shield me from the scene, as they were all too busy trying to discover what had happened. Dr. Proctor lifted the little bottle from the floor after listening to mam's chest. He sighed as I heard him say,

'Aspirins. Enough to do the job.'

P.C Clayton wrote something in his book. I remember Ethel putting her arm around me and telling me to go with her next door where I sat with a shawl around my shoulders shivering. I heard the siren of an ambulance on the road outside and voices, which I instinctively knew were the neighbours on both sides of the street wanting to know what had happened. Then William came up and I had to go past a lot of staring faces before getting into his car. He took me to gran's, and I slept in gran's bed for the rest of the week. It was comfortable to feel her big warm buttocks pressing against my back and to be not alone.

So it was I became an orphan in just a few short months. I didn't see mam again, as Mrs Winterbottom thought it best not to, after what the post mortem did to her. She didn't lie in the front room like Mr Grace, but stayed in the Chapel at the hospital, until her final resting place in the churchyard.

I didn't remember the funeral too much. It was dismal in the church and the service was quick. The drizzle was constant and we filed two by two over the worn flagstones, past sombre grey stones etched with green moss and glass covers that held artificial white lilies. We stopped by a long oblong hole with dirt and clay piled up beside it.

I stood with gran who was looking very old and fragile these days. Rev. Swindells said a few words and mam was lowered into the hole. I watched the coffin descend and couldn't believe mam was really in it. The only thought that helped me cope was that the deed she'd done would never have to be faced on earth. I prayed God would not be too hard in his judgement of her and I kept reminding myself what the Rev. Swindells told us: 'God is merciful'. But I have my doubts when I think of all us orphans left to face the world alone.

No one really talked about my mam like they had done about my dad, apart from Annie who would put her thin arms around me.

'Poor lovey,' she'd say. 'You must miss your mam something awful.'

I wished it was possible for me to go and live with her and Uncle Joseph, but it was all just an idle thought. My meagre belongings were put into Aunt Ada's old room, and I inherited her twin bed. As gran said it best to sell most of my mam's stuff, which didn't amount to much as it was. Our house had been rented so there was no money as such, to make much of a difference. What savings mam had went to pay for the funeral.

My depression was back again and, at the worst period I wondered if I'd end up like mam, but somehow I coped. I would lie on my bed listening to the voices drift up the stairs. My name came up often along with mam's but I wasn't interested. Gran said she'd knit me something, but it was usually baby wool that hung on her needles as Aunt Ada was always remarking how Charlie grew out of his things so quickly.

Some of the furniture from my home was taken by horse and cart to Uncle Joseph and Annie's house. The big Westminster clock my dad's parents had left him found its way to Aunt Ivy's front room, which they had taken over at the Big House. The horsehair settee was burnt in the back garden along with some of my mam's clothes. I thought this was such a waste with the war still on, but Aunt Ada said nobody would want them seeing how what had happened. Some of the kindnesses I once remembered had gone out of Aunt Ada, and she'd now become quite bossy and bitter.

Chapter 15

A letter came for Aunt Ada. It sat for a whole day on the sideboard before she eventually opened it and, after she had scanned her eyes quickly over the contents, it was left half sticking out of its envelope on top of the button box.

Having the house to myself the next morning and seeing it still there proved too great a temptation, so I quickly read it with my ears trained on the back door in case someone came in.

Poor Frank. The letter was obviously quickly scribbled and spoke of his longing for a hot bath and clean underwear as he was always dirty, tired and had knots in his stomach all the time. Lots of his mates had been killed or wounded and he hoped he could get the letter to her more quickly by giving it to one of the wounded being taken from the battlefield. There was a good chance it would reach her. He couldn't say very much apart from it being Hell. The bottom of the letter was covered in crosses and words with daft meanings and ending with lots of hugs for his beautiful little son.

People were still talking about the Normandy invasion and who was left a widow, or whose son was missing or killed. The headlines in the newspapers that were hanging outside the newsagents shop were bold and filled most of the front page. The man who stood on the corner by the Co-op with his newspaper bag over his shoulders shouted all the latest headlines in his singsong voice. There were so many casualties.

Just a week after D-day the first of Hitler's new secret weapons were dropping on London. It was a frightening thing, full of explosive and without any pilot. It was called the V1 and was quickly dubbed the buzz bomb from the incessant drone it made before its engine suddenly stopped and it dived down. A few seconds later it would hit the ground with a tremendous explosion. Although the range of the buzz bombs was far too short to reach our town, it nevertheless meant people's nerves were badly shaken and more and more children were being sent up north to be looked after away from the devastation.

We listened in awe to their experiences as they all recounted their tales of being crowded into the underground stations for safety. Too many had witnessed the smoking remains of their homes when they emerged. Some had lost all their family in the raids.

A new wave of evacuations had started again and more children began to appear in Danesbury, especially in the houses just on the edge of town where help was needed with the land. Sometimes I heard horror stories of some children being cruelly treated as evacuees, and how mothers had come up from London to take them back there to have them brave out the bombs instead.

There was young boy staying at the Crown and Anchor who looked happy enough. The landlady had had a brood of her own and had lost two sons in the war and now she lavished her motherly nurturing on her new charge. I guess he was lucky. At another house the police had to take away two young sisters who complained they were being abused by an old man who also lived in the house. Gran said he'd been at it before and it was a crying shame the authorities weren't more careful.

As the months passed, I still lived in my unreal world and showed little emotion of the tragic things that had happened to me. My gran would often remark to the neighbours that I was a cool one without a doubt, and her friends, usually members of the Mother's Union, would smile sympathetically as gran often offered her explanation.

'She's been through a lot for a girl of her age. It's not easy for any of us, let alone the youngsters, to have to grow up so quickly these days,' and sometimes adding, 'look at Joseph, he'll never be able to see the young bairn that Annie's carrying.'

We heard there had been a bomb attack on Hitler's life and Rommel had committed suicide, leaving Germany without one of its best Generals. We had a world map on the classroom wall and each morning after assembly our teacher would draw on it thick blue lines for the Allies, yellow ones for the Germans and red ones for the Russians, all in chalk of course so he could rub out and change the positions of the colours as the allies advanced.

It was a good job Ernest Heath wasn't in my class anymore as I was afraid the whole map would have looked totally different, especially as there wasn't a cane or strap in sight. We tended now to get detention instead, but as the nights drew in mothers fiercely opposed that idea, objecting to their offsprings having to walk the streets in the blackout. What cars and buses there were still had their headlights covered by shades and it was considered all too easy for children to get knocked down.

Christmas came and went that year. I got a pair of hand-knitted mittens, the same colour as my gran's old cardigan. Aunt Ivy brought me two books, the Dandy and Beano annuals. I lay on my bed all Boxing day reading the books and was fascinated at the snow that was drawn on the top of the fences and the huge cow pies with horns sticking out that Desperate Dan ate. It all seemed something that dreams are made of; holly on the big round Christmas pudding, jellies shaped like castles, and steaming turkeys, large red socks hanging over bedposts and filled with all sorts of toys and Christmas trees, all lit up with coloured candles. My Christmas that year was lived through those books and those dreams of the perfect Christmas time with a mother, father and happy children all around.

Nobody made much effort apart from Annie who tried to put on a dinner for all of us at gran's house. It couldn't have been easy with her large stomach and Uncle Joseph's constant needs. The only person, who appeared to benefit from Christmas, was young Charlie. Where Aunt Ada had got his new outfit from and his wind-up car I don't know. It must have taken a whole lot of coupons. I never appeared to have enough when my blouses were too tight as Aunt Ada kept a tight hold on my coupon book.

Aunt Ivy and Uncle William fared better at the Big House and I did receive a very welcome present from them. It was a pen and pencil set in a long wooden box that when you slid the top off held compartments for pen nibs, a pencil sharpener and even a rubber eraser. The first thing I did was to write my name in large black letters along the top of the box, which in doing so caused me to ruin two of the fine nibs. But it was well worth doing, as young Charlie had already got his eyes on it. I didn't enjoy church that year, as my voice was held somewhere within the hard lump that stuck in my throat whenever 'Onward Christian Soldiers' boomed out. Sometimes I think the lump will burst one day and my whole body will break up into a zillion pieces, but it never did.

Around the middle of spring there was uproar and public outrage as the Russians liberated Auschwitz and other concentration camps in Poland. The reports at first were heavily censored, so horrible were the images coming out. The headlines screamed of the conditions being found in the camps and the pictures eventually released left nothing to the imagination. Corpses were found in huge piles, whilst thousands were dying of starvation and disease. It hung over us all like a dark cloud and nobody complained about our shortage of food. Mothers were thankful their children were receiving school dinners and milk, as well as regular supplies of orange juice and cod liver oil capsules.

We heard old Mrs Grace had died. She just fell down in the garden it seems, and that was that. I did wonder how Doreen and Ethel were managing but I never went anywhere near our old house. Aunt Ada listened to the radio a lot. Gran knitted and I tried to do my homework as we all huddled around the only warmth we had coming from the fireplace. Now and then gran would cackle with laughter, as Mrs Mop in ITMA would say:

'Can I do you now sir' and Colonel Chinstrap, who thought every remark might have a drink in the offing would say,

'I don't mind if I do.'

Tommy Handley was always a great favourite of gran's and next came Kenneth Horne and Richard Murdock with their program 'Much Binding in the Marsh'. Aunt Ada liked anything American, comedians like Bob Hope and Red Skelton and she would close her eyes in a dreamlike state whenever Glen Miller's music was playing. She would often romance about the good old days when the GI's were around the town, and a tear would form.

'They knew how to treat a lady,' she would tell me, her mind very much in the past. I knew she wasn't just thinking of the tinned food they passed around, but of the chocolates and cigarettes. Not to mention of course those nylons. Once she tried to teach me to jitterbug when a band was playing on the radio, but that ended in disaster when my awkward body hit a solitary vase that had been in the family since any of us could remember.

Those American catchwords, or 'slang' as many called it, disappeared too, apart from that detestable phrase 'Hi-yah'. I myself made quite a profound effort to always greet people with, 'How do you do' instead of with the more usual town greeting of 'How-do'. I guess there were a lot of people in the town who missed the yanks, apart from the one I tried not to think about. The others were generally very good to the children of the town and seemed to miss their own families being around. I also knew some of the women that had actually married Americans and were wondering, like the wives of our lads, whether they would ever see them again.

In the dark recesses of my mind, I hated part of myself that had started with so much and left me now with so little. The mirror told me I'd changed. I'd grown up quickly and my features were beginning to take on a more adult look. It was my eyes I hated to look into. It was if they reflected my true self, the one that had led me to my punishment of losing all I loved.

If I felt any affection at all it was probably towards Annie, and I would call around to see her at her small terraced house as often as I could. It was a tiny place, set in a long street of what looked like a long wall with each house presenting a door and window to the pavement, all equally spaced with only paint colours making the difference to set them apart from one another. But even then, it was mostly only the difference in shades of green or brown. The front door steps were cleaner than the pavement after rain, always yellow or white, whichever stoning tablet was chosen for their weekly cleaning. Net curtains framed every one of the windows. It was too dark and small to see the heavy black curtains that were hung inside. Number 11 was Aunt Annie and Uncle Joseph's. The next house was number 15 instead of number 13. I guess that would be really asking for trouble during air raids.

Uncle Joseph hadn't much furniture. He'd sold some of ours to make ends meet, and what they had left was pushed against the side of the walls to give better access. The front door opened into what was usually called the parlour, then a door into a living room and another door into the tiny scullery, from where you could enter a closed-in yard.

By the solid wooden gate in the surrounding brick wall of the yard was a small building just big enough to hold a WC, which stood for water closet as it was then called and held the only flush toilet. Most parlours were hardly ever used and the best of what people had was displayed there and polished frequently, although it was customary for the visiting doctor or vicar to sit and drink tea in there from the best china that most people had for those special occasions.

Not so at Uncle Joseph's. Instead a bed filled a good half of the room, with an old washstand and chair taking up a great deal of the rest. Annie was afraid her husband might fall down the steep stairs that led up to the two bedrooms and she was not taking any chances.

It suited them well enough and they managed on the pay Joseph received from the army, although Annie did take in washing to help out. That meant on Mondays, the whole house was full of steam from the boiler. Tuesday wasn't much better as the kitchen and dining room were filled with drying clothes. On Wednesdays she ironed.

I did make a habit of visiting on a Saturday morning and, whilst Aunt Annie did her shopping, I would guide Uncle Joseph along the alley at the back and around the corner and back along the fronts of the houses to number 11. Often someone would stop and talk to him and, like as not, offer him a cigarette, which Joseph would take gratefully and put into his cigarette case.

He had been trying very hard to roll his own cigarettes but hadn't yet mastered it. I'm sure he soon will, because he used to be such a dab hand at it before his accident. We didn't say much and it didn't really matter for we were just two souls within a shadowy world, but I know he looked forward to my Saturday visits and I knew Annie was grateful.

Chapter 16

Optimism was now building in the town and other changes were around the corner as the Germans took defeat after defeat and people began to look forward to the future again.

Mr Chadwick, the principal at our school, always supervised the early morning assemblies; led prayers and gave out important notices in the assembly hall. One day at school we were in the playground during morning recess when our principal came into our midst with all the teachers and blew his whistle. Now seeing Mr Chadwick away from his desk gave us a clue immediately that something had happened or was about to happen that was beyond the normal. We all stood rock still waiting a climatic announcement, while some of us were anxiously scouring the skies above, expecting the sirens to go off any minute.

One of our teachers, Miss Taylor, prim as ever with a face that gave nothing away, said:

'Mr Chadwick has something to tell you all.'

But before he could open his mouth, church bells blasted out in a full peel

We all jumped, as they had not been heard since the start of the war. Mr Chadwick looked quite put out and glared in the direction of the church. We all stood in shock wondering if the bell-ringers now peeling all the bells would be chastised. Mr Chadwick wasn't going to wait anymore for the bells to stop and bellowed at us,

'Victory has just been declared in Europe.'

You could see the look on all the teacher's faces breaking out into huge smiles and Mrs Green started to cry. It took a moment or two for it to sink in, before someone yelled,

'The bloody war's over.'

I think it was Paul Dunn. I looked at Mr Chadwick to see if he'd heard Paul swear, but he was hugging Miss Stewart, a little too closely I thought. One of our teachers started to both cry and laugh a little hysterically and was taken back into the school. She had recently been informed that her husband and brother were both missing in action and presumed dead, so I suppose it was understandable.

All of us ran around, flinging hats and even shoes into the air. Mrs Bratt, the school cleaner fetched out a huge Union Jack on a long white pole and stood there in her pinafore and hair turban waving the flag 'til someone pushed the pole into the ground near the air raid shelter. Jerusalem, our school song was sung, followed by Rule Britannia. Mrs Bratt started to do 'Knees up Mother Brown' 'til her long bloomers started to show and someone told her. Then we were allowed to go home.

Our Prime Minister, Mr Churchill made the official announcement at three o'clock that afternoon.

'The war with Germany is at an end.'

The eighth of May is one of the most memorable of days for me. It is akin to a bright light seeping into my grey depressed world, although that day started grey enough, with that damp continuous drizzle that is so normal to our fair island. The sun did manage to put in an appearance in the afternoon, although it wasn't that that brought the people outside.

Everyone wanted to be together. Celebration was high on the list with displays of excitement and relief. Some people sported red, white and blue rosettes on their chests or in their hats, made out of paper. Strings of bunting quickly began to make their appearance and the Union Jack flags came out like magic. I hadn't realised so many people had these things tucked away in their houses. Then the most exciting thing of all happened. All the available lights went on in the evening after dusk. The floodlights and searchlights lit up the skies and everyone it seemed took a great delight in opening their blackout curtains, although no official permission to do this had yet been given.

People began to build bonfires and when I went upstairs I could see the flickering lights for miles. We, that is gran, Aunt Ada, Charlie and I walked around to Uncle Joseph and Annie's. We passed the pubs, whose doorways were already packed and the noise of singing drowned out everything else. Then the deafening sound of bells started ringing out again, their different tones echoing across the town as many people were making for the open doors of the churches.

Annie had put Uncle Joseph in a chair outside the front door and was holding her tummy with one hand and brushing away silent tears that trickled down his cheek with the other. Gran said Annie shouldn't overdo it, and then made for the kitchen to put the kettle on. Charlie was left with me while Aunt Ada popped around to the Black Boar for something stronger than tea. We waited and waited for her 'til gran took off herself to find her. Charlie was fast asleep when they returned a little worse for wear, but gran's arthritis seemed to be much better as she kicked her heels with the best of them that were dancing in the street.

On the radio it said the princesses were mingling with the thousands of people that were around Buckingham Palace. The broadcaster's voice was excited and it was hard to visualize people jumping into the fountains in Trafalgar Square. Apparently the Houses of Parliament and Big Ben were bathed in searchlights. It must have quite a sight indeed.

Then Churchill reminded us all there was still fighting going on in the world with Japan. After the celebrations had gone on for a few days, everybody started talking about the real celebrations yet to come when all our lads would be coming back home. Apart from the lights, now visible around the town and the removal of the anxiety of air raids, things were still going to be rationed. Life didn't change overnight and there was still a lot of bitterness too, as for some there would never be a homecoming to look forward to or their not knowing whether those missing would turn up.

Annie had her baby three days later, and although Annie had been very big, the baby was quite small and didn't cry very much. The doctor had to be called to help deliver it with instruments. Annie was in bed longer than the normal ten days and gran proved to be a godsend to have around. She did everything for Annie and the baby and looked after Joseph's needs too. It was as though she knew she was truly needed and took on the task at hand with a strength I was unaware of. I was pleased to see she talked less and less of her medicinal whisky.

Annie's baby died one month and a day later. It was all so sad. Gran made Joseph and Annie come over to our house and the baby's little coffin was placed in the parlour. It was such a small coffin, lined with white satin. The baby had the long christening gown on that William was christened in. It was a mite too big but nevertheless, the baby looked like an angel. A little cross had been placed in its hands and all around the coffin lay flowers.

Annie sat for the whole three days by the baby and some times I heard her talking to it. It hadn't been christened and she was frantic with worry that it wouldn't go to heaven until the Rev. Swindells blessed it and assured her it would go straight to heaven and be an angel as it had done no wrong. Uncle Joseph remained very quiet and, although I witnessed his shoulders shaking, I didn't see any tears from his scarred eyes. Gran's pains must have come back as she needed twice as much medicine as before.

Everyone was concerned for Joseph and Annie especially Aunt Ivy. Then William offered Joseph a job at the factory. I don't know exactly what it was but obviously Uncle Joseph thought he could do it, and every morning one of the vans from the factory came and picked Joseph up and later in the day, I often saw it standing outside their house on my way back home from school.

'Best thing for them is to try for another,' Gran confided to Aunt Ada who didn't seem very interested in what was best or not. Aunt

Ada had got fed up at the factory with everyone talking about their men folk coming home.

'Frank will be home soon,' I said, helping gran put on Charlie's boots as he wriggled a lot.

'More's the pity.' Ada almost spat out the words, then fiddled with her scarf after realizing it was a wicked thing to say about someone returning home from the war.

'You should be grateful you've got a man,' gran snapped back. 'You were glad enough of his name.'

Aunt Ada just sniffled and let her blue eyes roll back in her head. Annie did get pregnant again soon after the baby had been buried and Joseph was far more talkative since he'd begun to bring money home. At times I caught a glimpse of the old carefree uncle I once knew.

In August of that year the first atomic bomb was dropped on Hiroshima. Then a second one was dropped on Nagasaki. We all heard of the horror these bombs had created. Far worse than anything the Germans had thrown at us. In the local cinema the newsreels were showing pictures of naked bodies that were swollen with their skin peeling off. The flesh burnt and their poor bodies just thrown about by the force of the blasts. It was something I had a hard time understanding and lay on my bed at nights, sometimes in total darkness, questioning the very existence of God. What did I really want to know of Him? It was then I stopped going to church altogether and, against all the wrangling and wailings of my devote gran nothing would budge me. The Rev. Swindells sat patiently with me and tried to explain the reasons behind man's cruelty to man, but it was all so wasted on me, so he joined gran in a tot of whisky and tried to be of comfort to her instead.

'It's her age,' he said with conviction. 'She'll come back to the church when she's ready.'

This seemed to ease gran's worry of me going to Hell permanently, and gran told me later his predictions were based on great wisdom and his own understanding of teenager behaviour. I could never figure this out because he wasn't even married.

Every Sunday, gran donned her black coat and pulled her hat on over her tight curls that had been tied up in a scarf in curlers all through Saturday. She would look at me questioningly, hoping I was maybe going to get ready also. Then she'd shrug her shoulders and pick up her handbag making sure she had enough for the collection. Funnily enough she'd also given up on Aunt Ada who hadn't entered the church since Charlie's christening.

Chapter 17

Young Charlie was getting big, toddling around on his two chubby legs and examining everything within his reach. More and more stuff was piled on the sideboard 'til it looked like a table at a church jumble sale.

Aunt Ada went back to work at the factory whilst gran looked after her grandson. I thought it too much for gran, but Charlie was a good baby with an affectionate smile that more than made up for his attention needs, and gran truly adored him. Aunt Ada's job at the factory didn't last long before she got fed up with her sister Ivy swanking around, giving herself airs and graces and prancing around like lady muck. Those being Aunt Ada's words and not mine, for I thought my Aunt Ivy looked extremely ladylike.

When a vacancy came up in the Council Offices, Aunt Ada applied right away and was delighted to get it. Not as much money she said, but a far classier place to work in. She was certainly much happier, for she was less agitated at my presence and began to accept I actually lived in the same house. I was allowed to iron her dresses and carefully line her legs when needed, in return for which she gave me an old pair of slacks and a jumper. These were the first clothes I ever wore that made me feel as if I was beginning to be an adult.

I had one year left at school and, because I was one whose birthday was late in the year I would be one of the oldest to be leaving. I was beginning to look ahead and think of where to work.

One thing was for sure it wouldn't be painting china in any of the pot banks in Stoke–on–Trent. It was bad enough having to do my art schooling in the Potteries, but to breathe in that smoky atmosphere everyday was not going to be for me. It was the grimiest place I'd ever known. Even the privet hedges left black soot marks on your hands if you touched them. It was no wonder the buildings in the towns that made up the Potteries were all black as there were always some of the many coal-fired bottle kilns billowing out thick black smoke every day. Coming from the greenery of the Cheshire plains was quite a contrast.

The service men returning from overseas slowly began to filter back into our town and there was always time for celebrations when our very own came home sporting his medals. Today the main street was thronged with people as lorry load after lorry load of soldiers passed through. One of our local heroes arrived in an open staff car and the crowd waved flags frantically as he passed by. He was standing holding onto the frame of his open transport and waved to everyone, sometimes taking off his beret and twirling it around. Two officers sat behind, obviously high ranking, for they wore lots of gold braid. I cheered and waved too, that is until I saw who was following in the next car. Mrs Potts and Barbara smiled that fixed smile of royalty and waved formally like our Queen. I went home after Barbara spied me in the crowd and gave me a very haughty glare of superiority.

I was trying very hard to save and had opened a post office book with a one-pound note gran had said was left over from mam's things. The rest she said had to go into keeping me. I suppose that was fair enough. William took me on one side one day and told me to remember when I was twenty-one; the War Office would give me money for my dad being killed. I said I would remember but twenty-one was still along way off.

When Aunt Ada offered half-a-crown for baby-sitting on the nights gran went to Mothers Union, I jumped at the chance to add to my savings, little as it was. Some nights I'd wished I had held out for more because there were many times she would come home late, very late indeed. I'd even heard gran accusing her of being irresponsible. That was the thing that lit Aunt Ada's flame right away, for anything to do with Charlie heated her up. She raged on about needing to have some sort of a life for herself but had never neglected her son; picking him up for all to see what a healthy child he was, which no one could deny. But since she got out more, she did treat me more like a friend and many's the time she'd come home, flop into the big chair, examine her stockings for any ladders if she was wearing them, and checking her suspenders would often say:

'Put the kettle on duck.'

Once she painted my nails a nice pink, but gran made me scrape it off which took ages. Those few months were becoming more like having a family around again and me really belonging to it. I was beginning to think of her less as my aunt and more the big sister I'd always wanted.

I forgave a lot of past hurts and admitted that gran was probably right. Ada was missing Frank and a proper family unit. A lad needs his father around. I had to agree, for now I knew my own dad was never coming back and he had become a hero to me. I had his photo by one side of my bed with mam's on the other side. When I lay down at night in my bed, I didn't recite the old verse about angels guarding my head and feet anymore. Instead I prayed that my mam and dad would always guard over me. It seemed far more practical as angels had far too many people to divide their time over and mam and dad only had me.

Frank came home for good one Saturday afternoon and from the moment he stepped over the threshold I knew I'd been very wrong about Aunt Ada missing him. Aunt Ada had just taken out the last of her curlers and was getting dressed up to go out, when I opened the front door. Frank stood there grinning. I was about to yell my head off that Frank was back when he put his finger to his lips and winked. Bending over he whispered,

'Where is she?'

I nodded in the direction of the living room and watched him as he crept down the hall. Then he put down his bag, stood in the living room doorway and yelled.

'Watcha,' his arms extended ready for them to be eagerly filled with a loving wife.

By this time I was close behind him hoping to witness the joyful reception. Aunt Ada turned around with large unbrushed curls on top of her head and a curling iron in her hand. She looked as if she'd seen a ghost.

'Bloody hell,' she cried. 'Why didn't you let me know when you would be home?'

Frank laughed.

'I thought I'd surprise my beautiful wife,' he answered, his arms still waiting for his prize.

'Bloody hell.' Aunt Ada said again and looked confused as to what to do next. But Frank was certain of what he wanted and moved closer for the embrace. Aunt Ada was having none of it and side stepped him.

'You should have written.'

She was now clearly quite annoyed. At that moment gran came in with young Charlie, who stared at the strange man and hid his face into gran's apron. A car horn was heard outside, and Aunt Ada glanced out of the window, clearly in a dilemma and not knowing what to do. But the dilemma didn't last long as Frank had started to pull parcels out of the bag he'd got me to bring in. Charlie got a teddy with glass eyes, which he took to at once and even let Frank pick him up and kiss him without any crying. I think he thought the teddy was well worth not making a fuss over. Aunt Ada got a lovely silk blouse, some scent and a little gold brooch in the shape of two hearts with an arrow through them both. I got three Dandy comics that I'd already read and gran got some whisky. Gran fussed and asked questions about fighting, which he tried to answer between mouthfuls of sandwiches she'd made. Aunt Ada said she just had to nip around the corner for some fags and refused to take the Players Frank had brought her. Woodbines suited her better she said, which was a down right lie for I knew she always smoked Players.

The honking of the car horn seemed to stop and Aunt Ada came back with her Woodbines. Then gran insisted Frank and Ada went around to see Frank's parents and take Charlie with them as a surprise, which I think it would have been quite a big surprise seeing as Aunt Ada and Charlie had never once been around there since Frank left.

Having Frank back took a load off gran's shoulders. She didn't have to bring in the coal bucket any more and was clearly relieved to have someone help look after Charlie. Frank was looking for work, but then so were hundreds of other service men too and, as most of the women folk were not willing to give up their newfound freedom from household chores, the jobs available were few and far between.

The local Council had begun to build estates of prefabricated houses. There were rows and rows of them, each one looking the same with a square of garden at the front and the back. All the roads were given names like Churchill Road, Britannia Close. There was even a Potts Avenue. The houses were built mainly of asbestos and someone referred to the new estate as Toy Town and the name stuck with the locals.

In spite of this, the council houses generally had three bedrooms, inside toilets and everything was modern and new, but the waiting lists for them were as long as your arm. Aunt Ada put her name down for one and told me on the side they had a very good chance as she had all the right connections, and how it all helped if she worked over and on Saturday mornings. Her job couldn't have been too stressful however, because I often saw her in the local café with a man I think worked in the council offices along with her.

I went with Aunt Ada to look at one of the houses on the new council estate. I saw a fight going on outside the Stag public house at closing time and a crowd had quickly gathered. Apparently a sailor had broken the front teeth of someone who hadn't been fighting in the war. I heard the sailor had called him a coward and all hell had broken loose as a result, that is until the local bobby appeared and restored some semblance of order.

Some of the town's lasses who had wed Americans were leaving for New York. It was about this time that Aunt Ada and Uncle Frank had a big row and Aunt Ada sulked a great deal for some reason. Frank took out his frustration of her unreasonableness on the garden and dug a huge patch, which he filled with cabbages. I'm dreading them getting full-grown, as gran won't waste anything. Mr Oats in one of the terraced houses grew tobacco in his allotment and got a summons for it. At least he didn't have to look forward to cabbage with every meal.

Our vicar at the church changed and now we had the Rev. Tooley who is quite young. As gran said, 'he's still a bit wet behind the ears.'

I hadn't realised that there had been a problem with the Rev. Swindells until gran came home after arranging flowers as part of her alter duties. She was in a right state and said she'd had enough of the vicar's Catholic ways.

He'd brought back the use of holy water and had introduced the use of incense during some of the church services. Gran was quite angry about his proposals to introduce confessions into the church's routine.

'Enough is enough,' she said. 'Even if the people in our church only confessed to their sins half of the time, the church would be empty,' she said, looking very wise to the fact.

Until now, I'd never appreciated that the Reverend Swindells had leanings towards the Oxford movement in the Church of England. The Rev. Tooley soon brought things back to a more moderate level, which started yet another wave of discontent with the Mothers Union and gran in particular. She thought all vicars should wear long black robes all the time, and even missed the use of incense and holy water. There was no pleasing gran sometimes.

Chapter 18

It happened quite suddenly, gran collapsed among the cabbages. The day was unusually warm for an English summer and for once all clouds had been swept away leaving blue skies and the full force of the sun. A neighbour found her, still holding the cabbage in her hand, which I gave to the kind man for being there. Gran's face was pulled to one side and she had drooled out of her lob sided mouth. It was quite awful. The knowledgeable neighbour told us he'd seen it before with his own father.

'Stroke,' he said simply.

Frank was fortunately at home trying to make sense of our bills but couldn't make head or tale of them, which I'm afraid, none of us excelled at either. We were always behind in some of our payments, especially after Aunt Ada had gotten her hands on the coupon books.

Our neighbour and Frank managed to lift gran into the house and up the stairs to her room, which was no mean feat as she wasn't the lightest of persons. I took charge of young Charlie who kept calling for his nana to wake up.

The doctor arrived and I felt sorry it wasn't Dr. McKenzie, as he'd always taken such an interest in our family. The doctor confirmed it was indeed a stroke.

'It's a major one I'm afraid,' he stated very professionally, as though he came across a case every day. Maybe he did, for it was often said around town that some of our lads would be good stroke candidates if ever they got wind of what their wives had been up to. Gran and her friends from church gossiped a lot during their get-togethers and, as I had good hearing, was kept quite well informed on these matters.

After a quick examination the doctor said,

'I doubt if she'll come around. It will just be a matter of time before she goes.' He took his stethoscope from around his neck and placed it on top of his other medical things in his black bag; before adding, 'I'll send the nurse in to make her comfortable and I'll pop in from time to time myself. But if she shows any signs of distress call someone at the surgery right away.'

The newspaper boy, who just happened to have completed his last delivery at our house, took a message for us to Aunt Ada. For sixpence, he pedalled off furiously down the street on his sit-up-and-beg bike. Aunt Ada came home in a car driven by a sandy haired man. She was weeping and blowing her nose on a man's white hankie. I'd never seen mascara wet before and it looked almost comical running down from her eyes.

'Is she?' she whispered, letting Frank put a protective arm around her shaking shoulder, 'gone,' she finished. He shook his head.

'Now, now lass. Whilst there's life there's hope.' He was taking charge and knew it, and a very capable Frank was now emerging. 'We shall have to think of your mother now; she'll need all the care we can give her.'

Ada nestled into his chest, and then slowly untangled herself as he led her upstairs where the sobbing began all over again.

If ever I found anything admirable in Aunt Ada it was the way she looked after her mother those three days before gran passed away. With the air of a district nurse, she changed and washed gran's bedding, bedding I might add, that reeked of urine and such. She washed gran and combed her hair and sat up all that night before taking on long caring shifts with Frank. Charlie was not allowed to see his nana, so I didn't get much opportunity to do any share of the sitting with her.

Gran passed away peacefully in the early hours of the third day and, after Dr. Proctor had signed her death certificate, Mrs Winterbottom came and laid her out before the funeral people arrived to put her in the coffin that was now resting on a purple draped trestle table in the front room.

I didn't know gran had so many friends, for there was a continuous stream of people to see her before the lid was fastened down. She was buried with the grandpa I never knew at St. Anne's, the Mother Church on the edge of town among graves; some of which dated back to the eleventh century. I'm glad she was buried there with her ancestors, for in the following year the field next to the church was consecrated and began to take the overflow.

There is no doubt Aunt Ada missed her mother for I often found her drying her eyes after a private weep. The house was left equally to gran's four children. The will had never been changed, even after my own mother had died. It stipulated though the house couldn't be sold as long as a family member was living in it. Thoughts of a new council house were quickly forgotten as Aunt Ada said she couldn't leave her old home and, as they now had no rent to pay, it would be silly. Aunt Ivy said she didn't care, but would like a few of gran's things, like the cupboard with the mother-of-pearl inlays and the silver tea service that had been her own grandmother's. I noticed a lot more silver and china left the house with her.

Joseph and Annie got nothing apart from gran's large shopping basket and the bed sheets she'd died in. But Annie didn't complain when I said it wasn't fair. She just shrugged her shoulders and said she and Joseph had all they needed and just patted her stomach. Annie's baby was born the day I left school. A big bouncing boy they called Joey after Joseph. How they managed I don't quite know. I think Annie's mother had a lot to do with helping out, as she was there quite often; padding around in her worn slippers and paisley apron that she wore all the time. I'd even come to the conclusion she wore it instead of a dress.

I thought it would be so easy to get a job when I was at school, but now I was faced with it, I found my dreams diminishing as the reality of the situation took hold. London all at once appeared a strange and frightening place, so I put it on the back burner. Most of the art school students quickly found positions in the pot banks, painting designs on the biscuit chinaware. But then the majority of them lived in the Potteries and it was a natural follow-on to their training. Only one of the students had decided to teach and two others became hairdressers. I didn't want to brush gold around plates, cup and saucers, or paint flower designs. So I applied for a job in a small business, which designed and made badges. They needed a designer.

I packed my folder with my best artwork and took the long bus ride to arrive at a run-down building. I made my way up some rickety stairs to an office. A slick spiv-like man, dressed in a pin-striped suit with large padded shoulders and brylcreemed hair, eyed me up and down especially my long legs which I had crossed, lifting my skirt higher than I would have liked. A blond woman brought in a tray of tea, gave me a dirty look and slammed the door behind her rather sharply as she left.

Dave, as he asked me to call him, looked over my work and said he could see that I could draw well, but designing badges was a little different and that I would need to spend some time with him to train me. He thought I had good potential and offered me the job. Then he came around his desk to put his hand on my shoulder and give it a squeeze. I froze and don't know what got into me but jumping up, I picked up my drawings and told him to stick his job. I could see he was about to turn nasty and I made a hasty retreat for the door, almost knocking the blond over behind the door and who had obviously had her ear pressed to the keyhole.

I sat, still seething on the bus ride home, wondering how much of a fool I made of myself, and if I'd got the situation totally wrong. But by the time I neared home I'd convinced myself I'd been very right in my judgement of the so called Dave and wished the blond all the best with him.

Aunt Ada wasn't pleased.

'You have to think what you are getting out of it,' she said. 'It could have been a well paying job and there are always men who try to come on strong. That's life my girl.'

I knew she had now realised I was a potential moneymaker, and seized every opportunity in telling me I had to pull my weight like everyone else. She was without a job herself at present and was quick to tell all and sundry she thought a mother's place was at home with the children. Someone had already taken her job at the Council offices, and the sandy haired man was often seen chauffeuring a young dark haired girl around, not much older than me.

For weeks I scoured the local paper, my inexperience showing, as I was still hoping for that perfect job where I could apply something of all I had learned at the art school. But the only advertisements were for jobs involving domestic chores and cooking. Since many women had been in the work force during the war and had managed to bring up families too, they were not about to let their new-found independence go. Nobody wanted to clean anymore, especially the younger ones, and domestics were hard to find.

Uncle William came to my rescue as he had done for Uncle Joseph. He said if I was really stuck and didn't mind working on a machine, he would find me a job at the mill. Because he understood my dilemma, he said it would probably be only temporary 'til a proper job that fitted my skills came along. Cotton and silk production for clothing had now taken over from the war demands for parachutes and barrage balloon fabrics, and the town's manufacturing slowly resorted back to what it always had been. Although most of the mills had restarted, many were still only operating at half capacity and others were already being forced to shut down again and again because of fuel shortages.

From the very first day I knew I was going to hate it, but had very little choice with Aunt Ada demanding I brought my share of money into the house. The floor of the mill was covered with machines and large baskets. The noise was incessant and very often unbearable. It wreaked havoc on my nervous system. Music blared out, machines rattled, and voices shouted constantly at each other in attempting to be heard above the din. Many of the girls I had seen around the town and who had gone to the local Secondary Modern school, had that 'I told you so' look about them. They had often told me in the past that they considered my education a waste of time, especially since I had now ended up just like one of them.

However, my supervisor was friendly and patiently taught me to run up seams on the cotton dresses. If the truth be known, her kindness was more than likely to be because I was the niece of the mill's owner. I was nevertheless grateful and proved to be a fast learner. Ada took the majority of my pay packet and suggested me doing some overtime which would help pay for some rose patterned curtains she'd had her eyes on. Not that Ada had proved herself house proud in any way since she'd decided to stay at home.

The house carried on in the same old muddle and perhaps had even got worse with more of Charlie's toys appearing frequently all over the place and with the absence on my part of any daily tidying up. Frank tried and would look at me apologetically, especially on Saturday mornings, whenever I appeared with a dustpan and mop in an effort to regain some semblance of order. Today Frank was clearly annoyed

'Give the girl a hand will you,' he cried in exasperation as Aunt Ada lounged around on the settee reading magazines.

'I'm giving her a home, she should be grateful,' Aunt Ada lashed back. 'It does a young girl good to keep busy instead of hanging out at the cinema.'

'Wouldn't do you any harm to get yourself moving either. I don't know what you find to do all day,' Frank answered back.

At this Aunt Ada sat straight up and went on to define the role of a mother and how it wasn't easy looking after a child that was bright and needed a lot of looking after. Aunt Ada then reminded him of the time her mother had a cleaner in when they were young, and, as if to add to Frank's humbling, went on to explain how her father brought enough money in to keep his whole family and was considered a real man. At that Frank slammed the door and picked up his bike by the outhouse.

He pedalled straight for the Crown and didn't reappear until closing time. He rolled in and straight away fell into gran's old rocking chair and was soon snoring and quite oblivious to the world around him. Charlie, still not in bed, looked on with a puzzled look and sat quietly watching at Frank's feet. As was usually the case on these occasions Frank often woke himself up by his own snoring, making a funny noise in the process. I think it was at these times that Charlie seemed to like him the best, for his father would pick him up and the two of them would just laugh together.

I don't know why Aunt Ada hated Frank and Charlie being together so much, for she generally grabbed him off Frank's lap and gave some feeble excuse about Charlie being up way past his bedtime. This always ended up with Charlie screaming and Frank and Aunt Ada just yelling at each other again.

I would have liked to say it all got better as time passed but it didn't and many a night I would hear raised voices coming from their bedroom through the thin plaster walls. Times many some one would get up and I'd hear the bedroom door bang shut followed by gran's door being opened. I think it must have been Frank, as Aunt Ada wouldn't go into gran's old room anymore. I hated those nights and would cover up my ears with the eiderdown.

Chapter 19

I grew up very quickly during those years working at the mill and had just begun to feel accepted as one of the workers, for I was good at what I did. But the opening to being accepted didn't last long as a number of the mill girls were being handed their cards due to the continuing fuel shortages. There were more and more murmurings about the unfairness of it all. I knew I was the target of their frustrations as my length of time at the mill was very short compared to theirs. And then their hints about my being in the family started.

It all ended up by me being "Sent-to-Coventry" and everyday entering through the mill gates quickly became a nightmare. I handed in my cards. Uncle William seemed to understand and I think was somewhat grateful that I had relieved him of yet another mill headache. Aunt Ada didn't see it that way at all and hit the roof, bringing in Uncle Joseph as an example of toughing it out.

'Our Joseph's got more balls than the lot of you,' she shouted. 'He doesn't just leave and expect his family to survive on the dole.'

I sighed, mostly from the comparison she was throwing at me. Uncle Joseph was an ex-soldier and was blind, and many in the town thought he had risked his life for them. No one would want Joseph to lose his job at the mill. Frank in his way, tried to come to my defence.

'Leave the girl be Ada,' he said wearily. 'She'll come up with something and we can manage if you curb your spending.'

That did it. Any reference to Aunt Ada's spending created a torrent of unrepeatable words, which sent Frank back to the pub in quick time and Aunt Ada to gathering Charlie up in her arms as if he was her only comfort. After a week of heated rows and Aunt Ada's sullen face, I made my mind up to leave altogether. I had no idea where to. I was still a few weeks short of my eighteenth birthday and had neither any experience of the world outside the town nor had anyone that I could relate to.

Annie, bless her tried her best to listen but had too many responsibilities, and looked a little nervous in case I asked if I could live with them, although the idea had crossed my mind. William and Aunt Ivy never offered. I knew they were living in a different world to mine and it wouldn't have been easy with William's mother and father still being in control of the family affairs. I gathered from Aunt Ivy's remarks that she herself had to fit in and not cause waves within the established family circle she now found herself in.

An advert in the local paper caught my eye.

Nurses Training School.
Tuition starting September.
Anyone interested in
becoming a Qualified Nurse,
should apply to: The Matron,
Danesbury District Hospital.

It wasn't so much the desire to become a nurse that drove me to apply, but the room and board that went with the training plus the regular pay packet at the end of each month. I knew that every hospital had a nurse's home and, at that desperate time in my life, it appeared to be a God sent refuge, not that God and I were on speaking terms very much these days.

I applied and three weeks later I received a letter, which I opened with trembling hands. I had an interview in three days time. I must have polished my shoes about a dozen times with Frank staring at me suspiciously. I scrubbed and scrubbed my nails and stole one of Aunt Ada's nail files to perfect their shape. Not a speck of dirt remained, for I knew how important clean hands were to a nurse.

The interviews didn't take as long as I'd imagined. There were ten of us who had applied. I didn't recognise any of the others. I found out later they came from different towns and four were even from Ireland.

The matron sat at her large desk in a small office, the fire blazing up the chimney even though it was only the beginning of September. She was quite small and amply rounded, especially around her middle that was held in by a black belt that had an elaborate clasp buckle over a dark blue dress. Apart from her blue dress; black shoes and stockings, everything else was white. Her cuffs, a neat collar and a large cap that was folded into a triangle were stiffly starched.

When I was called in at last for my interview, I stood awkwardly waiting for her to turn around. But she took her time and went on adjusting piles of papers. I gazed at a photo of a man in a naval uniform in its frame on the side of the desk, and wondered if it was……

She turned, indicating I sat on the chair positioned opposite hers.

The first question was why I wanted to be a nurse. 'Why would anyone want to be a nurse?' The question floated around in my brain as if it didn't really apply directly to me. Just a general question I thought, so I gave a general answer.

'To help the sick and make them comfortable.'

It seemed to be the most suitable of answers at the time and was apparently accepted. She nodded and spoke about my education and I thought it only fitting to push my passing the eleven plus exam more than going to the Art School, but she insisted on me having to explain why I chose the latter.

'My dad died in the war.'

Where I thought that explanation would get me I didn't know, but it seemed to serve the purpose as she responded quite kindly to me whilst glancing at the man in the photograph.

'Yes, I know how that changes things,' she said.

I was to begin my nursing training at the end of the month. I would be allowed a room in the nurse's home, with uniform and meals provided. Laundry was done at the hospital, so sheets and towels were all marked and used only in the nurse's home. Providing notebooks and pencils were my responsibility together with a readable watch with a second hand. The last item threw me into panic. I'd no money and had never had a watch with or without a second finger.

I didn't want to do what I eventually did, but thought my mam would understand. I pulled out my mam's few trinkets that were tied in a handkerchief and looked through them, something I hadn't done before and was amazed to see the brooch she had so often worn on special occasions was gold, with little water pearls on it. So it was with her engagement ring, gold with a solitary diamond. There was also a thin gold chain and a gold ring with a broken band, a few other cheap items and a man's broken watch, which I think was my dad's.

I walked past the jeweller's shop in town six times, clutching the handkerchief with my precious treasure trove held inside. There was only one customer and he didn't stay long. Plucking up courage, I marched boldly in and placed my hankie on the glass counter top. The old man on the other side didn't even glance at me. His eyes were fastened on the contents of the hankie, which I was now fumbling to untie.

He poked his finger among the offerings and spread them apart, pushing anything that looked as if there was any value to it to one side and discarding the rest. We, the old man and I, hadn't said a word. We both had some sort of silent agreement. Out of his top pocket he produced an eyeglass, which fitted snugly under his heavy brows, then bent down to stare again at the ring he'd picked up. After glancing over the interesting pile once more he lifted his head and simply said,

'Thirty bob, the lot.'

My reply was,

'Can I get a watch with a second hand on it for that?'

He opened the panel to his window display that held all sorts of watches and picked out two. Both were plain, round faces with big numbers, had leather straps and both sported a second finger that ticked rhythmically around its circumference. I didn't see any price tags attached anywhere.

'Going nursing?' he asked. He was a man of few words.

'Yes,' I answered, looking as appealing as I could.

'Take your pick,' he said picking out the two and placing them on the counter, 'they're both one pound, two shillings and sixpence.'

I chose the one that had a black strap and he gave me the change from the thirty bob. I gathered up the rest of the valueless bits and pieces and, strapping the watch on my wrist, walked home with a step so light I could have flown. Aunt Ada spied my watch right away and was just about to open her mouth when I helped close it with my saying,

'I'm leaving,' and then went on to explain that I was going to become a nurse. I've never seen her so speechless, as the meaning of 'don't cut off your hand to spite your face' became clear to her. For once I felt so powerful and admit I used it to my best advantage by refusing to baby-sit Charlie anymore, not cleaning the house that Saturday and to turn the screw even tighter, I brought three pair of nylons in black with a lovely seam up the back and proceeded to try them on before her eyes.

Annie and Uncle Joseph were thrilled for me and Annie said it would be wonderful having a nurse in the family. Aunt Ivy congratulated me, saying in front of her friends, it was easy getting into nursing if anyone had a decent education, and how the family all had their fair share of brains. I think she'd hoped no one would remember Aunt Ada, who was never the brightest at figures or anything else for that matter.

It was the very same week I bumped into Ernest. We stood awkwardly for a moment talking about the weather. Then to my surprise he invited me into the café close by for a coffee. My heart was beating a little faster than normal and I'm sure my colour had heightened around my face. I was aware of his big frame as he opened the café's door. There was a smell of all male as I passed by his chest.

At first it was mostly small talk, then the conversation grew more natural and we were soon recalling our school days and laughing. I liked the way his hair fell in a curl across his forehead and his white even teeth peeked out from beneath his fine chiselled lips when he grinned. But most of all I liked the way his grey blue eyes had a mature gaze about them when he looked into mine over his coffee cup. I told him about my nursing and he said he was glad I was training in the hometown and didn't have to go to Manchester. He then told me he had applied to join the Police Force after he'd done his National Service. We laughed at that. I started it and he joining in, knowing we were both recalling all his exploits as a youngster.

'I reckon it will stand me in good stead,' he confessed. 'At least I will be a step ahead and should know all the tricks youngsters get up to.'

I didn't want the time with him to end. It was so good. I needed to talk to a friend so much and I found myself telling him all about my home life. He listened sympathetically and at one time placed his large hand over mine, then took it back quickly as though he had taken too much of a liberty.

I dreamed of Ernest that night. I dreamt we were walking hand-in-hand by the edge of the quarry when he fell and I watched him rolling over and over, the sand sliding over him until he was covered completely. I awoke sweating and developed a migraine, the first of many I would eventually suffer from.

Chapter 20

I gazed at the reflection of myself in the long mirror that hung behind the door of my small new room. It took a while to come to terms with myself that it was actually me.

My newly-cut hair curled under a stiff white cap; with an equally stiff white detachable collar circling my neck and fastened with a stud. The light blue dress stopped just below my black stockened knees and smart black sensible shoes completed the image. The crisp white apron was pinned by its square bib on the chest with the training school badge at one corner and a tiepin at the other. A broad Persil-white starched belt circled my slim waist and was closed with two more studs. Just above the apron bib peeked the top of a pen and the two ring handles of a pair of scissors.

I raised my wrist to display the watch, and over to my right I could see the reflection of my single bed backed up to the wall with a black cloak lined in red, and two matching long red fastening ties lying crossed over on it. I turned from the mirror to view my box-like living space.

A tall built-in half cupboard with a dressing table filled the wall opposite to the bed and under the window was a desk with three drawers and a high-backed chair. Last but not least, a tall wicker basket at the foot of the bed was provided to place dirty linen in. Three other items were placed in strategic positions to make it home-like and comfortable, a wastepaper bucket, an ashtray and a glass tumbler on top of a paper napkin on a tiny bedside table that also supported a reading lamp. The same floral curtains that covered every room in the nurses' home floated free with the cool air from the open window and outside the green lawns and flower beds of the hospital grounds greeted me.

I took to nursing as if born to it and realised the experience I'd had cleaning and managing young Charlie was a very good foundation to my nursing career. We spent the mornings in the classroom and the afternoons on the wards.

I felt for the first time in years I had a proper home and friends. The ten of us bonded, as did each class that followed us. Eventually two left to get married, one found she had TB and disappeared over night and the cleaners were quick to disinfect her room and seal it off. But the ones that remained worked hard and played well together.

I was like a cat let out of a house for the first time. I made my own decisions that were of course only those as far as any nurse-in-training was allowed to. But as long as you abided by the rules, life could be pleasant. Of course there was never any staying out after ten at night or bringing anyone back to your room. Studying was long and sometimes brought on my migraine headaches.

One Christmas, when I was on night duty, Ernest entered my life again. We had only two policemen on duty at night in the town. One was in the office and the other out on the beat. It was quite normal for the one out on patrol to stop by our hospital for a cup of tea and a warm-up by matron's fire, especially if it was very cold outside. We always used matron's office to sit in during the night hours as it was central to the wards and had a phone.

That night I caught myself glancing quite often at Ernest. He looked so handsome in his uniform and so official, sipping tea out of matron's best china cups. I think he looked over at me too, as he would glance away embarrassed whenever I lifted my eyes. I walked him to the main door later and I think he had something he wanted to ask me, but the chance was lost as an ambulance pulled in at that moment. I hoped he'd come again during that week and I kept walking the corridor to the main entrance door just in case I hadn't heard the bell of the side door. But he didn't come and I was soon back on day duty again.

It was that same week I first met Elaine. They brought her in after a dreadful accident on the main road. A lorry had failed to stop as she crossed the road and Elaine was hit. The lower parts of her legs were badly damaged and I knew from the start she'd never walk again. Elaine was younger than me and had so much courage that I was instantly drawn to her. She complained very little, although I knew from her pale drawn face she was suffering emotionally as well as physically.

At first a thin dark-haired young man came to sit by her side, holding her hand and talking to her gently as she cried. It was her boy friend Eric she told me. Then Eric came less and less and Elaine turned her face to the wall pretending she was asleep if anyone looked as though they might ask her about him. I think it was because I never mentioned him that Elaine and I were comfortable in each other's presence.

When she was given a wheelchair, I would spend my off duty afternoons wheeling her around the grounds. Her parents greeted me with great respect and, when Elaine eventually left the hospital, our friendship remained firm. It wasn't a friendship about what we did together or what we got from each other; it was simply the enjoyment of trust and understanding. She never once, in all the years I knew her, mentioned Eric again, although I'd seen his wedding picture in the local paper a year after the accident and had seen his wife later pushing a pram.

Elaine would laugh at my tales about Aunt Ada and it made me feel as though there had been some fun in my life, even though I couldn't see it at the time. I had considered going around to Aunt Ada's house and to try at having a pleasant conversation with her, for I missed young Charlie and would have liked to see him again, but I didn't.

Instead I got all the news from Annie, whose brood by now had grown to three. How she managed will always be a mystery, but the kids were always clean and well mannered. Uncle Joseph was learning brail and Annie would look at him with such pride as his fingers skimmed across the groups of raised dots. It is said that time is a great healer of things past and I was even beginning to believe in the possibility of a good future for myself.

My final exams were now over and I graduated with the Theory Prize. No one came to my graduation, although William and Aunt Ivy sent me a card. It didn't really bother me because the Irish nurses didn't have any family in England at all. These girls always amazed me in the way they gained at least ten to fifteen pounds every time they went back to Ireland for a visit and then came back to lose it all again.

'It's the amount of potatoes we are given to eat over there,' said Bridie, going on to explain how her mother's favourite meal for her family of eight was stews with very little meat but lots of 'tatties'. It explained a lot why Bridie's servings of potatoes were always pushed to one side of her plate whenever she came back from her holidays.

Some of the nurses would go to the Saturday dances at the Town Hall when they were off duty, and although they could never stay to the end, it was nice to take off the uniform and don a pretty dress. Often we'd sit in each other's room and listen to the beginnings of romances that had begun at these dances. Maybe for the nurses it became more of a challenge with their restricted hours. Much of this I would relay to Elaine.

'Why don't you go Rita,' she asked me questioningly. 'Can't you dance?' She lifted her eyebrows in a manner daring me to lie.

'No,' I stated bluntly.

'Then I'll teach you.'

I looked at her in surprise and she caught my drifting glance to the wheel chair.

'Don't worry about that,' she told me practically, 'I still got my voice.'

We set about making patterns of footprints from newspapers, which she instructed be placed on the hall floor. She switched on the music in the dining room loud enough to send her parents for a grateful drink at the local and Elaine had me placing my own feet into the footprints as she tapped her hand in time to my movements. Returning from the local, her dad, caught up in the enthusiasm, offered to lead me in the final practices. We had a great time and I promised Elaine I would go to the next Town Hall dance just to tell her all about it.

I did go to. The very next Saturday in fact, dressed in a borrowed but fashionable dress of Bridies. The band was marvellous and I managed to get around the floor without too much of a mishap. An hour before I had to take my leave, a familiar voice from behind me said

'Can I have this next dance?'

Why does the world around you threaten to collapse when the situation you want most to happen suddenly happens? I found myself saying

'I'm afraid I can't do the foxtrot.' I couldn't even lie properly and felt so unworthy.

'Neither can I, so let's just shuffle around the best we can,' and with that Ernest pulled me into his arms, which seemed to be the most natural place in the world to be. We danced in our fashion for three more dances and it didn't really matter what the dances were; for our steps were designed to bring our bodies together in an intimate embrace. It was the happiest time of my life. When I knew I really had to leave, Ernest insisted he walked me to the hospital gates. Without asking and in total union he held my hand all the way. He didn't say much, but before I had chance to reach for the big iron gate he'd pulled me gently to him, and with one hand just pushing away my fallen curls from my forehead and looking right into my eyes, he bent down and kissed me long and tenderly. We clung together for a moment, neither wishing to be free of the other, 'til he pushed me away and nodded to the lights in the nurses' home.

'You'd better go. I'll phone,' he said quietly.

I didn't sleep a wink that night and yet felt little tiredness the next day, but strangely finding each chore a joy. Besides the phone in matron's office, there were only two other outside phones in the hospital, and each was at one end or the other of long corridors. I'd tried to hover around them as much as I possibly could. True to his word, Ernest phoned me. I knew it was from the police station as I could hear some drunk shouting in the background.

'When are you off duty?' he said straight to the point.

'Thursday at 6.00 pm,' I answered just as briefly.

'Good, I'm off then too. I'll pick you up at 7.00 pm outside the gates.'

'Alright, I'll be there.' I was just about to put the phone down when I heard in a half whispered tone.

'I'm looking forward to it very much.'

'So am I,' I answered just as softly before hearing his phone click off.

Months before I'd made a promise to Annie I would visit Aunt Ada sometime, even if it were just for Charlie's sake, as he often asked why I never went there. I'd made a feeble promise with no real intention of keeping it, but today I wanted a perfect world around me and nothing, not even Aunt Ada, was going to spoil the joy I felt at that moment. I had three hours off this afternoon and was in such a good mood, I walked through the town with a bunch of flowers in my hand and, before I knew it I was standing on my gran's front doorstep.

It took me a while to recognise the swaying figure that opened the door. The whisky reeked from her breath as she too stood and stared back.

'Well I suppose you'd better come in,' she said eventually, and padded into the living room that had changed very little from my time there.

I noticed my favourite picture was no longer hung on the wall. A half empty bottle of malt whisky stood on the sideboard by the same box of buttons I used to thread together, and no doubt they were the same buttons. I had hoped to see young Charlie as he must be quite grown up now and I still had fond memories of him as a little boy.

'Want a drink?' She shuffled over to the sideboard and took hold of the whisky bottle's neck.

I shook my head.

'Please yourself,' she said, unscrewing the top of the bottle that held half an inch of the amber liquid in the bottom and refilling a glass that sat on the table. She slumped herself down in the old chair that had been my gran's favourite and didn't even bother to invite me to sit down also. She just gazed over her glass at me. For all her sloppiness and neglect with the black roots of her hair turning to blond, there was still a look of a very attractive Ada as she was, and certainly could be again with a little cleaning up.

'How's Charlie?' I asked finding not much else to say, even after three years.

'My Charles is fine.' She'd always called him 'Her Charles' as if it only took one to make a baby.

'And Frank?' It was the next most obvious question to ask. She shrugged her shoulders and took a long but shallow breath. I sat down still uninvited both hands on my knees and wondering if this were what health visiting would be like.

'Gets work here and there.' Aunt Ada crossed her long shapely legs, pulling at the wrinkle around her ankle where her stockings had slipped down.

At that moment Frank came in. He looked a little older and stressed.

'So did you find any work?' Aunt Ada asked before I could greet him

'They are thinking of opening the old sand quarries and I went there to put my name down.'

It didn't register at first but when it did I felt a blackness come over me and heard a distant voice saying

'Hey are you OK?' it asked.

The blackness passed, and I waited for the contents of my stomach to settle.

'Did you mean the quarries at the back of our old house?' I managed to collect myself and stop the nervous trembling I felt in my throat.

'They're the only quarries I know of.' Frank looked at me as if I was some sort of fool.

'And they're going to open them?' I questioned, hoping beyond hope I'd heard wrong.

'There's talk of it, but then there's been talk before.' He leaned forward to get a better look at me. 'Are you sure you're alright?'

I think he was more concerned with the possibility of me collapsing in their house than the state of my health. It was difficult maintaining a semblance of composure, but following a little small talk with Frank; I said I'd call again sometime. Aunt Ada didn't say anything and I thought for a brief moment that she was going to be sick she had gone so pale. Her drinking seemed to be getting out of hand.

It was a dreadful period I went through following my visit to Aunt Ada's. I couldn't speak, think or do anything. I was diagnosed with severe depression and sent to a psychiatric hospital for a while to recover. I never knew what Ernest thought as he must have waited that Thursday night. As for me I don't even remember that night and was somewhere in a dark void; not daring to allow myself to think any further about it for fear of what I'd find.

It took me a good three months to recover, and although I was asked to return to my old hospital as a staff nurse, probably because of the shortage of nursing staff, I now had other plans, plans that didn't include Ernest or any members of my family in them. I would be sorry to leave Elaine. She had written to me regularly despite my refusal to answer any of them 'til I was good and ready. She just kept being there for me the whole time. Sometimes I was tempted to tell her everything, but couldn't bare the thought of her horrified face.

They didn't reopen the quarries. A brand new one was established on the other side of town, but it was all too much for me to take in.

Ernest, I'd somehow blotted from my fragile mind, knowing there could never be a future for us. I applied to the General Hospital in Toronto and was accepted into the nursing staff.

By the summer, I was flying over the Atlantic to start my new life and a fresh beginning in Canada,

PART 3

England 1996

Chapter 21

A man's voice brought Rita out of her deep sleep and for a moment or two she felt disorientated. She'd caught a few of the words about air turbulence and a request from the captain for passengers to prepare for landing and fasten their seat belts. However it still took Rita a few minutes to come to terms with the fact the aircraft was heading for England not Canada.

Rita pushed herself to a better sitting position and looked out of the window. The jumbo jet had already commenced its slow descent to Manchester airport and was heading into cloud from the bright sunshine. The cloud cover over Manchester was in distinct layers; the daylight outside darkening through every layer and the aircraft experiencing a number of jolts in the process. At last the airport lights and runway came into view. The plane landed and started its manoeuvres to its assigned gate.

It was still raining when Rita stepped out of airport on the outskirts of Manchester. The rain wasn't anything like the warm downpour followed by bright sunshine that glazed the streets and the flat high–rise roofs of Toronto. Rita turned her collar up against the damp cold that crept into her bones. The sky was nothing but grey cloud and the drizzle constant.

She shivered. Everyone on her flight had departed quickly and not a taxi in sight. Alone and bedraggled, she stood beside her heavy suitcase feeling extremely alien in her homeland.

'Taxi luv?' A cheery voice poked out of the open window of a car that had crept up from behind her.

With a sigh of relief Rita nodded and went to pick up her suitcase. But her gallant rescuer was out of his seat in a trice and had his hand firmly on the case's handle, almost daring her to oppose him.

The taxi was warm inside and Rita sank gratefully down in the wide seat at the back, whilst half turning her head to watch the boot lid slam down. She was surprised the word 'boot' came to her so naturally instead of 'trunk'. She wondered if there was something deep down inside oneself that reverts back quickly to one's upbringing no matter how long you'd been away.

'Where to luv?'

Her driver had positioned himself behind his wheel and had turned his mirror to an angle to see his customer.

'Danesbury,' she answered without a second thought to the distance. Rita was used to thinking in terms of time not miles. The driver swung his head around to see her better, needing her expression as well as her confirmation.

'Twenty pounds,' he said flatly and, when he saw no surprise on his fare's face, he turned back and adjusted his meter.

Rita had already done the exchange rate in her head and settled for the worth of having an easy ride to a hotel, a meal and a hot shower. What unsettled her more was how far twenty pounds would have gone in 1954; it was more than a month's pay in those days.

The drizzle brought on a misting up of the car windows. Rita wiped her side window with her arm to get a glance of the English countryside. They were already joining the ring road at a speed that exceeded anything she would have done. Cars seemed to be coming from all directions and Rita had forgotten the English love of roundabouts. She was beginning to find it unnerving being driven on the other side of the road.

She closed her eyes and tried to visualise her hometown. The thought struck her that the traffic would be so much more than it had been, so she mustn't think of it being a quiet town any more.

The road noise lessened and her driver broke into a whistled rendering of 'Singing in the Rain'. She guessed he was a Gene Kelly fan.

When Rita peered out of the window again; there was a growing familiarity. They were now off the motorway and were travelling along an older road that ran through Wilmslow and Alderley Edge. As they turned onto the Danesbury road, Rita began to recognise certain places. A house, whose garden gate now almost opened onto the road itself following a recent road widening. The house was old and had probably been standing there when Cromwell's Army passed along the same road during the Civil War. It had seen so much change but was still there.

Rita spotted a pub she remembered. It had been modernized but the sign remained the same. They were now almost entering the outskirts of the town, for the pub was a landmark that divided the Manchester road from the Macclesfield road. She felt a quiver of excitement.

'How long have you been away?' The voice came out of the blue and took her so much by surprise that she didn't immediately answer.

'How many years have you been in Canada?' The driver asked again, his eyes holding her's in the mirror. Rita found her voice.

'Forty two.'

He whistled with surprise. 'Well you will no doubt find quite a few changes, but not as many in the country. It's mostly the new roads, but the towns themselves don't change much,' he informed.

'Houses too old in many cases; them's the ones they can't pull down because of them being heritage sites.'

It seemed there was no stopping him and he went on to tell her the problems of trying to cross roads in places like Prestbury, where the streets were so narrow and the traffic so continuous.

'Do you live in Prestbury?' Rita enquired trying to be polite.

'Oh, not me, that's where the posh live.'

He never did tell her where he lived but she guessed it was somewhere in Manchester for the next topic of conversation was Manchester United and did they play much football in Canada?

'More ice hockey,' she imparted.

He shut up and started to whistle again.

They had now slipped onto another ring road with familiar structures along the way. An old mill that used to belong to the Moseley's, and St. John's church that appeared isolated, although the churchyard looked well occupied.

Rita's memories of her hometown roads were shaken and it was quite disturbing to her, especially as she realised these changes must have happened many years before. Part of her knew where she was, the other part remained confused. She felt she was in some sort of time warp.

'We're in Danesbury miss,' he must have noticed the absence of any wedding band. 'Where to now?'

'The Black Boar Hotel, do you know it?'

She hoped he did because for the life of her she couldn't remember the name of the street it was on and she didn't dare to say it was just across from the pharmacist. Rita realised that she was thinking like a Canadian again and had to remember to call it a chemist in England.

'The Black Boar, nice place.' The taxi driver replaced her confusion with relief. 'It's very popular with the Americans,' he continued taking a sharp left that made his wheels scream.

'They like the haunted ones.'

'Haunted?' Rita sat up and leaned forward in her seat.

'That's right.'

He at once became an authority at the goings on at the hotel

'Some seventeenth century bloke sits in a chair in a certain room with a pen in his hand and moans like you wouldn't believe. You wouldn't get me sleeping there for all the tea in China.'

Rita leaned back and half smiled. She had never heard of the Black Boar ever having a ghost. It must have appeared about the same time the American holidaymakers started arriving.

The taxi wound its way through a variety of streets, some vaguely familiar, but it was now getting dull and the rain was still coming down, glazing the taxi windows outside.

'Here we are Miss.'

They came to an abrupt stop. Instead of parking outside the main entrance, they were in a cobbled courtyard to the side of the hotel. Rita paid the taxi driver, giving him an extra two pounds and reminding herself to find a bank to exchange her American Express cheques as she'd only cashed a little money at the airport.

A light illuminated a sign over a side door. It read 'Entrance'. Inside the full force of the Elizabethan architecture welcomed the guests. The room she was taken up to by a small rotund man with longish hair tied in a ponytail, was perfectly in tune with the rest of the building. Its beamed ceiling and white-washed walls being enhanced by a slightly sloping floor. Rita was certain the bed however was a reproduction. The wood was too polished to be original and had been deliberately distressed, but it added to the room's overall charm with its tapestry curtains hanging from the bed's four posts and matched by the window curtain drapes.

The wardrobe was naturally reproduction, as even she knew the Elizabethans didn't have them. But the high backed carved chair looked interesting, and for a second Rita wondered if she'd been given the haunted room on purpose, after all the English generally didn't find much difference between Americans and Canadians.

She didn't ask and he didn't say.

She was told dinner started at 7.00 pm, but she could always get a coffee and sandwich in the lounge. This Rita decided to do before unpacking. She also needed to stretch her legs. She did think of phoning John, but then found she needed some time alone before facing any of her family.

A fire was lit in the stone fireplace downstairs in the lounge. The surround of the fireplace was carved with fruits and grains centered on some sort of game bird, its head hanging down, and around its scrawny neck twisted a vine. Over the keystone of the fireplace was carved 1604. 'So much for it being Elizabethan,' mused Rita, knowing Elizabeth 1 died in 1603. She drank her tepid coffee and then decided the drizzle outside was better than the occasional back draught from the fireplace that smelled of soot.

Borrowing an umbrella from the manager, Rita went outside, this time via the great oak front doors and descending six wide steps to the pavement below. She paused to get her bearings. Part of her brain knew exactly where she was; the other part searched wildly for some order to her past memories.

Rita quickly realised what was wrong. The hotel was standing alone with a road on either side of it where once stood houses. Certainly it was an improvement, for the beautiful Elizabethan structure of the hotel had at last come into its own instead of being just another town building that wasn't really noticed. It was then Rita could have shouted with delight, for there right in front of her was the old chemist's shop she used to take her jar full of rosehips to for sixpence, and it had hardly changed. The gold lettering 'Est. 1780' in beautiful writing still adorned the stone mullioned windows at the top. The old stone wall that ran beside it had been taken down and a small garden with flower tubs had taken its place. It was tastefully done.

All at once and not being quite ready for such an intrusion, a wave of emotion hit Rita like a bolt of lightning. She wanted to cry. Tears welled up in her eyes and her throat constricted. There were so many things she wanted to cry for, but most of all for herself and who she really was. Not a Canadian, even her Canadian citizenship didn't elucidate who she really was. Her heritage was too deeply steeped in her genes with hundreds of years claiming her for their own.

At that moment she felt a dreadful loss, not so much for the physical absence of her mam, dad and gran, but for what she could have been if they'd lived. She needed them and they had let her down by dying before she'd grown up. For so long Rita had steeled herself against intimate relationships, and that barrier had cemented itself around anything to do with normal family expectations. The feelings that gushed up inside her were from a multitude of images she had been denied; a father walking with her down the aisle, a mother's confidential talks over pregnancy, sharing, helping, birthdays, Christmas, and family festivities. Then the sudden sadness laced with anger subsided leaving her drained.

Rain lashed against her face, the umbrella had remained unopened. Straightening up her shoulders and taking a deep breath, Rita turned and climbed the steps back up to the hotel door.

'Bad evening,' acknowledged the manager, not waiting for any reason for her return.

He was used to colonials finding the English weather disturbing. They found it contrasted sharply with the hot summer days and freezing winters in Canada.

Today the grey, damp monotony of the rain and drizzle got to her too. Shaking her hair and leaving her coat and umbrella in the entrance hall, Rita made for the lounge, picking up the local paper from a small round table that wobbled on its legs.

A dour-faced girl hovered around waiting for Rita to sit down. As soon as Rita found a table that was positioned by the window, the girl came rushing across, pad and pencil in hand.

'A glass of Pinot Noir please.'

The waitress looked at her dumbfounded, pencil still raised. Rita was about to re-order, then gave in.

'Red house wine then.' The girl's face broke into a big smile and she scribbled down the order, making Rita wonder why she just couldn't remember. 'Still the English have a reason for everything,' she mused. Just as she was beginning to wonder if the girl had forgotten her, she appeared with a well-filled glass and a bowl of crisps. Sipping on the pleasant but unidentifiable wine, Rita opened a newspaper, to be faced with large bold headlines:

AMERICAN SKELETON, FURTHER CLUES FOUND.

Rita's eyes blurred slightly and she felt a little faint. She looked around and was thankful there was no one else in the room. Part of her was ready to leave quickly, taking the paper to her room to read, the other part of her; namely her legs, seemed grounded to the floor. Another long sip of the wine smoothed the way as Rita read on.

'Facts are emerging from the Police Forensic Department about the body found in the sand quarry. Caucasian male, 18 to 25 years of age, 5 feet 9 inches tall and, from the pieces of clothing found, an American serviceman, the cloth samples dating from 1940 to 1945. Detective Heath of Manchester Homicide Division stated it was likely one of the American soldiers that were billeted in the town during the war. Murder is suspected as forensics found a large fracture in the skull made by a heavy instrument. Accidental death resulting from a fall and the head hitting against stone has been ruled out.'

Rita's hand began to shake and the paper trembled.

'It's the damp. Gets to you.' A voice came out of nowhere.

Rita looked up, placing the paper on the table and coming face to face with the manager sitting opposite her holding a bottle of wine and one glass. He leaned over and filled hers before helping himself.

'See you are reading about our murder,' he said indicating at the paper. 'Brought in a lot of trade it has. Nosey parkers I call them. All us old uns around here remember the yanks during the war and there's many a tale to be told.'

'Really.' Rita reached for her drink, willing her hand not to tremble.

'Funny that there's nowt to say who he is,' the manager's face grew rounder, his collar disappearing under his neck as his body slid further into the chair.

'They are bound to find out who he was, surely.' Rita voiced her hidden fear.

'Now that's the thing, who ever bonked the chap on the head took all his identification.' He was warming to this topic of conversation and refilled his glass again. 'Even his identity tags are gone. Now that tells me there must be a good reason and it wasn't no accident.'

'Did you say someone had taken everything?' Rita was leaning forward, the image of her note clearly in her mind.

'The lot.' The manager leaned back tipping his chair a little dangerously on its hind legs, and then went on with his own theories.

'The Americans must have their records of who was billeted in the town. No doubt they thought him just another doing a runner. But they will be able to at least narrow the search down, given time.'

Rita murmured in agreement and seeing the man might stay much longer as the hotel was quiet, made excuses about her jet lag and gathered up her things, half wondering if he'd let her borrow the newspaper but he was already picking it up.

Half an hour later, after struggling with a dribbling shower, Rita curled up under the thick cosy eiderdown. She'd no intention of phoning any of her family 'til she was ready. Images of the quarry still played in her mind as she closed her eyes, but the effects of the jet lag soon blotted them out and she slept long and heavy.

Chapter 22

Rita awoke with a headache, the sort that begins in the shoulders and ends up throbbing over one eye. She wondered if it was the beginning of a migraine, which made her instantly feel worse. A migraine was something she really couldn't be bothered with today and, recalling the instruction she'd had at a Yoga class, was determined to give it all she'd got.

Rita stretched out so that all her muscles could relax, then went through the deep breathing exercise, remembering to breathe from the diaphragm and concentrating on letting go of the tension with the out-breath.

Starting at her feet, she clenched her toes while breathing in, then slowly relaxing them as she breathed out. She was well aware of the advantage her knowledge of anatomy and physiology had given her as a nurse, so it wasn't hard for her to go methodically through her body structure. She relaxed her mouth, eyes and forehead and released the tension from her scalp and behind her head, feeling a sense of detachment in time and space. Her body now felt heavy and totally at ease. She'd no idea how long she lain there, but when a knock on her door brought her back into focus, her headache had lessened.

Only the English wake you with a cup of tea, even if it was never ordered. It was the universal picker-upper, and what better time to have it but first thing in the morning before the day started and work began. Rita poured the nectar out of its small china pot. She touched the small china milk jug with its gold rim; the milk looked like real milk, not the 1% fat reduced variety she had been using for years because of her cholesterol concerns. Life used to be so much less complicated before the plethora of present day dieting fads had taken hold. After two cups, Rita's headache had begun to subside totally and she knew it wasn't the beginning of a migraine after all but rather tension.

Pulling back the curtains, she rolled her head around her tight shoulders and peered outside. The sky was still grey as if holding on to the rain before the next burst, but the pavements were dry. A few people were about. One young woman was pushing a high pram; something Rita rarely saw these days. The mother was in a hurry and, following her at a distance, was a little lad crying as he tried to catch up. Rita watched as the mother stopped, scooping him up and plonking him on the cover of the pram, before disappearing around the corner. Rita remembered young Charlie with his cheery smile and little plump arms. He had been a lovely little boy, but she had never kept in touch with her Aunt Ada and so had no knowledge of his growing up.

'What was he like now?' she mused to herself, letting the curtain drop from her hand.

After forgoing the pathetic excuse for a shower and sorting out something from her case warm enough to stop her shivering, she began to think about what she should do with her day. One thing for certain was that she wasn't ready to stay with any of her relatives just yet. She needed time and privacy to think. Aunt Ivy meant meeting her Cousin John and then she would be taken over. Mentally Rita shied away from meeting with Aunt Ada at her gran's house; she wasn't quite ready for that emotion either. No matter how hard she tried to remind herself that her aunts were now quite old, she still had difficulty replacing their faces with older versions in her mind. By the time Rita had fixed her face with a little light make-up and had tried to tame her hair, which had curled more from the damp weather, she came to the realisation that she too might look like a total stranger to them also.

She elected to visit Uncle Joseph and Annie by noting the comfort feeling that came over her at the thought of meeting them. Rita believed very strongly in her own comfort level, and so felt much better. She even ordered egg and bacon for her breakfast and was pleased she had done so, for the bacon was lean with hardly any fat and the eggs freshly laid. She had three thick slices of toast with thick-cut marmalade and enjoyed the whole meal; she let cholesterol take a back seat.

The manager nodded as Rita slipped by and walked out of the hotel. He was too busy to speak as he bent his head and returned to his accounts. She coughed a little at first, as the chilly atmosphere entered her lungs and then, taking a long deep breath of English morning air, found it quite bracing. She wouldn't make straight for Uncle Joseph's, as she reminded herself it was too early and she really wanted to walk around awhile and see familiar buildings.

She stood for a few moments contemplating which direction to take. There were three possibilities for sightseeing, but the one facing her led into town and she needed to find a bank. The first surprise when she entered the main street was that there was no traffic and not even a road as such for that matter. It was one wide walkway of brown interlocking bricks, with occasional seats and flowerpots.

Rita strolled down the town's unfamiliar centre. Some of the architecture of the shops had remained much the same, although they were now stocking different merchandize. Boyce Adams was now a dress shop, the old butcher's a computer shop, but Rita's heart leapt as she saw the Woolworth she remembered still displaying its sign.

She walked through the glass doors to discover the inside was quite alien with rows of checkout counters and piles of wire baskets that could be filled with everything from artificial flowers to apple pies. Rita let herself indulge in the past for a moment, recalling the motto that used to be displayed over the entrance door, 'Woolworth's. The Three Pence and Sixpence Store' with its counters filled with steel nuts, bolts and screws and everything else imaginable.

A large plump woman bumped into her, interrupting her daydreaming. They stared at each other for a moment searching their brain cells for some figment of lost memory, but neither could put a name to a face that looked vaguely familiar. It wasn't 'til Rita was standing in the Westminster Bank later that it hit her.

'Barbara Potts.'

She wanted to run out and find her, just to find out how Barbara's life had turned out, but the moment of opportunity had gone.

'Sign here.' The pretty blond pushed Rita's American Express cheques across the counter and started to count out the pound notes.

Leaving the bank, Rita walked the full length of the main street, passing the ancient grey stone Town Hall and many other familiar buildings until she came to the Cenotaph that had been built in town. She strolled over to the stone cross with the names of the local war dead carved into the marble stonework. Her eyes travelled down. She had already picked out three familiar names before stopping at her father's name:

Sidney Goodwin 1913 –1944

Rita stood for a while letting the wave of sadness travel through her before tracing her finger over the lettering.

'Took the best, the war did.' A voice shattered her meditation. An old man in a woollen cardigan and cloth cap had walked up behind her and stood looking at the list of names. He must have been in his nineties, his skin wrinkled in a thousand creases.

'Your dad?' he said, nodding towards the list.

Rita nodded back, afraid her voice would break if she spoke. He seemed to understand and silently drifted away, leaving a trail of cigarette smoke that only invoked more memories for her. After a while, Rita pulled herself together and strolled back along the route she'd already taken, to find a wine shop and to purchase flowers for Annie.

The area was now filled with more people and Rita couldn't help wondering if she would recognise anyone, or for that matter if anyone would recognise her. The problem was two-sided as she now understood they and she had changed. It took awhile for her to adjust to the insight that she wouldn't know anyone under sixty. As for mothers with young children, they would have been but a twinkle in their parent's eyes. She continued searching for any vaguely familiar face around her, but now looking more at people her own age. Maybe deep down, she was still hoping to see Ernest Heath.

'Silly woman,' she told herself. He's probably left the town, married with grandchildren. But that didn't stop her from claiming the phantom youth as her own, and that last kiss still lingered in her head.

'I'm getting sentimental,' she told herself and quickly brought herself back into the real world. She sighed.

Whatever made her think Uncle Joseph still lived where he did when she left England all those years ago. Why hadn't this possibility ever occurred to her before now? All at once she felt as if she was a stranger. No one knew her, and the houses she'd known in her past were now probably owned by others. Loneliness began to creep over her like a dark cloud. She'd lived too long with past memories and the town she'd grown up in had moved forward. She just had to move on and accept all the changes.

Leaving the town, Rita walked westward towards a more familiar environment. It would mean passing gran's old house, but that couldn't be helped. A car squealed to a stop, as she was about to cross the road. The driver waved his fist at her. Badly shaken, Rita reminded herself to be more careful. She was used to looking for traffic coming from the other direction.

She passed the cricket ground, which really hadn't changed much, apart from the clubhouse and a new fence that now separated it from a council housing estate on the right. Something appeared very different about her old church. It looked smaller and more isolated. Rita saw that her old school was no longer there. Even the stone wall around it had been taken down. The area had been grassed over and the small height of the few planted trees suggested the change was recent.

On impulse, Rita pushed open the iron gates of the churchyard and walked up the worn path to the large oak door of the church. It was locked. She tried again, still found it firmly locked and then, as her eyes travelled the side of the church, she noted frames supporting an iron mesh over the stained glass windows.

'How times have changed,' Rita mused, walking around the circumference of the church 'til she found herself looking up at the window where St. Barbara still stood, but now screened from the outside world and looking very neglected. Rita gave her a little salute and thought St. Barbara smiled but it was only the sun catching the glass.

A number of headstones were leaning and others had fallen or had been deliberately pushed over. Rita guessed the latter as a number of these gravestones had been defaced with paint. There was little there of the past, just a shell that no one seemed to care about. It was sad after centuries of reverence and respect to find this generation had seemingly forsaken its heritage.

Rita wondered if she'd done the right thing coming along the road that passed her gran's, but it was quicker than going all the way around the cricket ground. At first she barely recognised her gran's house; it was dwarfed by large detached homes that had taken the place of the terraced houses on either side. All now stood back in line with gran's, each having a decent garden in front. Gran's house looked totally out of place with its Victorian architecture and grey stone. The stables had been taken down and a prefabricated garage stood forlornly in its place. The gates were still missing since the war effort claimed them. The stone wall on the other side looked the same, but the trees leaning over it were heavy and thick with growth for the want of pruning.

Rita walked briskly past, imagining someone was peering through the curtains like her gran always did. She was finding it hard to think of gran being dead so long and an older Auntie Ada living there. Twice she turned around to look back at it, part of her wanting to touch the familiar parts of her childhood, but she walked on.

She was quite tired when she reached the bottom of the road where Uncle Joseph had lived and began to feel her own age. With a sigh of relief she saw the houses were still lined up like soldiers, although much smarter than they used to be. The brickwork had been cleaned for a start and many had modern windows and doors. Gone were the nets, and pretty curtains now framed the new windows. Rita's heart began to pump and a slight dizziness caused her to stop, but it passed quickly. She began counting the house numbers. It was no use relying on her memory and the countless times she'd ran up this road and found the house without thinking.

Suddenly she was facing number eleven. A brass knocker in the shape of a lion's head was full centre and above it a small stained glass window. Reaching out her hand to knock, the thought again entered her mind that maybe someone else was living there and then what would she say, but she didn't have time to come up with anything for the door opened.

A tall slim middle-aged woman was standing there with an enquiring look. Rita felt an instant letdown and fumbled for words.

'I'm sorry; I was looking for someone called Foster who used to live here.' She turned to walk away.

'We are Fosters,' said the woman looking interested, especially after catching a slight accent she couldn't quite place.

Rita looked at the woman closely trying to see some resemblance to her family at the same time asking,

'I'm looking for Joseph and Annie Foster.'

'Them's my mam and dad,' answered the woman opening the door a little wider. 'Who shall I say wants them.'

'I'm Rita Goodwin, your dad's niece,' said Rita as there simply wasn't anything else to add.

'Best come in then,' the woman was now very curious and kept eyeing Rita's clothes, and then shouted, 'Someone here called Rita Goodwin to see you.'

Rita stood pushed against the wall of a small hall, not quite understanding why it wasn't the front room she remembered. The floor had a thick Axminster carpet and the wallpaper embossed.

Somebody was standing in the doorway at the end of the passage. She was small and slightly bent, her white hair neatly permed. Soft blue eyes gazed out from the delicate lines of her face. The change was bewildering but Rita knew it was Annie; just a much, much older edition.

They both stood there, taking in the changes but recognising each other. Without saying anything and, to the watching woman's surprise, the two older women clasped each other in a light embrace.

'Rita. Rita,' said Annie half crying. 'I'd know you anywhere. This is wonderful. Joseph!' she yelled.

Joseph came and there were more hugs again, and laughing too, 'til Annie sensed her daughter was being left out.

'This is our Susan.' Annie slipped her arm around her daughter's waist. Rita smiled at her then turned to her Uncle Joseph. She was surprised how well her uncle had aged. He looked fit and, apart from the scarring on his face, she would recognise him anywhere. His hair now white but still thick and his frame a little bent. Rita quickly realized that neither Annie nor her daughter treated him as if he was blind.

The house had undergone alterations; the back yard had been used to add a room downstairs and upstairs. It had been modernized with a false fireplace with an electric fire and a new kitchen. Rita now knew why Annie would never leave this house. It was her nest and always would be. Annie was talking ten-to-the-dozen whilst preparing dinner, which she insisted Rita shared with them.

'We've got two grandchildren, both boys. Our Joey married and has two nippers, Ted and Peter and both are at university and our Susan is a nurse.' There was real pride in Annie's voice. Rita looked with interest at Susan.

'I was also a nurse and trained at the local hospital,' said Rita. Susan looked surprised and a little confused.

'I'm at the Manchester General. I didn't know there used to be a training hospital here in town,' she added and went on eyeing Rita's sweater that had a North American Indian design around the bottom.

'The old hospital has now been converted into a medical centre,' enlightened Uncle Joseph. 'Such a pity as we now have to go miles for operations and such, and if you ask me, the whole medical field wants a good turning around.'

Annie nodded.

'How about our murder love?' asked Annie, changing the subject?

'Murder?' exclaimed Rita having all her attention

'A body or skeleton more like. It was found in the quarry back of your old house. Seems it was one of those yanks that billeted here during the war,' Annie went on, shelling more peas as she talked; the kitchen door open to the living room.

'Do they think they can find out who he is?' asked Rita, her heart beating quickly again.

'I reckon them's all doing tests,' inserted Uncle Joseph lighting a cigarette. Rita wished someone had read him the riot act on smoking, but what use would taking the only pleasure from a blind man be.

Annie came into the room wiping her hands on an apron.

'You remember young Ernest Heath don't you Rita,' Annie said enquiringly. 'He's the detective in charge of the case.'

Rita was taken completely by surprise. Ernest Heath, a detective. Uncle Joseph blew a cloud of smoke her way.

'Aye lass, the boy did well for himself. Joined the police as soon as he could, and went up the ladder fast: He's bright that one.'

Rita felt a little sick. Too much was happening. She had seen the name Detective Heath in the local paper, but never in a million years would she have guessed it was Ernest. A silly thought popped into her head.

'Is he married?' Having said it she wished she hadn't, for three sets of eyes turned to look at her.

'Funny you should ask that,' Annie said her voice lowering.

'His wife died last year, no children.' Annie shook her head. 'Lingered she did with cancer and he did everything for her. It's harder for a man without his wife.' She was looking at Uncle Joseph as if wondering what the future would bring.

Rita stayed for dinner and told them all about Canada. They politely listened but Rita could see they had little interest. Their world was England and the people who decided to leave their homeland were now just other 'colonials' to them. Rita promised to visit again and insisted on walking back to the hotel instead of getting a taxi. Her brain was working overtime from all the information on her aunts, cousins, half cousins, and Ernest.

She found herself thinking of Ernest quite a lot and tried to push it away, but it kept coming back.

Chapter 23

After enjoying yet another cholesterol-loaded breakfast the next morning, Rita returned to her room and sat on the side of her bed. An old fashioned black telephone faced her on the bedside table. Rita stared at it for a few minutes then turned on the bedside lamp to get a clearer view of the phone's outside line instructions. The number she wanted to call was written in a notebook balanced on her lap. Whilst struggling to stop the notebook pages from turning with her elbow, she lifted the phone and dialled the number. She heard it ringing out a number of times, and then a 'click' interrupted the dial tone and a man's educated voice said:

'This is the Taylor's residence. We are afraid there is no one available to take your call at present, please leave a message and your telephone number, and someone will get back to you.' Another 'click' and an automated voice repeated the familiar question. 'After the beep, please leave your message.'

Rita slammed down the phone. She felt all her old irritations coming back. She hated answering machines. They were so impersonal and had often been in friend's homes where the ringing of the phone was totally ignored. The frustration passed as Rita perceived that the answering machine could be used to her advantage. She dialled again and waited for the peep, then in a controlled voice stated:

'This is Rita Goodwin from Canada. As no one appears to be home, I'm taking the opportunity to sight-see. I am staying at the Black Boar Hotel, should you wish to leave a message.'

She felt empowered and her spirits were rising. Now she had another day without being taken over by relatives. Rita lifted her suitcase onto the bed and rummaged through it. She hadn't taken much time in packing and suddenly felt quite dowdy. She hadn't even packed a skirt, just one dress that was grey. It was for the reunion and it would have to do for the funeral service also. The rest of her things were pants and sweat shirts. She'd been very conscious during the previous day in town, that track-pants were not worn as much as they were in Canada. In fact, she noticed her age group here generally looked very smart and many wore hats.

Rita went over to the oval mirror behind the wardrobe door and studied herself. Grey flaked her temples and in the parting of her hair. She tried to visualise herself as she was forty-two years ago, but apart from the facial structure and eyes, there wasn't much left of whom she had been. Ernest kept popping up into her mind. He too would have aged, probably now quite grey or maybe even quite bald. Although Rita would never have admitted it, the vague possibility of meeting him pushed her into her next manoeuvre. Flicking through the phone-book she found a hairdresser.

'Yes,' purred the receptionist. They could manage a colour and cut at 10 am: as they had had a cancellation.

At 9.45 am and eager to be off, Rita left the hotel giving the surprised waitress a big smile. It wasn't difficult to locate the hairdresser's, as Rita knew the directions to the salon. At the corner of Market Square where the old bicycle shop once stood, was a modern frontage with a large pair of scissors swinging above the doorway. The shop was called 'SNIP& CLIP'. Rita hoped she'd made the right choice and wouldn't come out looking like a punk.

Two hours later and lighter by more £'s than she'd expected, Rita left the shop well pleased with her new look. Her hair colour had been lightened to add softness to her complexion and the cut and blow-dry framed her face admirably. So pleased was she, that she stopped at a number of shop windows just to look at her reflection.

One shop had a display of lovely stylish clothes in good materials, and the next moment Rita found herself inside happily trying on a number of them. Everything in the shop pleased her. The jumpers were made of beautifully soft Scotch wool and the skirts in good quality tweeds and plaids. She ended up buying two tailored skirts, three pure wool jumpers in bright colours, a couple of silk scarves and earrings to match everything.

Rita's walk through the town was suddenly brightened by the clouds lifting and the sun breaking through, only weakly however, compared to the full brightness of Canadian sunshine, but never-the-less much welcomed. Her steps became much lighter and she started to hum to herself, 'All things bright and beautiful'. Why that old hymn came to her mind she'd never know.

Rita's spirits were so lifted that she almost laughed out loud when she spied the tiny black and white café. It was the same one she used to go into during the war. The same heavy door creaked open above the same worn doorstep that led down into the dark low-beamed room. The sign standing outside advertised the place as The Tea House and, looking around, she knew why. Copper kettles, pewter jugs and ancient tea caddies filled every nook and cranny, with many hanging from the aged beams. Over to one side was the only modern piece of furniture, a glass display cabinet with mouth-watering tarts and pastries.

Rita sat by the lace-covered window, placing her packages on the carver chair opposite. She ordered tea and two custard tarts, which reminded her of gran's. A number of small tables were occupied by groups of women, and Rita marvelled at how smart they looked in well-hosed stockings and decent shoes. She realised she was subconsciously looking to see if any were wearing sneakers. They weren't and Rita pushed her own feet further under the table. One of the women smiled at her and while Rita's heart leapt in anticipation of recognition, it passed just as quickly as she realised the age gap between them was too wide.

Rita wasn't sure why she felt so high. The feeling wasn't anything to do with why she was here. It was something more primeval that made her search for something that had been missing all her life.

She had a dreadful urge to walk past the police station and might even have submitted to it, if it hadn't been for all her carrier bags and the nearness to her hotel that forced the more practical side of keeping to her schedule.

Back in the hotel, Rita stared at the waitress; daring her to make any remark about her new hairstyle. The waitress, never deterred by looks, smiled back innocently saying:

'Gosh you look years younger.'

Because the remark was so genuine and meaningful, Rita retracted and patted her new haircut.

'Thank you, I like it too.'

Lunchtime brought other admiring glances from the manager, which made Rita hurry her meal in case he joined her at the table. He didn't, but did manage to wink at her as she left the hotel and said,

'Meeting someone special?'

Rita smiled to herself. It would be rather nice for once to hear someone say 'Have a nice day'. Even though the words were said so automatically in Canada, it made one feel a sense of belonging. Rita remembered the pretty waitress's look of surprise in the café when she was told, 'You're welcome' after thanking Rita for her generous tip.

Back in her room, Rita debated about the clothes she was wearing. She decided to keep the sneakers on and pulled out her crumpled jeans and overly big sweatshirt with a cat and flowers printed on the front.

The place she was about to visit was going to be hard and would be tough on her emotions but it was something she had to do, just the once and then leave it forever. She was going home. The home that had really been hers, even if only for a short while. A home where once a family had lived; a mother, a father and herself. She was now the only one left to have such memories.

Rita didn't want to pass by gran's house again or Uncle Joseph's, so she took the road that ran around the back of the main street into the town. She was thankful for keeping her sneakers on for she knew it was a long walk and she would probably have to find her way through; where new houses had been built. Rita turned north by the side of the cricket field. The council houses stood like square boxes, every one the same. Reaching the top of the road, Rita turned to the left following a somewhat neglected road with prewar built houses. Houses that now had double drives and lean-to or prefabricated garages that looked somewhat dismal and generally unplanned. How had she ever thought that this way home was not too far when she was young. Rita noted her legs were getting tired.

Finding a road that led down to the main road again was no problem. Nothing had changed. It was like the street that Uncle Joseph lived on; just two rows of flat-fronted terraced houses. Reaching the main road reminded her that she had just a few yards to go and she would be at the bottom of the road she'd lived in all those years ago. Before she had time to wonder what it would be like, she was there, standing looking up at it. The road looked narrower and the houses smaller, but very much the same, just a few small additions here and there. She stood for a while one reason being to rest her legs; the second to just look.

'I'll walk up and just accept how it is,' she told herself firmly taking the first step.

But it didn't work out that way. Each house she passed she recalled its former occupants, who had leaned over those same gates and had pushed their prams up and down the road. Ghosts of the past flitted here and there. Some hedges had been taken down and others planted, garden shapes altered and again many garages added. A couple of new houses had been erected beside those homes that once had very large lots.

She was now nearing her old home and felt almost a fear that she wouldn't know it. She knew she didn't want it to be changed in any way for if it was; her memories would have cheated her all these years and she would feel a great loss.

Reaching Vera's house, part of the garden had been concreted over and double gates erected. The tiny postage stamp lawn that was left looked pathetic. Could she stand in front of her old home next-door and just stare? What would the owners think? I'll look as much as I dare Rita thought, then come back on the other side of the road slowly and look again from across the road.

The first thing that struck her was that pebble dash no longer adorned the walls, which made her sad for the sunlight used to catch the pebbles and make them twinkle like diamonds. There were no double gates. She wondered where they parked their car. They must have one. Everyone had these days. The front door had been changed. Gone was the stained glass and all the windows were new, but without the net curtains. Then Rita was past her old home and hardly noticed the Grace's house next door. The dirt lane that used to be at the top of the road was gone and a hedge now barred the way. Some one had claimed their property.

Rita turned and walked down the other side of the road. She could just about see through the gaps between the houses opposite parts of the old quarry. She had almost come opposite to her old house again and had slowed down, when the front door of the Grace's house opened and a very old lady stood looking at her. There was something about the way she stood, the neck bent and the head pushed forward just like Ethel.

'It can't be.' Rita's adrenaline welled up. 'But why not?' she mused. 'She must be in her nineties now and it is just possible she never left.'

Rita took a chance and crossed the road, her eyes searching the old woman's face, but before she could pick up courage to enquire, it was done for her.

'Rita, young Rita Goodwin.' The old lady's voice was shrill, as if it needed a lubricant

'Ethel, is that really you?' Rita wanted to laugh.

'Aye, 'tis me alreet,' crackled Ethel opening the door wide as an invitation for Rita to come in.

'How on earth did you know it was me?' asked Rita in amazement and let herself be led into a cosy but dated house.

'Know thee anywhere,' chuckled Ethel, pulling her by the sweater and almost pushing her into an armchair. 'It's your hair, those beautiful curls and that walk of yours, just like your mam's.'

Rita didn't have to ask about Ethel's family, for Ethel never stopped talking. So different from that shy introverted person Rita once knew.

'Our Doreen went to her maker, three years past.' Ethel rambled on popping in and out of the kitchen whilst making tea. 'She's buried with our mam and dad,' stated the old lady in a tone suggesting they had gone away on holiday. 'We'll all be together when the Good Lord fetches me,' she continued. 'Our plot's at St. Anne's, quiet and such a nice view.'

Rita listened in amazement to Ethel's conversation and rather envied the simplicity of her old neighbour's life. She'd learnt a lot from her over tea and Dundee cake.

'Vera and her family left after the eldest girl married, and young Jessie went to university to study medicine. Old Mr Clayton, the bobbie, died way back of brain cancer. Mrs Winterbottom went to live with her daughter in America after her husband passed away. Then next door in your old house are young-uns.' Ethel looked a little sad. 'They don't need neighbours like we used to. Both working, never see them from one day to the next. But the ones' before them were alreet. Nice kids, all left home and married now. Get a Christmas card regularly from their mam.'

Ethel was going further and further back in time and Rita wondered if she remembered she was still there in the room, as Ethel's eyes were now closed and was obviously in a world of her own.

'Rose, poor dear, killed herself. I pray every night the Good Lord will forgive her.'

Rita nearly spilled her tea and sat up quickly gazing at Ethel's fragile face that seemed locked in a trance.

'I'm sure God will understand why some people take their own lives.' Rita found herself on the defensive, but Ethel now seemed unaware of her presence.

'She'd got a good man. Never could understand why she wasn't content with one and that lovely little girl to bring up too.'

Rita felt icy cold and was about to hyperventilate before forcing herself to breathe normally again.

'Ethel.' Rita was now aware her voice had suddenly become urgent and demanding. 'What do you mean about not content with one?'

Ethel's eyes flew open and she looked blank and dazed. It took a few minutes to register she had a visitor. Rita posed the question again. This time a little more softly, but Ethel seemed vague and changed the subject.

'I should make you tea,' she said, pushing herself up and making for the kitchen. Rita tried again to get Ethel to tell her what she knew, but it was obvious Ethel's memory came and went with pieces of information that were completely forgotten seconds later.

She left Ethel with a promise to call again, but Ethel seemed to have forgotten who she was and asked her how much she owed for the eggs. Rita's reasonably happy day had turned into depression. She forwent dinner at the hotel and lay on her bed recalling her mam's death, and with Ethel's words still ringing in her head.

Chapter 24

Rita awoke suddenly to a repetitive knocking on the door of her hotel room. She struggled to push away the bunched up eiderdown that covered her head before sitting up. A voice called from the other side of the door.

'Seven o'clock Miss Goodwin.' A pause, then 'Would you like tea?'

Rita squinted at her watch. The hands were dead on seven-o'clock. She swung her feet over the edge of the bed and called back to the unseen person.

'Yes please.' Then, as an afterthought, she added 'Thank you,' pushing away some uncomfortable curls that were blocking her vision.

'God I feel awful,' she muttered, and just wanted to sink back onto the pillow and sleep. She guessed her sleep time couldn't have exceeded more than a couple of hours before being awakened by the loud knocking and the arrival of her morning cuppa. She'd lain awake for hours pondering on Ethel's remark about her mam. So many questions had drifted through Rita's fertile mind during the night.

'What did Ethel know and more to the point what had Ethel seen?' Daft Ethel, the one person no one took much notice of, but Rita remembered Ethel as always hovering in the background, listening, watching and not saying anything. In the end, whether it was from her reasoning or the need to sleep, Rita had convinced herself no one would take much notice of Ethel's ramblings anyway.

Rita shrugged her tight shoulders up and down. She had to pull herself together. When she'd returned to the hotel yesterday there had been a message from her cousin John, telling her he'd pick her up at 9.00 am sharp. An hour to pack her things, shower and have breakfast pushed her into action. By 8.30 am she was sitting down to breakfast trying to eat and answer the manager's questions. He seemed to think he had some sort of right to accompany her at her meals.

'Are you staying in the town?' he asked, helping himself to a piece of toast.

Rita pulled the remaining toast by the side of her plate and with her mouth full told him,

'I'm staying with my relatives at The Mill House,' she mumbled and, looking up at him, asked innocently, 'Do you know it?'

The rotund manager's eyes lit up.

'Oh, indeed I do, it's one of the town's nicest property.' He leaned forward eager to form some bond of familiarity. It was in the hotel's best interest to be acquainted with the wealthy patrons of the town. He was about to ask just what her relationship was to the mill owners, when he was interrupted by a tall well-dressed gentleman.

'Rita?' The newcomer said, gazing down at her.

Rita thought at first she as seeing William, so alike were father and son, but his eyes had an odd twinkle that made her like him right away.

'John,' Rita couldn't think of anything else to say apart from, 'how did you know it was me?'

He laughed and his eyes crinkled, lighting up his whole face.

'No mystery, I confess I wouldn't have known you if I hadn't asked the young girl at the desk. She pointed you out to me.'

Despite the fussing of the manager, John managed to put Rita's luggage in the boot of his British racing green sports car, and whisk her away through the narrow streets to the ring road and finally to the home of the Taylor's.

They didn't talk much, but Rita felt the instant bond of their liking for each other. Approaching the gates of the Mill House, Rita instantly understood the hotel manager's behaviour. The stone pillars, topped by ornate lanterns, beside the huge iron gates that guarded a wide drive. Rita sorted through her memory, but couldn't visualize the high hedge or the stone pillars. All she could recall was a big stone house standing on high ground. John pressed a device in the car and the gates swung open. He turned and looked at Rita.

'I imagine it's all changed since you left England,' he said with a smile. 'When Grandpa Taylor died, dad and mum brought some of the surrounding land and had new gates and the hedging planted.'

Rita nodded, confirming it was all quite new to her, but as the car drove towards the house, the past and present merged. Apart from more ivy growing up the walls, the well-kept appearance of the Mill House remained the same as the day it was built. Splendid in its height and well-proportioned architecture, it boasted three floors plus attics.

John helped her out of the car, insisting he carry her cases. Rita wondered if she should have brought gifts for everyone. Someone was standing by the front door and Rita knew her at once. Older, thinner, but never the less her Aunt Ivy in every way even down to the dark hair, well styled and dyed. The old lady stepped carefully down the two large steps and opened her arms.

'Rita, is it really you? Come here dear, let me look at you.'

Allowing herself to be clasped and hugged, Rita noticed tears gently following the wrinkled contours of her Aunt Ivy's face.

'I never watched our Rose grow older, she must have looked just like you if she'd lived,' said her Aunt Ivy. Rita hadn't the heart to say her mam would have looked twenty years older than herself. She felt touched with the softness in her aunt's eyes and remembered that they had been pretty close sisters.

'How's Aunt Ada?' Rita ventured, whilst being led into a well-furnished hallway. Aunt Ivy remained silent for a moment as if struggling for the right words.

'Not well, some days are a little better than others but she refuses to get help.'

Rita caught John's glance and understood her Aunt Ada had a drinking problem as he cupped his hand and raised it a couple of times to his mouth, then rolled his eyes. Rita wanted to giggle, but knew it wasn't the thing to do in front of her aunt.

The lunch was very tasty and well cooked. Rita soon found out the house had paid staff, although they didn't live in but came from town each day. John explained his wife Daphne was in London visiting her ailing mother and his two sons were at university. There was a photograph of them on the sideboard.

'Mother still entertains a lot,' explained John and then, as if reminded of something he'd forgotten, quickly told her there were a few people coming around that evening, just for drinks he assured her, as if apologizing. Rita began to wilt and begged forgiveness for she really needed to rest. The jet lag seemed a poor excuse but it was accepted with understanding.

She was given a room whose sole window looked down over the River Dane at the back of the house. The river meandered through the fields below. Rita was amazed the land hadn't been built on and that cows were still grazing on the grass.

She leaned against the window frame and let her vision rest on the very English scene: Fields, oak trees, the river, cows, cloudy skies and the great feeling of timelessness. She thought of Constable and his paintings. She almost wished it were Sunday when she would hear the sound of church bells ringing out across the town summoning the parishioners to worship. Taking off her shoes, she was asleep soon after her head hit the pillow.

When she awoke the daylight had faded outside and the room was dark. A soft tap at the door and Aunt Ivy came in with a cup of tea on a tray, the bone china delicately patterned and almost too fragile to use.

'There are a few friends of William's coming this evening; do you have anything to wear?' It was delicately put, but Rita was English enough to know that her aunt was telling her a dress or skirt was more acceptable than the slacks she'd been wearing.

'I've got a rather nice skirt I brought in the town yesterday.' Rita volunteered, noticing the relief that softened her Aunt Ivy's tense features.

Rita wondered if the Taylor's were living in today's world, or keeping up with some past protocol of the house itself. Later she was quite surprised when a tray arrived carrying cold meats, salad, bread and butter and a slice of lemon meringue. The woman who brought the tray must be one of the living-out domestics thought Rita.

Although she was beginning to feel she was back in a hotel room again, she quickly decided it wasn't the right thing to offer a tip. But where were all the mod cons she now needed? Will the maid go downstairs again without her being told of the amenities available? Her dilemma was quickly paved-over however by the domestic telling her,

'There's a bathroom just down the hallway, third door on the right.' She then ventured to explain the family never use it and it's provided solely for the guest's use.

'Bits and bobs will be served in an hour.' The woman gave Rita a big smile as if having given the same patter many times before.

After eating and unpacking the necessities and forgoing the shower for a hot bath and large fluffy towels, Rita tried on her new clothes. She surveyed herself in the long mirror that hung in a rosewood mount. Tilting it forward to get a better view, she was well pleased with the returning images. The skirt had been skilfully tailored to take emphasis off the hips and, with her long slim legs the effect was one of shedding of a number of unwanted pounds.

Rita left her room feeling refreshed and well groomed, which gave her an air of confidence. She would by choice prefer not to partake in small talk with strangers, but couldn't think of any excuse for not being there.

William was the first to greet her as she entered the room. He had changed a lot, and of course it added to her understanding of why John had seemed so much a part of her past memories, whilst William was almost a stranger. Time is a constant companion but left alone it becomes almost a traitor. White haired and thinning to almost baldness and without the moustache he once grew, William was now almost like his own father, the old man Rita had once met at the Big House in her childhood. Rita had a warped feeling of knowing and yet not knowing. Even the Mill House had changed in some way just by being called the Big House years ago.

People looked like the parents of the children she remembered, and it was these memories she now tried to cling to. No doubt he would be thinking the same of her she thought. Looking for telltale signs on William's face, she was delighted he gave none and said he'd recognise her anywhere, which she knew was probably a lie, but being polite was so very English.

She was introduced around as a relative from the colonies, which made her wince a little. The family doctor and wife asked her questions about the cold winters and bears as if the two tended to go together and, by the time she had explained she'd never set eyes on the latter in her part of the country, others were telling her that the Chinese were slowly taking over in British Columbia. They were totally surprised when she said she'd never been there, as it was almost as far away going west as England was going east. By the time everyone had given her their account of life in Canada, and not being particularly interested in her version, she found herself alone pouring out a drink in desperation for something to do.

'Make that two.' Someone had come across to her and was holding a glass for her to fill.

Rita filled it to the brim, and then looked up to see who she had been accommodating. The bottle she was holding nearly slipped from her fingers and her legs felt like jelly. At first she really did think she'd had too much to drink and was hallucinating.

Ernest Heath was watching her with a slight grin on his face. He'd changed as age merits, fuller in the face and body, and grey around the temples. Lines etched where once the skin was fresh and smooth. Glasses covered the blue eyes that held hers for a moment 'till Rita found herself getting hot and her face flushing. With a desperate voice she said,

'What are you doing here?'

He put his hand over the bottle she was holding and lowered it to the table.

'I could ask you the same.' He smiled his old lob-sided smile that still made her heart leap and before she could answer he had lifted her left hand and was gazing at it.

'Not married or divorced?' He looked right at her daring her to give him the correct answer.

'Never married,' she answered weakly, and then feeling further explanation was necessary, added, 'never came across a man who could put up with me.' Rita experienced her control seeping back and found herself laughing, when he responded quickly,

'But you let the one who was willing get away.'

Although said jokingly, Rita knew there was a hint of truth behind it. Ernest moved her to a couple of chairs which gave them a chance to talk without interruption, then explained to her he was a golf partner of William's and, although there was quite an age gap, they both enjoyed the game together. He went on to tell her about the death of his wife and his nearing retirement from the police force and not relishing the thought of it. Rita in turn told him about her life in Canada and how she'd thought of taking up golf.

The next two hours slipped away far too quickly, so engrossed were they in each other and Rita was so thankful she'd spent some time and money on herself, vowing never to fall into track-suits and grey hair again, at least while she was in England. The conversation eventually got around to the sand quarry investigation, although Rita never could remember later who had instigated the topic first.

'I'd like to finish this case before I retire' confessed Ernest. 'It's going back a long way, but with the new scientific methods, we should be able to at least find out who the blighter was who bashed his head in. There's a chance we may still be able to apprehend a person, although we admit it's quite a long shot.'

'Couldn't he have slipped down the quarry and just hit his head,' she asked going out on a limb and hoping against hope there was chance of it happening that way.

'Not possible.' Ernest's voice changed. He suddenly became knowledgeable and a person to be listened to.

'The angle, depth and splintering of the bone suggests he was struck from a standing position by someone behind him.'

'How come he wasn't found earlier?' She nearly gave herself away by saying he couldn't have been covered too deeply by sand.

'Whoever killed him must have been lucky because a slippage must have occurred shortly afterwards, as he was buried fairly deep under the sand and the quarry was never used until it was reopened last year.'

Rita knew it could have happened that way. Sometimes a sand slippage often triggers another if the top's unstable and there certainly was a great overhang at the quarry top, held back only by the roots of bushes and grass. As a kid, Rita often stamped on the edge just to watch it slide taking the soft silky sand with it.

'How can you possibly find out who he is?' asked Rita almost trembling and having to move her hands from her lap and fiddle with her hair.

'DNA, although it depends if the relatives of the guys who went missing whilst stationed over here are still alive and can be traced.'

'So there's a possibility you will never know who he is.' Rita's questioning was now taking on an air of urgency to find out all he knew.

'Oh, we will narrow it down and if not me, someday someone will find out who he was,' Ernest chuckled suddenly. 'But there are still people around that know more about the war years than they are willing to tell, but given time and their curiosity, they will. I'm banking on that.'

He sounded more than confident he'd find the truth and it was the truth Rita needed more than anything to know about. So when he asked her if she'd have dinner with him later in the week, she said yes. Although she told herself that her friendship with him was the only reason.

She only later confessed to herself she wasn't being totally truthful.

Chapter 25

After spending three days at the Mill House, Rita had had enough. She felt imprisoned by routine, etiquette and having to fit in with everyone's plans. It was almost like living in the Edwardian era; a time for this, a place for that. Rita began to feel frustration taking a tight grip of her.

Frequently she found herself heading to her room on some pretext or other. This seemed to suit the rest of the household with a sense of relief, by not having to deal with someone who didn't understand that tracksuits were not an acceptable attire to every meal; especially dinner.

John was the only one that appeared to accept the period he was living in. He took a lot of interest in social programmes as an active Rotarian and board member of the hospital, or 'The Medical Centre' as it was now known by. That of course is how he came to know Rita's friend Elaine. He'd been instrumental in the building of flats for the disabled and Elaine had taken on a lot of the responsibility for the needs of the handicapped. Both had had a great respect for each other and John was genuinely sorry about her untimely death.

Rita had felt a little disturbed by her own lack of emotion and, although she knew the day and the time of the funeral service, she had not really mourned for her friend as she thought she would have. The more Rita tried to conjure up Elaine's face, the more it eluded her. Letters had kept the contact, but the actual physical person had long been gone. She'd miss Elaine's letters, but would she miss the person? Rita reflected on the books of philosophy she'd read and agreed with the 'concept of maya' or illusion. She made a mental note to study the philosophy of Buddhism. Not that detachment would have done much good regarding Ernest, for feelings for him still arose and created the emotions that she found she wanted to indulge herself in. She pondered on the fact that fear and joy are produced by the same chemicals that always leave the adrenaline activating the nervous system.

Later, when John suggested he could drop her off at her Aunt Ada's for the afternoon: Rita jumped at the chance to get away and be herself, even with the reservation of what she might be letting herself in for.

During the drive across town Rita asked John why the cousins have a reunion when they all live fairly close by. She'd often thought to ask but never 'til this moment got around to it. John concentrated on his positioning on a traffic roundabout for a moment, and then glanced at her with a boyish smile.

'It really started years ago. Charlie took me for my first drink when we were eighteen and, by the time I'd got well and truly sozzled, we'd vowed to meet again once a year and do justice again to another bottle of Johnny Walker.' John didn't need to explain Johnny Walker was whisky. Rita remembered her gran having a liking for it too.

'But that's just Charlie and you,' stated Rita looking puzzled.

'Ah, well yes,' began John, swerving to avoid a swinging caravan being towed, then continued to explain.

'As soon as each of the cousins reach eighteen they join us. Then someone suggested we all have a meal, Susan I think it was.' John laughed. 'It sort of mellowed with the women folk and then, when we got married and the kids started arriving, they insisted on coming along too.'

Rita grinned, as she thought of the strong women in her family. It was good to be part of ones own family after being only the guest at the Thanksgiving and Christmas festivities she'd experienced in Canada.

She was now beginning to look forward to the reunion, and belonging in her own right, she being the eldest to boot. John did a sharp turn and pulled up behind another car in the drive of her gran's old house.

'Charlie must be here,' he said opening the car door for Rita to step out. Before she could take a quick look around, John was hustling her around the back of the house.

'No use using the front door. No one answers it,' he assured her in a matter-of-fact manner.

Before Rita had time to say anything she was pushed through the back door into the kitchen and John was yelling,

'Charlie, Charlie. Look who I've brought to see you.'

A tall well-built man appeared in the doorway that led from the kitchen to the hallway. He was holding out his hand in greeting. Rita's feet felt glued to the floor. Her own arm refused to move. Standing there as large as life before her was an exact replica of the yank. Not stiff and cold, buried under sand but alive, vibrant and speaking.

'Cousin Rita, we've waited a long time for this day.'

He was walking towards her and, as his long arms enfolded her to his chest. She couldn't help remembering little Charlie whom she had looked after and loved. Rita relaxed and allowed herself to be drawn into the hall. The black and white floor she used to mop loomed up at her. Then the hallstand caught her eye, still standing in its same place but with a heavy coat actually hanging from one of the pegs and not being just draped over the staircase banister. She was being ushered quickly into the living room and led toward a big armchair where a wisp of a woman sat wrapped in a shawl.

'Aunt Ada.' There was almost a question in Rita's acknowledgement. It was after all a guess, not a recognition.

The first thing that struck Rita was how very small her aunt appeared. Small, frail and older by far in appearance than her sister Ivy.

Rita glanced at John, but he was leaning against the doorway and digging into his pocket for a cigarette. Charlie stood behind his mother and rubbed his hand on her frail shoulders.

'Well Mother,' he said, more to Rita than to the person he was addressing. 'Look who we have here to visit you.'

Two sharp eyes peered at the visitor then a sound so shrill erupted from her mouth. It had an edge of sarcasm echoing with the words.

'Young Rita, not so young anymore eh.' It was more of a statement than a question.

It didn't take much of Rita's nursing experience to realize her aunt had, at sometime, suffered a stroke, although she had recovered sufficiently to function, there were still visible signs in her facial movements. Ada was talking again, whilst beckoning her son to fill her glass that was sitting on a small table beside her. Charlie looked a little embarrassed but did his mother's bidding.

'Never married I hear,' Ada chuckled, then with smothered spite added, 'never found anyone good enough for you then?'

Charlie had come back in and was pouring whisky into the glass. Aunt Ada grabbed at it and drank quickly, letting some dribble down from the corners of her mouth in her eagerness. Charlie glanced at Rita with an almost apologetic look, whilst John raised one eyebrow and put on an expression of utter resignation. There was no doubt in Rita's mind that her aunt had a long standing drinking problem, far more serious than her gran's occasional tipple.

'Get yourself a glass girl,' her aunt's voice commanded. 'We have to celebrate your homecoming.' Rita was on the verge of refusing but was smart enough to not want to start any trouble so she nodded to Charlie.

'I'll drink to that and it's lovely to see you Aunt Ada.' Rita bent down to give the old lady a kiss and inhaled a lung full of stale whisky vapour in the process.

Her aunt now began to relax and started asking questions about Canada. She genuinely seemed interested and it wasn't long before Rita realized her aunt thought Canada and America were the same. She even joked and told Charlie they must go there one day and see it for themselves.

After an hour, Rita found her aunt fast asleep snoring loudly with her glass still in her hand. John had put the kettle on and Rita joined him in the kitchen to help make coffee.

'Poor Charlie,' his cousin said as the kettle boiled. 'She keeps him on a tight string and expects him to come over right away whenever she phones.'

John explained that after Charlie had married, his mother had had a small stroke. Charlie's wife Janet refused point blank to go and live with his mother or having her live with them. Janet wasn't the most sympathetic of women and wouldn't have anything to do with her mother-in-law. In return, Ada had no interest in Charlie's only son Michael, nor he in her.

'Can't say I blame them if she's always into the bottle,' Rita muttered, pouring out three cups of coffee.

'It's not easy for old Charlie,' John said defending his cousin. 'He looks worn out, but he can't get anyone to give him a break even for a day or so. It's a good job he's got his own practice'. Rita was surprised to learn Charlie was a lawyer, but didn't say anything.

Rita suddenly realised what John was getting at. He wanted her to stay with her aunt. Rita's hand shook as she lifted the cup to her lips, her mind rebelling against the underlying suggestion.

John went out to go to the toilet and Rita found her eyes focussing on more and more on the familiar objects around her. Even the teacups were her gran's and she had a strange but distant feeling of coming home.

'Was it such a bad idea of John's?' she thought. At least she wouldn't have to be part of the structured life at the Mill House, but free to make herself a sandwich whenever she felt like it. She would be near to town and, because her nursing instincts were still very much part of her. Rita knew she could be a great help to her aunt; her compassion overriding the drink problem and the state of the house. When John came back Rita was the first to speak.

'I could do it,' she said.

'Do what?' said John looking surprised.

'Look after Aunt Ada for a while.' She watched the relief on his face, and then Rita guessed her Cousin Charlie had already conspired with his cousin.

'Great, oh great,' he was obviously very fond of Charlie. 'I'll take you home to pack and bring you right back.'

Rita hadn't envisioned such an immediate evacuation from the Mill House, but agreed to do as he suggested and she knew she'd made the right decision when she told Charlie of her plans.

'Bless you Rita.' He must have repeated it three or four times and even kissed her. Rita wondered what her aunt's reaction would be.

John was as good as his word. He drove Rita back and waited whilst she packed and talked with his mother. Rita's Aunt Ivy just took everything in her stride and said Rita must do what she thought fit, although it wouldn't be easy with Ada taking a liking to the bottle and all. Rita wasn't quite sure what the 'and all' meant but said she'd manage and explained how she'd had plenty of experience with the likes of her aunt.

Just at that moment her Aunt Ivy took off the mask of being the lady superior of the household and began to lay bare her inner soul.

'Ada was never the same after Charlie was born,' she said, her thoughts flying way back in the past. 'We all thought she would settle down eventually with Frank, but even he couldn't take it and walked out one day.' Her aunt stopped for a moment before adding, 'she used to be such a nice kid and fun to be with too.' Then the moment passed and her aunt was looking at her watch.

'Must go; have to meet some ladies for lunch.' A quick peck on Rita's cheek and she flounced out of the room.

Two hours later and very hungry, Rita was dropped off and was back at her Aunt Ada's. Charlie took her upstairs and showed her to a bedroom that had had its bed recently changed and the room tided. Charlie must have been working very hard since they had left earlier in the day. Rita knew the room and its furniture well for she'd slept in it before; the same room she had had before leaving for nursing school.

She sat on the small bed, the case beside her, just looking around and half expecting old feelings to come flooding back through her body. There was nothing, but there was a sense of foreboding, interspersed by fleeting but pleasurable thoughts of seeing Ernest again.

Later, after assuring Charlie she'd be fine and telling him to take a break and enjoy the time with his family; Rita began to check the cupboards in the kitchen for food and was delighted to find them well stocked. Charlie had been busy. Her aunt appeared indifferent to her staying and all was accepted, as long as the whisky bottle was within her reach and Rita fetched and carried as ordered.

Rita prepared a couple of chops with potatoes, peas and gravy for dinner, which her aunt ate with relish. It was followed by ice cream and fruit. Rita refused another whisky, but poured herself a small sherry. Her Aunt Ada mellowed as the drink and the fire warmed her body and the evening passed pleasantly, mostly talking about Ada's childhood, which included her sisters. Rita heard tales of her mam she'd never heard before and listened intently. Now and then, when the conversation dried up, Rita caught her aunt looking at her.

'More like your dad,' she announced to Rita, at the same time holding out her glass. 'He was a fine looking man and you take after him.'

Rita was just about to say 'thank you' for the roundabout compliment, when her aunt spoiled it all.

'Didn't know when she'd got a good one.'

Then she began to drift off, but the nastiness in her voice couldn't be mistaken. Rita looked at her aunt, the head rolled off to one side and her mouth opened. It was no use pushing her for more information; her aunt was too far-gone. She sat looking at her aunt and didn't quite know whether the feelings she felt at that moment were of pity, hatred or revulsion. She picked up the glass and went into the kitchen, walking under the stag's head that looked down at her with its one and only glass eye.

Chapter 26

Strangely enough Rita found herself enjoying putting her skills into action once more and it made her realize she actually missed nursing. There was something extremely satisfying in making someone comfortable.

The first thing she did was to get her aunt up the stairs and into a warm bath. It had been a struggle and as not easily accomplished with her aunt refusing to cooperate at every stage. But bath her Rita did and even shampooed her matted hair. Wrapping her aunt in the only clean towel she could find, Rita was aware of how painfully thin she had become and felt sad, remembering the vibrant young woman she used to be, whose figure had been better than most. Ada stared at her, defying any comments and made for the stairs as soon as she had her nightgown on. Rita hovered behind her; fearful of her aunt's balance, but Ada just pushed her aside.

'I'm not addled yet,' she snapped and proceeded to inch her way down the stairs holding onto the banister for support.

The fire was banked up sending out a pleasant heat. Ada pulled her dressing gown closer around her legs and, reaching for the whisky bottle by the side of her chair. As the drink and the warmth took effect, she became mellow and more interested in the world around her.

'Who does your hair?' she asked as though her niece had a permanent hairdresser in England. Rita told her about her shopping trip in town, and then gently posed a question.

'Would you like me to trim your hair?' she asked.

Ada lifted her glass and sipped, then answered in a tone that suggested boredom.

'Do as you like, you seem to have quite the knack for it.'

Rita sighed, but inwardly smiled to herself. She was used to this sort of behaviour during the time she was working with geriatrics and had learned to accept the fact they hated asking for assistance.

Rita was pleased with the result of the trim. She'd cut it around the ears and had brought down a little fringe so it resembled a pixie style. Ada looked in the mirror being offered and hummed and ahhed, but was visibly pleased with the result and asked when Charlie was coming around.

'He's just got some catching up to do at work,' lied Rita so as not to explain why he needed time away from his mother's demands.

'He'll think you're real pretty,' Rita went on and watched her aunt's cheeks glow a little. She really does love her son thought Rita and warmed a little to the aunt who had held out no love at all to her parentless niece.

Making a list for some cleaning materials, which she would give to Charlie, Rita spent the next two days cleaning the house, especially the fridge and stove, The bathroom was tackled in the same way as she got down on her knees and rubbed the Vim into the grey tide line that ringed the bath. Next she emptied the medicine cupboard, checking each prescription for dates and was mortified to discover a bottle of tablets with her gran's name still written quite clearly on it. Rita struggled with the top of the bottle before flushing the contents down the toilet bowl. The last act prompted her to have a serious talk with Charlie and get him to get in touch with her aunt's doctor. Her aunt's drinking was another problem that needed professional help. Rita knew she hadn't the time or dedication to get involved, so only concerned herself with those basic needs for which she was trained.

Now was the time for Rita to remember one of the reasons why she had come to England and to concentrate on Elaine. The funeral had been arranged for the following day at her old church at 2-00 pm followed by a small gathering in the church hall afterwards; put on by the Mother's Union. Rita wondered if Elaine had any relations, as she knew her parents had long passed away and her only brother lived in Australia.

What to wear had also been playing on her mind? All at once her grey dress seemed too old fashioned. Rita had attended a number of funerals in Canada where the wearing of black or grey was not seemingly a prerequisite. In fact people there tended to dress in just about anything, from shirts without ties to summer dresses in pastel shades of any colour, particularly if it was hot. Still Rita couldn't get the images of an English funeral she'd recently watched on TV out of her mind. Some English dignitary had died and the mourners had all been wearing very sombre attire. There wasn't one man present not wearing a black tie.

'Did she need a hat?' she asked herself. This was now her most pressing question after she'd decided on wearing a grey skirt with her new maroon top and, if it got chilly, she'd just have to wear her dark blue anorak over it. The idea of a hat with an anorak made her chuckle and that seemed to lighten her dilemma. No one would bother with what Canadians wore, she acknowledged, and if they did she'd be gone in a couple of weeks anyway.

John was going to the funeral too to pay his respects and had arranged to pick Rita up. There was no coffin as Elaine had expressed a wish to be cremated, which had already been done. So the service was really more of a celebration of her life. Rita was glad there was no body to view, as it wouldn't have done her any good to look down at someone she probably wouldn't have recognised anyway. No, it was far better to remember her friend, as she'd known her.

Rita tucked a piece of paper into her handbag. It held a few written references about her friend, just in case she was asked to say a few words about her.

Waiting for John seemed like an eternity. Her aunt became very demanding and spiteful even to the point of telling her she shouldn't wear maroon as it made her skin look sallow. Rita tried her best to ignore her aunt but found the tenseness in her shoulders building up, and for an awful moment thought she'd just have to scream and tell her to shut up, but she didn't.

Then John arrived dressed in a dark suit and wearing a black tie. Rita left with him after deciding to leave her anorak behind. Finding somewhere to park close to the church posed a bit of a problem and the two of them had to walk through a series of small streets. It occurred to Rita when the church was built, cars had not even been thought about. In fact no one drove to church even when she was young, apart from that is, the doctor and the undertaker.

People were already filtering into the church's doorway. Rita noticed a couple of wheelchairs, the owner of one manoeuvring himself, and the other being pushed.

When was the last time I'd walked through this archway? Pondered Rita, stealing a glance at the wall where the holy water used to be. The stone protrusion was still there, carved by some mason's hand long ago, but the pewter vessel it once supported was now missing. Something instinctively grabbed her. It was that the air in the church was sweet and clean. Not a trace of the sickly heavy incense that turned the filtered beams of sunlight blue. Apart from those small but unforgettable things, the old church remained the same as it had been over the years. Rita stole a glimpse at the font where she and all her family's ancestors had been baptized.

She let John lead her to a pew. After kneeling to say a short prayer, she let her past spread out before her like a tapestry. She thought of the many and various occasions she'd sat in this old church and all the emotions that had played out their time within her body. Rita tried to remember the old saying she had once heard long ago.

> 'When you come to church as a baby your mother brings you.
> When you come to church as an adult your father brings you.

When you come to church in your coffin your family brings you.
Isn't it time you came to church for yourself.'

Rita knew she'd not quite got it right but never the less had to admit she'd never come willingly to church in all her life. She allowed herself a brief moment of wondering if she'd married; how it might have all been different. Her thoughts were interrupted by the sounds of the organ. The vicar entered from the vestry door to the side of the alter steps.

'Goodness' thought Rita, 'He isn't wearing a long black cassock.' She was more taken aback by that fact than listening out for the number of the next hymn and had to glance over at John's hymnbook to catch up.

It was a nice service, the vicar was well versed in the right choice of sermon for a funeral and it didn't drone on and on like some she'd sat through. He spoke of Elaine as a courageous woman, much loved by all who knew her as a devoted member of the church. This surprised Rita. Elaine never really wrote of her spiritual self or her relationship with the church. One of the women who occupied the same pew as herself got up and gave a testament to Elaine's character, much in the same vein as the vicar's and mostly about her charitable works.

Rita clasped the top of her handbag tight, her actions demonstrating she was now unwilling to read from her prepared notes. What had she got to say anyway? Did she want to talk about the past when Elaine lay in the hospital bed or about her letters to a friend? Rita looked down at her hands tightening and felt tears struggling to find release. Elaine and her relationship with her were private. They had held each other up without personal involvement, sharing what they wanted the other to think of them. It was no place for intruders. A hand covered hers and, looking up, she saw John's comforting smile winning her away from her own imprisoned grief.

Afterwards everyone strolled to the church hall, where tea and sandwiches had been prepared. A group of people had gathered, mostly women, chattering and occasionally breaking into laughter. The vicar introduced himself and was more interested in the Canadian Anglican Church than Rita's relationship to Elaine. There was a moment when Rita nearly asked herself why she'd bothered to return to England at all. Things had certainly taken on a different twist since she had felt compelled to come. She felt somehow she had lost her way. John had gone to get some more tea when Rita found herself isolated from the rest and began looking through the church hall window to the place where her old school once stood.

'You went to the old church school didn't you?' The woman who had spoken of Elaine during the church service had come over to her side.

'Yes,' answered Rita, turning and getting a close up look at a small elfin shaped face surrounded by fair unruly hair which sported a black tam that angled dangerously towards the back of her head.

'Elaine spoke of you often,' she continued, looking across the grounds outside. Then, as if driven by a sudden burst of memory, started to dig down into her shoulder bag and held out a small packet of letters to Rita.

'I think these are yours,' she said, and then went on to explain that she was responsible for clearing out Elaine's apartment. 'John told me you would be here.'

'I work at the Health Department,' she explained to Rita, 'and during my visits to Elaine, we became great friends and she told me about her friend in Canada and how she always looked forward to your letters.'

Rita was looking down at the writing on the letters. It certainly was her name.

Miss Rita Goodwin.

But it was not in Elaine's handwriting. Rita turned them over and saw that they hadn't been opened. Who had written to her? Rita held the letters nearer to her eyes to see the handwriting more clearly. She had definitely never seen it before. There was no address, just her name. John came back at that moment and Rita slipped the mysterious letters into her handbag. The woman whose name was Lisa left after giving Rita an impromptu hug.

Rita asked John to show her where Elaine's ashes had been put. There were flowers she had brought in the back of John's car and Rita now wanted them placed on her friend's final resting place.

Part of the new churchyard had been parcelled off as a garden of remembrance, and John let Rita stroll through it alone to find the small plaque bearing her friend's name. Rita laid the flowers down. She had chosen a small wreath of rosebuds, realising a spray of flowers, needing more water, would not have lasted as long.

She stood for a few moments almost feeling Elaine's gentle spirit around her. A happy free Elaine no longer bound to a wheelchair. The thought eased all sense of sadness and loss. In its wake it brought a sense of happiness and fulfillment. Elaine's journey had ended and all the trappings and scars of human existence vanished. Her friend's true spirit could fly to any heights with no bounds.

John sensed a change in his cousin and suggested they find a country pub and have a proper meal with a bottle of champagne to celebrate Elaine's life. Rita agreed instantly and John's car left the boundaries of the town and headed out for the moors and an isolated pub that was built at the highest point. The scenery was wild and spacious and allowed the mind to let itself be, instead of hopping from thought to thought. The steak and kidney pie was excellent and so was the champagne that they did justice to.

It was now Friday and the reunion was planned for Sunday. John obviously enjoyed the planning and Rita had glimpses of a once lonely little boy who needed companionship. There was no doubt he was close to Charlie. Rita approached the subject that no one had talked of.

'What happened to Frank?' she asked when the time was right. 'Doesn't Charles ever see his father?'

John put down his glass, wiping the effects of the tingling bubbles off the end of his nose and screwing up his eyes.

'Rita,' he leaned forward looking at her straight in the face. 'Rita,' he said again, 'can you honestly tell me you can see anything of Frank in Charlie?'

He leaned back and waited for her answer, convinced she had to agree with him. Rita brought the memory of Frank to her mind and let it linger awhile. She already knew the true answer to Charles' parentage but had to somehow give Frank a chance and not to just dismiss any likeness out of hand.

'No,' she answered honestly, although never would she divulge the truth. Rita had known who Charlie's real father was the moment she'd seen him.

'Frank knew it too, I'm sure,' said John, 'and although we all thought he could have forgiven Aunt Ada, it was Aunt Ada who would never let Frank forget that Charles' real father had been the only true love of her life.'

John took another sip of his champagne. 'I guess that would be too much for any man to live with.' He shook his head as if siding with Frank. 'One day Frank took off and never came back.'

'Doesn't anyone know where he went?' quizzed Rita, feeling extremely sorry for the kind forgiving man she once knew.

'No, never heard a sound.' He replenished her now empty glass, 'although there was a rumour he went to Yorkshire with a lassie from the town, but it's just a rumour. No foundation for it really.'

Rita hoped it was true. She hoped Frank had found a woman who really loved him and had had lots of children all looking just like Frank.

Her Aunt Ada was rambling when Rita got back and was no fit companion to be with. After getting her aunt to eat, she had a little trouble getting her to bed but soon loud snores erupted from her room.

Rita made herself a cup of tea and sat by the diminishing fire alone. She shivered a little as the cold seeped in. Her handbag sat on the table and why she kept putting off reading the letters she didn't quite know. Rita sat there for the next two hours just letting the day's events drift by before opening the bag and taking the letters out.

She took the handle of her teaspoon and slid it under the first envelope and pulled out three pages of a letter. It began, 'My Dearest Rita. She didn't have to look to see who had sent them. The date on the top of the page and the contents told her all she wanted to know. They were letters sent to her by Ernest. Letters so personal that she just sat there almost in shock. They were written not long after she'd gone to Canada, telling her he loved her and would even come to Canada if she'd marry him. The other two letters bespoke of the same requests, pleading for her to write.

He'd obviously given the letters to Elaine to address them for him, as Elaine had promised Rita not to divulge her address before she left.

Rita read the letters over and over again. Why hadn't Elaine sent them on? Did she actually tell Elaine not to do so? Rita couldn't remember. Had Elaine assumed no contact should be made? Why had Elaine kept them all these years? The whys kept coming, tumbling over each other in anticipation of some clarification. Then came the self-accusations. Had she been right in denying herself a normal life? Did she need to blame herself so much for sending that fatal note to the yank? After all she was only a child at the time. But why she did, still remained an open question to which there seemed no answer.

Exhausted she fell asleep and awoke to find her aunt standing over her with a triumphant look on her face and, although Rita was convinced there had been three letters, now there were only two on her lap, but it had been a long day. Rita shook herself into reality.

Chapter 27

After tidying up, Rita took the afternoon off on the pretence of doing some shopping. Her aunt scurried around peering into the fridge and larder complaining she needed this and that, although Rita was well aware a big bottle of whisky was on the top of her required list.

Tucking the list in her pocket, she knew exactly where she was heading even before she'd left the house. The shopping could be done on her journey back for Rita wasn't heading for the shops at all but to the park. Her mind was in turmoil. Rita desperately needed to think, and think clearly.

The letters had disturbed her much more than she had realized. Had she been unfair to the man she respected more than anyone else, or was it something more than respect she had felt all those years back. Had she actually been in love with Ernest? The thought wouldn't go away and kept challenging her. Now all Rita wanted to do was to sit by the river that ran through the park and remember some of the sweetest moments from her past.

Her legs took her through the town as if they knew the way without any guidance from her and, before she knew it, the impressive iron gates of the park entrance confronted her. Walking through them, she followed the tarmac path that wound its way past the formal gardens of well-tended shrubs and flowers. Then, following a smaller path off to her right that passed the new tennis courts and pavilion, she made her way down a flight of wooden stairs that finished on a gravel path flanking one side of the river.

Iron railings fenced the river side of the path, releasing the council from any responsibility of children falling into the dangerous waters. About one hundred yards on or so along the path, a bench had been placed sporting a brass plaque bearing the name of the donor. Rita read it before sitting down. The bench had been dedicated in the name of a James O'Riley and she wondered if one of the Irish tinkers had risen to be part of the elite in the town.

It was nice to sit and just let the day unfold; no one to disturb her dreaming of what could have been and no one to remind her of the searching still going on in the quarry. She couldn't any longer deny that Ernest had always been the one for her. Even in his second hand clothes and uncared-for childhood, she had secretly laid claim to him. She sighed, and for once relaxed into a warm acceptance of her feelings. Was it too late to take some happiness back? Rita had no doubt the self same attraction was still there between them. All it needed was for herself to give a signal he could pursue.

'So what if the yank had been discovered, did that really matter?' she pondered. Her mam was long dead and no one would ever really know what had happened that fateful night so many years ago, not even herself it seemed. The vital question now before her was. 'Did she care how the yank had met his end and by whom?' Her mother couldn't have done it, for she didn't have time. Rita remembered the night she crawled home. Yes, her mother was already there at home, anxiously waiting for her, so what had it all to do with her.

Suddenly all tension eased, Rita's mind cleared and she got up and started to walk back. It was as if the constraints that had bound her for so long had now released their grip of her. She felt quite light-headed and carefree and would have danced by the river, if anyone had asked her at that moment. There was a steadiness in her heartbeat, a rhythm she hadn't felt in ages, since her electrocardiogram had shown atrial arrhythmia. Her medications since had always kept it in check but had never cured it. It was just a matter of not getting too stressed-out.

She listened calmly to her now steady heartbeat and reminded herself to get her prescriptions for her Warfarin and Digoxin tablets renewed and maybe even get another medical check up before returning home to Canada. She needed the Digoxin to slow down her heartbeat and the Warfarin to thin her blood to reduce its tendency to clot.

The lighter step and a feeling of youth and expectation embraced Rita though the park and into the town where she quickly picked up all of her listed shopping items. So good did she feel, she bought a large sized whisky bottle for her aunt, making the excuse that after she'd talked to the doctor about her aunt, the drinking problem could then be tackled, but just for now she wanted everyone to be happy.

Charlie was there when she returned and he looked a little startled at the size of the bottle but his mother looked happy and even told Charlie how well she and Rita had got on. Charlie was more than impressed by the clean if not totally tidy home. He then ventured on to tell his cousin in private, he'd never seen his mother look so cared for in a long time.

In the evening Ernest phoned, at first he sounded disappointed he couldn't see Rita the next day but cheered up as Rita explained she had to attend a cousin's reunion, but would be free all day on Monday.

'Done' he said with the authority of someone used to taking control. '11.00 am sharp then and we will find somewhere nice to talk our heads off.'

So, instead of looking forward to the coming reunion with the cousins and second cousins she'd never seen, Rita wished she could skip Sunday and just concentrate on Monday. But because Sunday has, and always will precede Monday, Rita was ready and waiting for John at the prescribed time.

'It will take us half an hour or so,' said John explaining the route and heading towards Leek.

Rita knew the name of the town well enough but had to confess to never owning a car and never having been there in her life.

'Nice hotel,' John said whilst giving her a running commentary on where they were going.

'Funny name, The Green Man, isn't it,' remarked Rita after taking in the passing countryside.

'It's a name that comes from way back.' John didn't sound too sure of his facts but tried to give her a rough explanation by saying, 'the name is steeped in folklore and mythology.'

Rita left it at that and found herself talking about Elaine.

'Did you get to know her well John?' Rita enquired, then without awaiting his answer that seemed a long while coming; ventured, 'she once had a boy friend you know. They were engaged to be married before her accident, but he couldn't bring himself to handle her disability.'

John let the silence between them last for a while then, out of the blue, gave his very frank opinion.

'Truth to tell, I got the impression Elaine was jealous of any good relationship between a man and a woman. It was as if she couldn't bear that someone should feel happiness with the opposite sex.' Silence again, before he asked, 'does that sound daft to you? if so, I'm sorry, she was your friend and must have confided in you during all these years.'

Rita was now searching her past to see if there were any clues to support John's admission. Yes indeed there were. Rita was surprised to find there were so many times Elaine had told her Ernest was not worthy of her. She had thought at the time that Elaine was being over protective. It had never dawned on her she might have been jealous. It would certainly account for her holding onto Ernest's letters. For one depressing moment, Rita doubted her whole life's beliefs and felt like banging her fist against the dashboard of the car. But she didn't, and became aware of an increase in her heart rhythm and the irregular pauses between her heartbeats.

She saw the sign for the Green Man Hotel before John had even started his manoeuvre into the car park. The sign was swinging lazily from its iron rings. It depicted a man with branches for his arms and legs that sprouted leaves, and hair of twigs with small flowers. The man in the sign was painted in shades of green and set against a black background. There certainly was something medieval and supernatural about it.

Charles was in front of them and just about to open the passenger door of his car. He turned and waved before helping a trim well-dressed blond woman out.

So this was Janet, Charlie's wife, thought Rita. No wonder that Aunt Ada didn't like her. It would remind her too much of what she had been, for Janet was so like the younger Ada; more than anyone she had seen. They were both coming across to her. Rita put on her best smile, holding out her hand in greeting.

'Rita my dear.' Janet made no move to take her hand, so Rita let her's drop.

'Charles here says you are a wonder with mother-in-law.'

Rita didn't get a chance to answer as a yell echoed across the parking lot, and there was no mistaking John's sons taking large strides over to them. A well-endowed dark haired woman hurried behind them, puffing to keep up. Rita took a liking to John's wife Daphne, before she'd even had a chance to speak to her. She had the open friendly face of her husband. John was obviously glad to see his wife back from visiting her mother and gave her a great bear hug, and then beckoned his sons over to be introduced to Rita.

Janet, who was standing beside Rita, frowned and took out her sunglasses from her handbag before saying;
'Tom and Rob, this is your second cousin straight over from the colonies.' Rita felt herself stiffen up. She was getting annoyed at the reference to the colonies as if it was some inferior part of the Commonwealth. She bit her lip to hide her annoyance but continued smiling. The boys were polite enough, but only too eager to get back to their own age group.

'Uncle Charlie,' Tom asked, 'where's Michael?'

'Michael will be here, his young lady is driving him,' Charlie answered. Janet smirked.

There were hoots and whistles from John's sons, now all the more eager to meet the said young lady that would be intruding into their family circle. A fresh face was always welcome with the younger set.

The roar of a motorbike turned everyone's attention to the entrance of the parking lot. A large machine skidded around the corner followed by a green sports car and a-not-so-new van that had more rust exposed on its sides than paint. Rita guessed correctly, the motorbike had brought Joey's boys, Edward and Peter, for as soon as their helmets were removed and their long black hair shaken free, the unmistakable oriental features of their mother were seen. It was much harder to assimilate the totally bald gentleman stepping out of his sports car as her cousin Joey, but the petite Korean woman with him verified his relationship.

The van slipped in between the sports car and the motorbike and Susan, jumped out. As Beryl, Susan's other sister, was in Australia, the whole network of cousins and half cousins, apart from Michael, now littered the car park.

Rita didn't feel as much at ease as she thought she might, as everyone knew each other so well. But that wasn't quite as uncomfortable for her as knowing that she was the eldest there by far. That made her alien in age and country to the rest; leaving her little to say unless asked.

No one seemed terribly interested Canada or her life there. England was for the one's that stayed and anything that went on beyond the fair island wasn't worth bothering about. After all the British had ruled over much of the world. Of course Rita knew she was being overly sensitive but would have once just loved to explain how tiny everything looked here, and drab for that matter. Even the birds looked nothing compared to the blue jays, cardinals, and yellow finches and had any of them seen the magnificence of the mountains out west.

She pulled herself together and let John and Daphne lead her into the old inn, which after all had been standing there long before Canada and the west had even been discovered.

There was no doubt the place was lovely in its old-world charm. White starched tablecloths graced the separate tables with card names inviting each guest to their place. A small rosebud lay across each side plate to welcome them. By the entrance a longer table was set out with a large open book, its blank pages waiting to be written on with the silver pen by its side. At the back of the table, three oversized blown up photographs in old frames were propped up.

Rita gazed at her gran's picture, her eyes filled with expectation and promise, as were the eyes of her grandpa. The thought immediately occurred to her that none of the others would remember these people. She was the only one who could talk with any authority about the apparent head of the maternal household.

Rita bent forward to look closer at the middle photograph, its brown sepia colouring visibly faded. It was a photo of her gran's parents, with her gran standing stiffly in a smock and a large bow in her hair. Rita wouldn't have known who these people were if it hadn't been for the scrawly handwriting on the bottom.

Martha with her parents,
1894

'You remember our gran don't you?' Charlie was standing behind her. Rita turned and looked at her cousin as memories washed over her in that fleeting moment.

'Yes,' she nodded. 'I did indeed; she thought the world of you.'

Charlie smiled, 'I wish I could remember her but I was too young.'

The meal was excellent, especially the lemon meringue, which melted exquisitely on tasting. There were two empty chairs that had remained so until the coffee was about to be served, when two more people arrived. Now all eyes were focussed on the late arrivals. It was Michael and his new lady friend, the cuckoo in their nest.

There was a hush as Michael claimed centre stage, an arrogant person who obviously liked the attention. Good looks from his father, but with his mother's haughtiness; he stood, his feet apart, almost awaiting a round of applause just for arriving. The woman, who had provided Michael's means of transport, was partially blocked from view. Janet leapt forward, almost knocking over her chair.

'Michael darling. Thank goodness you're safe. I was worried.'

They both gave each other a peck that seemed so rehearsed it hardly had meaning. Rita noticed Charlie never got up, but picked up his coffee and turned his attention to it.

As Michael moved aside, a tall woman dressed very elegantly; the taste and money so obvious from the material choice and cut of her dress; moved forward to greet Janet. Janet, for her part, whimpered and almost curtsied in admiration of her son's choice. The young woman was obviously more upper class than most.

Rita sat back witnessing the individual behaviour of each of her new found family. She decided however there was little she knew of them or really wanted to and wished it were all over. Tomorrow she would see Ernest and there were so many things to talk about; past, present and future.

Thankfully for her, the reunion did eventually come to an end.

Chapter 28

Rita had slept well. She lay in bed later than usual with no desire to get up. Golden streamers cast by the early sunlight flicked over the bedroom walls. Rita lifted a hand in a fantasy of catching one, but only felt the momentary warmth on her skin.

Downstairs could be heard the shuffle of her aunt in the kitchen, and a fleeting thought passed that she should arise. Yet the need to just be and let her mind wander at will down different paths was holding her firmly where she was. In the background was the constant hum of the traffic outside. That's how her life had been. She was so locked into moving fast-forward, she'd not had time to stop and take in the simple everyday things around her.

Was she to end up like her aunt, lonely and bitter? Rita couldn't get it out of her head that her aunt showed no interest in her grandchild. Aunt Ada had never asked her about the reunion and had turned away at the very mention of Charlie's wife. However it didn't take the mind of a Sherlock Holmes to detect why she behaved so. It was plain to see she resented anyone who took her Charlie's attention away from her. So instead of the grandchild binding the family together, Janet and Michael had pulled it apart just by being who they were.

It was Charlie's family that dictated the amount of time he spent with his mother. Rita pondered on her aunt's drinking problem and came to the conclusion it wouldn't do any harm to talk to a doctor to see if she could get something done about it.

Once Rita had seen a positive purpose ahead of her, she found it impossible to keep to her bed. She got dressed and joined her aunt at the breakfast table. Between munching on overdone toast and chunky marmalade, Rita asked her aunt who her family doctor was. Ada eyed her suspiciously,

'What do you want to know that for?'

Rita explained about her own arrhythmia and her need to get more Digoxin tablets.

'Them things can be dangerous, can't they?' said her aunt looking interested and Rita found herself explaining that a certain amount of the drug keeps her heartbeat steady and slow, but an overdose would certainly kill.

'It's made from foxgloves you know,' continued Rita, finding it pleasurable to be able to hold a semblance of normal conversation for once.

Her aunt nodded; adding

'We were not allowed to touch foxgloves or rowan tree berries as children. We were warned they could poison us.'

'Quite right.'

Rita went on to explain the different plants in Canada that children there were warned not to touch, plants like poison-ivy. Her aunt said she was thirsty and got up and made another cup of tea, bringing back her doctor's telephone number with her.

Rita phoned the surgery and was amazed to find that there was an opening that day. By eleven-fifteen am. she was sitting in a brand new waiting room built onto the side of one of the larger older houses in the most exclusive part of the town. As a young girl she had often passed these very posh houses, never dreaming one day she would enter one.

The receptionist called her name and ushered her through the surgery door. Rita knew straight away why she hadn't had to wait for an appointment. Although obviously qualified, as the framed certificates on the wall testified, the doctor was so young it must have been his first practice straight from medical school. Chubby with a baby sort of face, blond and blue honest eyes. Rita wondered who would have the most medical knowledge and Rita silently bet on herself, recalling from her experiences with the interns at her old hospital.

She explained she was running out of her medication and showed him her card; indicating the medicines she needed for her condition. She was pleased he didn't take her word as the go-ahead to fill out her prescription, but chose to examine her before doing so. Then and only then, giving her enough tablets to last her for three weeks.

Rita thanked him and then enquired about her Aunt Ada, telling the doctor that, as a nurse herself, she was concerned with her aunt's health and especially her drinking problem. Ada's file was brought in and the doctor studied it for a while.

'Actually I've never met with her,' he admitted. 'Her own doctor died six months ago and I've taken over his practice.' He glanced up and down and gave a cute smile. 'Name's the same of course. It used to be my dad's practice.' Rita murmured that she was sorry, but he waved her sympathy away and continued studying the documents before him.

'Seems the last time she was here, she was very depressed and Valium was prescribed, but there is nothing here about her drinking.' He wrote something down.

'Maybe you could get her to come in for a check-up?' He asked; scratching his head. 'As for her drinking problem, I'm afraid all I can do is to give you names and addresses of societies that devote themselves to getting people off the bottle permanently, but as you know the person afflicted must want to do it in the first place.'

Rita sighed. In her heart she knew that groups like 'Alcoholics Anonymous' couldn't do anything without the total commitment of the person needing help. Rita shook his hand, thanked him and left.

Dropping off her prescription with the chemist, Rita did a little shopping and managed a quick coffee before picking up her tablets and walking back to Ada's, realising she was no further ahead helping Charles with his mother's problem.

The afternoon hours dragged by. Ada was snoring rhythmically upstairs on her bed. Even the passing minutes appeared to have slowed down, and Rita knew the reason why. 'A watched kettle never boils' she reminded herself. Her mind was focussed on her meeting with Ernest and it made her restless. She nibbled at her lunch but couldn't force much food down and the cups of coffee she managed to drink only stimulated her.

Her aunt appeared later, her mood dark and broody. Rita tried to lighten the atmosphere by sharing the details of her meeting with Ernest. She knew her aunt would know his family as everyone who had been born and bred in the town were no strangers. Ada looked Rita up and down, which in itself made Rita feel uncomfortable, before her aunt uttered sneeringly.

'You used to run after him years back didn't you?' Rita was about to deny the forward accusation, but Ada went on, 'soon married someone else after you upped and left.'

Rita was taken aback at the tone of her aunt's voice and experienced a cold shiver running through her. But there was no time to retaliate, as a car horn sounded in the drive and Rita snatched up her bag and hurried out of the room.

'My goodness Rita, I'm delighted you can't wait to see me,' laughed Ernest as Rita nearly ran into the car door he was about to open.

Rita gave a shaky laugh back, more from relief at being out of the negative atmosphere of the house. As she buckled her seat belt, the curtain of the living room moved a fraction.

Relaxing into her seat she was acutely aware of the person beside her. She took a deep breath, catching a faint whiff of his aftershave in doing so. They didn't say much for a while, each more than content to be just in the other's company.

'Remember you getting me to buy you some chips because your mam didn't like the smell of the chip shop on your clothes?' He said at last turning his head to look at her.

'I remember you gobbling your share down as if it was your only meal of the day,' Rita retorted.

'It was,' he said simply, and Rita felt the same rush of compassion and the overwhelming need to look after him that she'd felt all those years ago. Suddenly his face became serious, the playfulness had gone.

'You were my first girlfriend.' Ernest waited for her reply.

'And you were my first and only boyfriend,' Rita answered truthfully and without any feeling of failure on her part.

'Why didn't you answer any of my letters?' A confidence was growing in his voice, allowing him touch painful areas within himself. 'I wrote to you many times via Elaine and your Aunt Ada,' he confessed, waiting patiently for the answer to this obviously long-standing question.

'I never got any of them,' Rita answered, a sadness creeping into her own voice. 'A couple were found in a box after Elaine died.'

'What,' the car nearly touched the curb and Ernest quickly and skilfully regained control.

'I have them now.' Rita explained what had happened after the funeral, but couldn't offer any reason for Elaine not sending them. She'd come to terms with Elaine's deception, but the fact her aunt had had letters also really angered her.

'Then you know I'd asked you to marry me and even said I'd come to Canada.' It was now out and Ernest felt a sense of relief. The answer was not as important as the fact she now knew.

'Oh Ernest,' Rita let out a long sigh and stared at the grey ribbon of road ahead. It appeared to go on and on without ending. There was a silence as they just followed the direction the signposts were indicating along the way. She regretted so much, but mostly the time lost with the only person that meant more to her than anyone else.

'Still you probably would have said no,' Ernest said at last giving a faint laugh to lighten the conversation.

Rita didn't say anything, but when he laid his big hand over hers, she didn't resist as their fingers entwined. They stayed like that until they reached a hotel overlooking Rudyard Lake.

A table had been reserved by the window, giving a wonderful view over the water. There were many people dining, but neither of them noticed anyone else. After dinner they strolled by the lake, watching the silver darts reflected from the moon over its shimmering dark surface. Ernest's arm stole around her waist and Rita's head found its resting place against his broad shoulders. They sat awhile with whispers each enchanted whilst silently the moon passed behind wisps of cloud. He turned and kissed her gently, the kiss of an everlasting bond from so long ago, still burning deep and meaningful.

Back in the car, their fingers intertwined again on their return journey. Even policemen break rules sometimes, not keeping both hands on the steering wheel, thought Rita. Here they were, both in their sixties and still behaving like teenagers. The goodnight kiss was longer with indications of passion to come at some later stage in their relationship. But she knew and he knew they could wait for the right moment; after all they had already waited for forty-two years.

'Give me a few days darling,' he said touching her lips gently. 'A policeman's life is not always his own, but I'll ring you the first break I get and we will work something out.' They looked deep into each other's eyes before he broke away and said with conviction,

'I'm not losing you again Rita Goodwin.'

Rita waited while he backed his car out of the drive, and then turned towards the house. A light was shining in the living room; the rest of the house a black shape.

Entering the kitchen, she closed the back door quietly and moved into the hall, slipping her coat off her shoulders after turning on the light. She hung it over the brass hook on her gran's hallstand and caught her reflection in its mirror. The face that gazed back at her was the Rita she'd seen in that same mirror all those years ago. It shone with vitality and youth. Rita grinned at herself and winked. She so wanted to share her happiness and, as only her reflection was there, it was better than no one at all.

She jumped suddenly as a voice shrieked out behind her.

'Just look at you, an old woman. A bit of attention from a man and you think you're young again.'

Her Aunt Ada stood by the living room door, holding a glass in one hand and a half empty bottle of whisky in the other. She was clearly unsteady on her feet as she kept slipping down against the doorframe.

'Face it Rita girl, he only wants a good fuck so don't you go getting any lofty ideas.' Ada raised her glass in a salute. 'Here's to men; bastards all.'

At first Rita went white as the blood drained from her face but then, as anger took over, her face flushed. Drink or no drink, how dare her aunt talk to her as if she was some common harlot. Ada turned and stumbled back into the living room. Rita hurried after her, her steps firm and purposeful and, before Ada could resist, Rita had snatched the whisky bottle out of her hand.

'Give me that, it's mine.' Ada screamed lunging forward and would have fallen if her hand had not landed on the arm of her chair.

Still whining after her whisky bottle, she twisted her body and sat down with a thud leaving Rita standing over her quivering with rage.

'How dare you talk about Ernest that way, you sad excuse for a woman. I could kill you for that.'

Ada's whining stopped and a crafty look came across her face. She knew she needed another way to get the bottle back and she still had plenty to draw on up her sleeve.

'You are as naive as your mother.' Her aunt was beginning to rally all the forces she had for her ammunition.

'Believed everything the pathetic doctor told her.'

Rita couldn't stop the racing in her heart. She could feel and hear it thumping in her chest and remembered briefly she was due for her medications, but the bottles were on her dressing table and her legs wouldn't move

'What do you mean?'

Ada placed a finger on the side of her nose and tapped it, her eyes never leaving Rita.

'The bottle,' she said holding out her hand.

The seconds passed, eyes still locked and each wondering what the other would do. At last Rita pushed the whisky bottle towards her aunt.

'The truth,' Rita demanded.

Ada nodded, grabbing the precious bottle and after refilling her glass; let the amber liquid warm her throat and slowly track through her body. What did she care about her niece, time she came off her high horse and know about the stock she came from.

'Your mam, our Rose and Dr. McKenzie,' she said slowly and deliberately, searching Rita's face for the shock and pain she hoped it would produce.

Rita thought she might faint, she felt warm and slightly sick and sat down to face her opponent.

'You are telling me they had a relationship?'

Her aunt laughed and it was genuine. Rita was as innocent as a new babe and Ada knew it was time she grew up.

'Call it what you want ducks, but they were having it off whenever they got a chance.'

Rita had flashes of the rides Dr. McKenzie would give her mam and the times he was at their house for no real reason now she came to think of it. She knew her aunt was speaking the truth.

Ada leaned back, watching Rita like a cat that had cornered a mouse.

'Looked down her nose at Ivy and me she did, 'til she got caught herself.'

Rita looked bewildered. What was her aunt talking about? Rita's look must have given her away, for Ada made no bones about anything as she continued explaining,

'Bun in the oven, husband dead and her lover miles away with his wife who had just dropped twin bairns herself.'

Horror swept over Rita, her mam's suicide then was nothing to do with the yank. It was all about her not being able to face up to the disgrace of her own pregnancy.

'That's why she topped herself.' Her aunt said the words for her, and the satisfaction of saying them was evident from the tone of her voice.

Rita was still having trouble and looked ill.

'Mam having a baby,' she said more as a statement than a question.

Her aunt nodded.

'Want a drink?' Ada could now be benevolent and offered to share the bottle with her.

Rita got up and almost in a trance, opened the cupboard and pulling out a glass, she let Ada's shaky hand fill it.

'Bottom's up.' Ada lifted her glass and took a swig. This was more like it, she thought. A drinking companion at last to lift the greyness of the day.

Chapter 29

The sound of the phone brought Rita's head up sharply from under the tap where she was washing her hair. She felt at the sore spot where she'd caught her forehead on the metal and winced as she wrapped a nearby towel around her head. Her dressing gown flopped around her bare feet almost tripping her up as she flew downstairs to answer the persistent ringing.

'Hello,' Rita shouted into the voice piece, trying at the same time to capture the towel sliding off her wet hair.

'Is it a bad time to call?' Ernest sounded slightly taken aback at her response, and then laughed when she described her semi-clothed state. 'Sorry old girl,' he apologized. 'I know it's a bit early in the morning, but I can't find much time for myself 'til the pressure's off with this skeleton business and wondered if you would mind sharing time with me whilst I worked a little.'

Rita wasn't certain whether her shivering was set off by the morning chill or his reference to the skeleton. She tightened the dressing gown around her.

'What do you mean?' she asked. Surely he didn't expect her to sit in his office whilst he went through paperwork, although truth to tell she would have done it just to be with him.

'I've got to go up to the old quarry. Something very important to our case has been found there.' He broke off and Rita heard him talking to someone.

She steadied herself against the stair banister, and then slid down to sit on the bottom stair, pulling the phone cord to its maximum length. In the background she was aware of muffled voices coming out of the phone, but her thoughts were concentrated on the awful possibility of her note to the yank surviving under the undisturbed sand.

Was it possible, her mind raced with images she'd seen on the TV of ancient artefacts discovered under sand after hundreds and even thousands of years, but paper….? Ernest's voice came back clear and loud.

'If you wouldn't mind bearing with me whilst I have a word with the chaps up there, we could have an extended lunch hour.'

Rita tried to keep the tremble out of her voice as she was about to answer.

'Are you ok Rita?' Ernest asked full of concern at her silence.

'Yes, yes. I'm just shivering, it's chilly here.' She struggled to sound light-hearted as she pulled her dressing gown closer to her.

'Pick you up, say in about an hour, ok?'

'I'd rather meet you at the bottom of the road that leads to the quarry as I need the walk,' Rita proposed, and then got confused at whether the old road still existed and was about to ask. However Ernest agreed and didn't mention any changes that might have occurred over the years.

Her Aunt Ada's tongue that morning was syrupy and condescending, asking Rita what time she would be back so they could have a drink together and talk over old times. She even suggested Rita look at some old photos of her mam when she was young and how much Rita looked like her. It was at that point Rita realized, with surprise, just how much she disliked her aunt and always had. It had only been Charlie that had helped her to bear her younger years at the house.

Rita pulled out a pair of dressy jeans and a warm sweater, as she'd lost some weight since being in the UK. They did her justice and were just the thing to wear, although Rita didn't really care anymore whether she fitted the English matronly image or not. She felt comfortable and needed to have one thing less to worry about.

The fresh air and the walk did her good and she felt her shoulders beginning to relax. Even the silly thought about a note surviving seemed ridiculous, and even if it did for some fantastic reason there was no signature; only the letter R, and her writing now was nothing like that of her writing as a child. The walk would have been totally enjoyable if it wasn't for the constant noise of the traffic that passed nose to tail, through the narrow main road. After a while it began to get on her nerves. It was strange how she'd never noticed it in Canada.

A car screeched to a stop beside her and it took some moments before she realised it was Ernest's car driving along the side of the pavement. He leaned over unlocking the passenger side door.

'Hi Rita,' he grinned, coming to a braking stop, that caused other cars to honk and tires to squeal.

'Hi yourself.' Rita grinned back their eyes locking in an intimate moment.

'Couldn't get away fast enough,' he said giving her hand a squeeze. 'This shouldn't take long then we can have some time to ourselves.'

If Rita had thought the road to the quarry hadn't changed she couldn't have been more wrong. The old concrete base where the Americans had been billeted had been pulled up and a small mall had been erected there. The car park was quite busy, but the old lane that now passed to the side of it remained pretty much the same, though much more overgrown. Trees of oak, ash and horse chestnut, that had once been saplings, now sported thick trunks and large spreading branches.

'You once gave me some conkers on a string,' Rita said, memories flooding back at the sight of the horse chestnuts.

Ernest smiled as he too remembered.

'Got a hiding from my mam too for using the pickle vinegar to put them in. I'd thrown away her pickles and she wasn't very understanding at all.'

Why did the man and the boy always bring out her nursing instincts? A great sadness swept over her and produced protective feelings towards him. How she would have loved to look after a child looking just like him.

'Penny for your thoughts,' his voice jolted her out of her dreaming.

She blushed.

'It's been a long time since I came along this lane' she remarked, keeping her eyes on the narrowness and roughness of the ground.

The pole that once rested across two posts was no longer there when they reached the old quarry, although part of one of the posts remained. A length of yellow tape now encircled a large area. Two other cars were already there, together with a number of plain clothes men as well as a couple of policemen and a policewoman.

'Shouldn't take too long.' Ernest bent over to release the catch of the boot lid.

Opening the car door to get out, he touched her shoulder gently, his eyes telling her he'd rather be with her than what he had to do. From the car mirror, Rita watched him lift the boot lid. A few moments later he came back into view, wearing a white coverall and gloves. Her eyes followed his tall frame, his footsteps long and purposeful.

Hands tightly gripping the car seat her body leaned forwards straining against her still fastened seat belt. Rita felt as if she was watching a movie. It was unreal, almost ridiculous to the point she wanted to laugh, not just an ordinary laugh, but more like a hysterical scream. She wanted to tell them what idiots they all were, thinking they could really know what had happened. But she did know and who it was was. How stupid could they be? They had the only witness right there, sitting in the police inspector's own car. She felt her nerves beginning to fray.

What on earth was she doing here? Was it curiosity or fear? There had to be something else she still didn't know. Rita took three deep breaths. How had the yank really died? The question burned deeply into her psyche and she needed to know before she went completely to pieces.

Rita pulled at her seat belt, grappling with it in desperation to get to her handbag. Once she had the bag on her knee, her fingers rummaged through it 'til she found the small bottle of pills her Canadian doctor had given her to take off the anxiety of flying. The little white top came off as she pushed down on it and turned. One tablet was too much, as it had made her sleepy on the flight over. Rita broke one in half with her teeth and managed to swallow it with the little saliva she had remaining in her mouth.

Ernest took longer than he'd thought and when he came back Rita was breathing quietly and seemingly quite relaxed. He pulled off his plastic gloves and, tapped the car window indicating for her to open the boot for him again to dispense of the rest of his forensic attire. Rita glanced at him as he sat down in the car, his hands caressing the steering wheel without turning the engine on. It was a habit he had got into whilst thinking through an investigation.

'Looks like we have the murder weapon,' he said. 'An iron bar, rusty as hell but it is the murder weapon all right.'

Rita listened through a veil of calmness that was now numbing her previous anxieties.

'What do you think happened?' Rita asked, her hand going to place its palm on her still slightly turbulent stomach in a comforting gesture.

'Someone clobbered the poor old soul from behind.'

'How can you tell, surely any blood on it would have long gone with weathering.' Rita's logic now began to surface.

'Oh, we know what we were looking for by the shape of the injury in the skull. Dr. Levenson over there,' said Ernest pointing to a small long-haired man in the group, 'is convinced the bar found is what we are looking for and with all our modern equipment there will be other traces on it that can be identified.'

'You mean someone hit him over there and killed him.' Rita heard her own words coming out as she nodded in the direction of the group of people.

'Right, and we think we know who he was too.' Ernest made no attempt to drive away. He was watching the movements around the yellow tape and knew he had a captive listener.

'What?' Rita turned sharply towards him hanging desperately on his next words

'We were right about him being an American that was billeted here around 1944. Our guys have contacted the US Defence Department and have narrowed down the ones that may have gone AWOL.'

'They' said Ernest, referring to the US Defence Department, 'have records of two servicemen missing from their unit in Cheshire and one of them was here in Danesbury.'

'Oh' was all Rita was capable of saying.

'We have to find out all we can for the sake of English – American relations you understand, but it was a long time ago and the chance of finding the murderer is slight. But the victim's family would welcome the remains back and some account of what happened, so we have been given orders to do our best.'

'Nothing else found?' Rita ventured, and then turned to look outside her window as if the question was of little importance. Ernest didn't hear the anxiety in her voice as he answered.

'Not a thing, no identity tags. It is most likely they were taken off at the time of his death.'

The effects of the tablet had started to wear off a little and Rita's mind began to sharpen and spin. Ernest put the key into the engine and turned it on. The car engine started and the engine purred over.

'Are you all right Rita? He said, glancing at her pale face, and thinking how sunken her eyes looked against her skin.

'Too busy to eat breakfast, I feel a little faint.' Rita rattled off the excuse, trying to look cheerful.

'That's soon remedied. Let's go for lunch.' He was in charge again.

Steering the car out of the quarry, he made for the Manchester road. Ernest did most of the talking, with Rita adding to the conversation with only a comment or two now and then; on how the landscape had changed. She noticed a sign to Prestbury. She pointed to the sign.

'My grandfather had a butcher's shop in Prestbury. That's where my family comes from, I think.' Suddenly her memory jolted her back in time as she recalled sitting on her dad's knee and listening to him telling her about his childhood.

'Ernest,' said Rita suddenly sitting up. 'Let's have lunch in Prestbury.'

She had a need to feel her roots again, grounded in something tangible. Ernest swung around a sharp corner and Rita now understood why her taxi driver had remarked that Prestbury was where the posh lived, for a lot of the houses and grounds around them were big and affluent.

The winding road that went through the centre of the town was nose to tail with cars, the streets far too narrow for so much traffic. Ernest indicated a left turn and turned into a car park that backed up to some very old stone terraced houses. She mused to herself that the early occupants who had once lived there would never have seen a car in their lives.

The lunch was very tasty, and two glasses of good wine with the pleasant surroundings helped Rita settle down and turn her attention to her companion, and they gossiped about all manner of things.

'Rita,' Ernest said at last, turning the general topic of conversation around to themselves. 'I don't want you to go back to Canada.'

There was a prolonged silence. Rita looked at him over the top of her glass and felt all the love and security his eyes offered and realised what she desired so much was now within her grasp. Yet still she couldn't commit, not until her past was cleansed or buried forever. Play for time her instinct warned her.

'Canada isn't that far away these days,' she said with a laugh. 'I have to pay bills and things there first.'

Leaving it at that gave the impression she was willing to come back permanently and Ernest cheered up and started talking about what they would do in the future.

Rita wasn't emotionally ready for his vision as yet and, in desperation, asked Ernest if he would walk around the churchyard with her to see if she could find some of her ancestors.

'Sure, why not,' he said jokingly. 'It seems to be the day for having skeletons around.' He didn't notice Rita's flinching.

There was something timeless about walking among the old moss covered gravestones. It was the sort of thing they had often done after school in their own churchyard, but then Ernest would have climbed up on one of the tombs and danced or even tried to lift the stone lid. He grinned at Rita, they both remembered. Suddenly Rita stopped. There in front of her was a gravestone with the simple inscription,

Thomas Goodwin, Died 1846.

Ellen; wife of Thomas, Died 1850.

Then close by Ernest found a William Goodwin, wife Elizabeth and a child of six months; who had all died in the same year, 1831.

'Probably they died of something like scarlet fever or TB,' suggested Ernest, his mind examining what evidence there was. They stood awhile looking at the grave, Ernest's arm around Rita, both quietly thinking their own thoughts. Ernest wondered how quickly he should proceed with his courtship and Rita, left thinking her ancestors must have had some happiness in their lives, short as they may have been. At least they had married and had a child.

Chapter 30

The migraine came with a vengeance, bringing blurred vision, throbbing headache and the nausea. The first time Rita vomited she had managed to stumble to the bathroom sink. Sitting on the edge of the cold bath to recover, she grabbed the plastic waste bucket and made it back to bed before curling up and shivering under the thick eiderdown. Time after time the nausea overwhelmed her, triggered by the cooking smells from downstairs. When there was nothing left in her stomach to bring up, she lay back exhausted and the headache throbbing twice as bad.

Once Ada asked if she wanted a cup of tea but then left hurriedly at the sight of Rita's face. Eventually the hours slipped away leaving nature to take its course on its healing journey. Rita lay staring up at the bedroom ceiling almost afraid to move. The ticking of her travel clock broke the silence as the dusk of the evening sent its lengthening shadows at will around the walls of the room.

'Funny how the body deals with things,' thought Rita. 'It's like I have to purge my body before I can think clearly again.'

Rita's tempestuous mind had let many ideas take form, but all now became much clearer, as in the aftermath of a storm. She knew from experience that too much, too quickly always brought on her painful affliction and was now glad it was over because it always left her calm, although completely drained. Maybe it's what myths are all about, considered Rita? She recalled the heroes of the old myths, people always travelling through the underworld or through a dark tunnel to emerge eventually into the light, every time enlightened with wisdom and truth or some higher state of consciousness.

Many times Rita analysed her problems over and over again; yet she still felt compelled to place them in some sort of order that didn't overwhelm her so much.

'What were her fears?'

She tried to be practical but found pieces of information would merge with something else that hadn't any foundation, like bits coming unglued. Determined to wrestle with it, it soon resulted in her making her first concluding statement to herself.

'I was afraid my mam had murdered the yank.' There it was said, though Rita didn't even know his name, so 'yank' it still had to remain.

'But I was wrong. It was no accident caused by my mam; someone else had deliberately murdered him with a piece of iron bar,'

Rita made an effort to let the pieces of the jigsaw stay for a while, before asking herself why she just couldn't leave it alone and walk away. What was it that always set her stomach fluttering and her heart racing? She pondered on the police evidence Ernest had shared with her yesterday. Nothing he had said could indicate the presence of her mam or herself at the scene of the crime that fateful night. The more time she took to let the threads of the mystery to be pulled out, the neared she moved to that piece of the fabric so thickly embroidered over.

Piece by piece, the process loosened the knots of denial and slowly unravelled them 'til the answer faced her. Suddenly she had moved out of the mythical tunnel and allowed herself to face the light. Someone else must have been there that night. Someone who had followed one of them, the yank, her mam or herself. But who? Someone had taken advantage of the situation.

'Someone else, think Rita think.'

For the first time in decades she sifted through the dark recesses of her mind with everything about that night. Once started there was no stopping. Painful as it was, not a cell of her brain was left unturned.

Ethel. Did daft Ethel follow her mother? She'd certainly hinted at something. Rita dismissed it, remembering how timid Ethel was; but couldn't imagine her roaming around the quarry in the dusk. Ethel had probably only stumbled on the truth about Dr. McKenzie and her mam.

Maybe it was some other serviceman with a grudge against the yank and took that opportunity to kill him? Rita mulled over that possibility and, remembering the absence of the identity tags, placed that scenario at the top of her list, as a lot would then start to make sense. Maybe some gambling debt, who knows, but if that were the case the murderer would either be back in America, killed in action or, as if to hedge her bets; had died naturally of old age.

A great wave of relief swept over Rita. Why hadn't she thought about the obvious before? The relief was so great, Rita allowed the highest of the brick walls she had mentally built around herself over the years to fall as she came face to face with the child she once was.

Tears trickled down Rita's cheeks as the consequences and relief of her finding her mam innocent seeped out. A child needs a mam that is good, kind and never wanting to leave her. Rita had been terrified of any character slight that may have harmed her mam's image. Instead of a mother shielding her child, it had been the other way around. Her mam hadn't really wanted to leave her alone and Rita was convinced of that. What had happened wasn't her mam's fault at all and she'd transferred the blame onto herself with the note she'd written.

Rita could no longer live a life of denial. She had to face all truths if she was to have any kind of life at all. She now allowed herself to see her mam in reality as a woman who had fallen desperately in love with another man, loved him enough to have his child inside her and had despaired when he left her. After her husband was killed, she was alone with all the guilt of bearing a child that everyone would know wasn't his. That didn't mean she didn't love her own daughter, it simply meant her mam was human, given to temptation and weakness. And hadn't Rita nursed and felt compassion all her life for those whose lives were so entwined with that of her own mother's. Rita heard herself saying,

'It's okay Mam, I know you love me wherever you are and I love you too.'

A light went on in the hall and its shimmer landed on the ceiling. Rita smiled, she had been an intense child remembering her escapades, but she now resolved to lighten up for the remaining years of her life. Tiredness crept over her and she was just about to drift off again, when the thought came to her as to why and how her mam had decided to go to the quarry that night anyway. After all, it was herself who had handed the note to the yank.

'God, Oh God,' she exclaimed to herself. 'Why can't I get everything to fit together in perfect order?'

She sighed. 'Well I don't know everything and don't suppose I ever will.' Rita pushed the problem away into her subconscious and drifted off to sleep.

Someone was gently shaking her and Rita opened one eye; the other seemingly still stuck down with sleep.

'Hi cousin,' Charlie was hovering over her with a cup of something hot, for steam was drifting up from its contents.

'Charlie,' the other eye opened and Rita propped herself up on her elbow.

'Mam said you were sick,' said Charlie sounding concerned and Rita had the momentary sensation of his hand reaching out to test her forehead for a fever.

'I get migraines,' stated Rita, sitting up and taking the welcoming beverage from his hand. 'It's gone now. Every year one doosey, that's me.'

She laughed trying to cheer him up. He certainly did look quite worried.

Charlie didn't ask permission but sat on the side of her bed and she moved over to make space. He couldn't explain it but he felt an odd but comfortable feeling just being with his cousin. She allowed him to be himself, unlike his wife and mother. He felt torn between the two of them, so much so that he often felt like jumping in the car and just taking off. Even his own son didn't seem to need him, for Michael was very much his mother's boy. However Charlie wasn't that type or just hadn't the courage to leave. So he soldiered on, always hopeful something better would come along.

He thought briefly about the woman who worked in the garage he took his car to. She always found time for him, asking about his mother and sympathizing in a nice way, not pulling him down like his wife did. Her name was Lucy, and her husband had left her to bring up her son on her own. There was nothing selfish about her and he often found himself looking forward to something going wrong with the car so he could talk to her again.

'What's Canada like,' Charlie asked out of the blue. 'Do you think I'd like it?' Rita stared back at him

'Don't see why not, big guys like you would soon master the ski hills.' Then being more serious asked, 'but why are you asking?'

'Oh, nothing really.' Charlie looked around the room as if feeling its claustrophobia. 'One day I'd just like to be in some wide open spaces on my own.'

Rita looked at him understanding his need, but to keep the conversation cheerful replied,

'Then you will have to visit Saskatoon and the wide-open plains of the Prairies. The sky and land go on forever there without a house or person in sight for miles.'

Rita realized Charlie's problem and offered the only advice she could think of.

'Get a cleaner to come in once a week Charlie. Your mam will probably go through all the pitying ways she knows to keep you coming here, but as time passes she'll be glad of someone to talk to even if it's not you. Get a health visitor to pop in too, to check on her medications and health, and have her talk to your mam about the problems of drink. They are trained for that sort of thing you know.' Rita went on to explain how Charlie was too close emotionally.

'You will enjoy being with her much more and she'll have someone else to talk about.' Rita continued, surprising herself at her experience of coping with others needs, but realizing her own needs had always escaped her.

'Tell you what Charlie,' Rita touched his bent shoulders. 'I'll go through the house, give it a good cleaning if you take your mam out for a day, then I'll help you place an advert for a cleaner.'

Charlie seemed to cheer up and asked if Rita wanted another cup of tea.

'No thank you Charlie.' Rita snuggled down again, her stomach still growling but not for the want of any more tea, which she found to be far too sweet.

'Maybe a glass of water before you leave.' Just as he was going through the door Rita said softly,

'Charlie, be kinder to yourself at home too.'

Charlie stopped for a moment, and then nodded. Descending the stairs, he thought he might ask Lucy out for a coffee sometime, especially if he could manage to get his car to breakdown during her lunchtime. That thought took the edge off having to spend the rest of the day with his mother.

Chapter 31

True to his promise, Charlie came to collect his mother the very next day. Although he had planned a partner's meeting, he had felt no qualms about cancelling it at his office. The talk he'd had with Rita made him take a real look at himself and he didn't like what he saw.

He had drifted into marriage, choosing a woman with the same overbearing possessiveness as his mother and he had almost given up the struggle for his own identity. Michael didn't need him and he really didn't understand his son. His cousin had forced him to reflect back on himself; although he didn't really comprehend how Rita could be so understanding when her own life seemed so lonely and uninteresting. He never-the-less blessed the day Rita had come back,

His mother was already awaiting him, looking better than she had for years in a freshly ironed pink blouse that Rita had done for her and a navy suit, which had been quite fashionable years ago, and still retained that tailored look. Her haircut, thanks to Rita, shaped her delicate bone structure and Charlie couldn't help the emotional lump from developing in his throat. He did love his mother and was more than grateful for all she'd done for him since his dad had left, but didn't want to feel quite so guilty all the time.

He was surprised his mother put up no argument in leaving the house as his other past offers had all been refused. Driving off, Charlie resolved to make a great effort and treat his mother royally that day before suggesting she needed help other than his. It would take some doing but he had to take the first step to kick-start his own life again, in which he hoped Lucy would eventually be playing a more meaningful role.

Yesterday, after leaving Rita, Lucy had agreed to have coffee with him sometime. He hadn't planned it, but servicing his car had taken him to the garage and he'd plucked up the courage to ask her.

After Charles and his mother left for the day, Rita was up and about, feeling much better and, after a good breakfast, was looking forward to cleaning the house. Order had always helped Rita survive. It blocked out things she couldn't do anything about or that caused too much emotion. She liked having a place for everything and everything in its place. A characteristic so deeply ingrained in every nurse's training.

'I'll make a start upstairs,' she decided, arming herself with the necessary cleaning materials. She got out tins of polish, bathroom cleanser and window spray, all unopened. Now dusters were a problem, there weren't any, so Rita took the initiative and cut two old tea towels down the middle, promising herself to buy some new ones.

She stood in the hallway for a moment. It was like being in a time warp and she was ten years old again, trying to help her gran by dusting the furniture in the hall, and how her gran would smile and say, 'put that duster down I've a nice custard tart for you'.

'Oh gran' Rita moaned out aloud. Letting the moment pass, she climbed the stairs. After cleaning the floor and all the bathroom fixtures 'til they shone, Rita tackled the spare room, which, apart from general neglect and bed sheets that hadn't seen a wash in a long time, didn't take her long. Her own room she just tided as she'd already made sure everything had been cleaned before she had slept in it. Piling the bedding on the floor of the landing, Rita collected her cleaning materials and opened her aunt's bedroom door.

It was the first time she'd been alone in the room since she was a child and Rita's eyes swept around it. It was the first opportunity she'd had to look around and to Rita's amazement nothing had really changed. It needed cleaning in the worst way. Piles of unwashed clothes slipped off the wicker chair as Rita walked by. The bed was unmade and the pillowcases soiled. The smell of whisky prevailed everywhere, old, musty and sickly.

Rita went over to the window and, after a lot of coaxing and banging, managed to open it. There was a rush of fresh air into the room and for awhile Rita allowed herself to breathe normally again, instead of half holding her breath. She looked at the wardrobe; the same one Ada had once stacked with fashionable clothes and high-heeled shoes. She opened it and was taken aback at rows of 1940's dresses still hanging there.

Memories flooded back when she gazed at the dressing table, where Ada once put on her makeup, sometimes putting a little on Rita's childish lips and telling her to look at their beautiful reflections.

Now there were the two faces of her aunt, one young blond and pretty, the other old and brooding. Rita let her fingers trail through the hairpins, jars of unopened face creams, and a brush that still had golden hairs bound in its bristles. It was weird and it reminded Rita of Great Expectations and Miss Havershall. How could anyone exist in the past like this? It was as if the room was a shrine to her aunt's youth. Why hadn't anyone noticed? Rita surmised that Charlie probably hadn't gone in there since he left home.

Rita kicked something by the bed and it rolled under it. She kneeled down to pick it up but a large object under the bed was blocking her view. It was a suitcase and, as she moved it to one side, it disturbed some dust making Rita sneeze.

What better place to start than under the bed decided Rita, dusting herself down as she stood up. She began pulling off the bedclothes before plugging in the vacuum cleaner, to sweep under the bed.

Bending down she felt for the case's handle and pulled. A green canvass case with a leather corners slid out. On the top in black printed letters was Frank's name and army number. Rita knew at once; as one of the old cases from the wartime. She recalled how she'd waited patiently so many times as a girl for her own dad to open his and produce some present for her when he came home on leave.

Obviously Frank hadn't taken it with him when he left and her aunt most likely didn't want it. They were hard and heavy and most had been thrown away when the much lighter materials came into use with the upsurge in air travel.

Rita lifted it up and plonked it on the bed, immediately wishing she hadn't as a fine film of dust settled over the mattress.

As if her fingers were a separate entity to the rest of her body, they moved on their own, sliding the locks to one side 'til each of the fasteners flew open with a loud click.

Rita lifted the lid and stared down at the contents. Three bunches of letters tied with blue faded ribbon lay on top of a neatly folded dress, a dress that Rita remembered her aunt wearing before she as married. There was underwear too. Rita lifted up satin knickers embroidered on the side with a butterfly, a silk slip slid through Rita's hands like the shifting of soft sand.

There was a photograph turned upside down, the photographer's name on the back; faded and unrecognisable. Rita picked it up and turned her body so the light from the window fell across the sepia print. A young woman with blond curls and wearing a pretty dress was laughing and looking up at a tall young man in an American uniform. There was no mistaking her Aunt Ada, no more than eighteen and with a figure that any woman would envy. Her aunt's happiness was directed at the person Rita had held in her mind for so long. Charlie could have been his clone.

The quicker Rita's mind raced, the more impulsive she became and couldn't stop herself from digging her fingers under the clothes and finding a small cardboard box. Rita prised the lid off and found herself staring down at an assortment of jewellery, not women's as she would have expected but, by the size of the watch and ring, definitely belonging to a man. At first she wondered if they belonged to the yank, maybe things he had given her aunt.

Lifting up a silver cigarette case with a scroll like design entwined with initials, Rita knew it all belonged to Frank Cole. She took the gold ring and wondered if he'd deliberately left his wedding ring behind when he left, although thinking it funny he should go without his watch and cigarette case as Frank, she remembered, smoked a lot.

Rita shook her head as if to clear it, and began putting the things back. She lifted the bundles of letters to smooth out the dress, when something caught her eye. It was a dirty piece of thin ball chain. She pulled and it slipped easily from under the material bringing with it two metal tags. She knew they didn't belong to Frank. Her instinct was correct. She read out aloud the name stamped into both the aluminum metal of the dog tags.

'Charles Haddon. USAF #6148391.' The latter obviously being his service number.

Thoughts were beginning to tumble over like a waterfall. A slight throbbing began over her left eye. Rita thrust the tags into the pocket of her jeans, tided the case's contents, and pushed the closed case back where she had found it. Then she did what she always did when she got confused, she went on with the job at hand, polishing and vacuuming as if on autopilot, her mind blank and her body just going through the motions.

She even went outside and picked some flowers that had managed to survive in the neglected garden and placed them on the table.

All this time she had been conscious of a mouse watching her from the corner of the room. What did it know of these things and other hidden secrets around the house? If only it could talk. Then Rita, realizing the mouse's limited lifespan, burst out laughing hysterically at her own stupidity and ended up half crying with tears rolling down her cheeks. She'd have to put a mousetrap down.

The bottle of whisky caught the evening sunlight, tempting the watcher with its amber glow and the promise of some much needed relaxation. However, Rita poured herself water instead and stood glass in hand, before reminding herself that she hadn't taken any of her tablets that day. Taking out the bottle of Digoxin tablets from her handbag, she opened it and carefully dispensed the required dose into her palm. A quick movement of her hand to her mouth was followed by gulp of water and the tablet was swallowed. She placed her bottle of tablets down beside the whisky bottle and, just as she was again reaching for her handbag, the phone rang. Rita moved quickly to the phone hoping it was Ernest. It was Charlie.

'I'm on my way home Rita.' His voice sounded odd.

'Are you alright?' asked Rita, holding the phone firmly with both hands and trying to breathe normally.

'Mother's taken it badly and I'm at my wits end. She'd started to drink in the restaurant and has become quite unreasonable.'

'Where is she now?' asked Rita, visualizing him trying to get her away from the bar.

'She's in the car and saying things I don't understand.' Charlie choked a little and went on. 'I need your help cousin, I really do.

'Charlie, bring her home, we will sort this out don't worry.'

Rita put down the phone and went into the kitchen to put the kettle on. She thought of her gran, that's what she would have done under these circumstances. 'Everything gets settled over a cup of tea', she'd often say.

'Perhaps Rita Goodwin you are more like her than you ever thought,' Rita muttered to herself, standing by the kitchen window and sipping her tea.

When Ada arrived she was indeed in a sorry state. She came bursting into the kitchen nearly knocking Rita down.

'So that's what I get for giving you somewhere to stay,' she screamed at her niece. 'Trying to bring strangers and nosey parkers into my house are you? I'll not have it, do you hear.'

She poked her face at Rita, glaring at her with blood shot eyes. Charlie hung back by the back door and Rita indicated with a hand gesture he should go. He left quickly giving her a look of gratitude.

'How dare you set up my own son against me,' shouted her aunt from the living room where the sound of a glass being brought hard down on the table sent a shiver through Rita as she poured out two cups of tea.

Rita took a deep breath and made for the living room and the challenge to come.

Holding her hand to her forehead, her aunt was sitting in her chair whining,

'Damn this headache, it's all your fault,' she was moaning.

Rita began handing her the cup of tea. Ada's hand flew out and knocked it to the floor, the liquid forming a brown patch on the carpet. Both stared at it for a second, and then Ada shouted,

'I need a drink, not that gnat's pee.'

Rita clenched her teeth and picked up an empty glass. She filled it up without remorse and if it would quieten down her aunt, then so much the better. But before she gave it to her, Rita picked up her tablet bottle and was surprised to find she'd left the lid off. Replacing it, she put the bottle back in her handbag.

Handing her aunt the glass of whisky, Rita stood over her, one hand in her pocket fingering the identity discs. Ada's eyes darted around the room, sensing something in the air.

'Quite the cleaner aren't you' she sneered. 'Well as long as you didn't set foot in my bedroom, I reckon we are quits. Pack your bags and leave me in peace.'

Rita stood her ground, then in one movement pulled out the two tags and dangled them before her aunt's eyes.

Ada screamed.

Chapter 32

Ada's eyes were wild as she sank back into her chair. She looked like a cornered animal fearing the final onslaught of death.

Rita moved in for the kill, dangling the clinking dog tags in front of her aunt's face. Ada made a desperate attempt to snatch them but her opponent was too quick and withdrew them from her reach. The two women stared at each other 'til Ada broke away and submitted.

'You have opened a can of worms my girl,' she spat the words out. 'Think you've been so clever snooping where you had no business to.'

She waited for Rita to step back a little then attacked viciously again.

'Your saintly mam killed my Charlie.'

Rita went cold, so cold she couldn't reach out and hit the dismal creature before her, but somehow her voice rang out loud and clear.

'What proof have you?'

Ada leaned forward, her left eyelid twitching in her excitement.

'Proof you want,' she yelled. 'I'll give you all the proof you need. You could have found it for yourself if you had looked more thoroughly through my private things. You would have found the note our Rose wrote to my Chuck, begging him to meet her.'

Rita's vision began to blur a little. She knew something didn't make sense but she couldn't put her finger on it.

'My mam couldn't have killed him' was all Rita could say.

'Oh but she did. She's to blame; she pushed him over the edge of the quarry.'

Ada was now sitting up straight, and then dared to stand and walk around the frozen Rita before making straight for the whisky bottle.

Rita watched her every movement, waiting for something, but she didn't know what it was. Some mistake in the telling? Something to reactivate the truth?

Ada was looking at the table with a puzzled look.

'Where the hell are my Aspirins?' She screwed up her forehead indicating pain, then shrugged and took her glass and bottle over to her chair.

'Sit down missy, and I'll tell you what really happened.' Ada's eyes glinted like those of a fox, the firelight catching them as she turned.

Rita sat down; the identity discs limp between her lap and fingers.

'Chuck was my chap. We were good together 'til I found out I was pregnant, then he got scared.'

Her aunt was clearly now in the past and went on. 'He just needed time to get used to it. He loved me you know, and even after I married Frank, he still wanted me.' She stopped, daring Rita to deny it, and then waited for some confirmation from Rita but found none. 'Then your mam took a shine to him. Wasn't enough that she'd seduced her own doctor, she had to have my man too.'

'I don't believe you' Rita said, her voice coming from behind her clenched teeth, her eyes like steel.

Ada's tone hardened.

'You don't have to believe me, I've got all the proof I need, and you with your meddling never found it.'

'What proof?' Rita was beginning to feel cracks in her own armour.

'The note,' said Ada, almost screaming at her.' She sent him a bloody note to meet her. Signed it she did, but I found it in his pocket.'

'She signed it with her name?' A little light was now beginning to filter through the haze.

'Signed it with a big fat R.' There was venom in Ada's voice again. 'I followed them to the quarry, and saw her lift an iron bar and kill my Chuck.'

Then Ada's face changed as if her personality had taken a back seat and another person emerged. She became frail, vulnerable and fragile.

'It smashed down on his lovely blond head. There was blood everywhere. My poor Chuck dead. Dead I tell you. He didn't move, just lay there he did.'

Rita realized something wasn't quite right but let her aunt continue.

'She ruined my life. If it wasn't for the likes of that bitch sister of mine, Chuck and me would have been together, instead of me having to put up with Frank's mauling.' She shuddered.

Her Aunt Ada had, in her torment, described the yank's death, Rita tensed as she now sensed the pieces of the jigsaw were at last together and all she had to do was to place them in the right spaces.

'How did you get hold of these?' She lifted the identity tags by the cord. Ada's eyes glued on them, a sly look was stealing across her face.

'Found them in your kitchen drawer I did.' Ada's eyes moved to her glass, her hands beginning to tremble.

Rita now knew she was lying. Her mam would never put a thing like that among her polished cutlery and Rita herself would have seen them. But before she confronted her aunt with the full force of her anger, she needed one more piece of the jigsaw that had always evaded her. Without threatening her further, she poured Ada another drink then quietly asked,

'Did Chuck reply to my mam?' Rita waited with baited breath.

'Oh she used her charms on him. He sent her a note back to say he'd meet her, probably to tell her to leave him alone.'

Rita breathed a sigh of relief.

'How did you know?'

'His buddy told me. Ray had a bit of a crush on me and thought to make me jealous.'

Rita got up and walked around the room leaving Ada to follow her actions with her own puzzled gaze.

Suddenly Rita turned and walked over to her original position standing over the old lady.

'I don't believe you.'

Her Aunt Ada looked startled, but Rita took command.

'Oh I believe you about the notes alright, but I don't believe you saw my mam kill your bloody yank.'

Ada made a protest and began to lift herself out of the chair, but Rita's hand went out and pushed her back, holding her imprisoned for a second, before stepping back.

'I'll tell you what happened.' Rita smiled a smile of victory. 'You see my version is the truth because I was there.'

Ada's mouth dropped, and fear seeped into her now stony expression.

'How could you be there? I didn't see you.' Ada clamed up afraid she'd already said too much. She was beginning to feel a little lightheaded and not at all well. She could hardly feel her heartbeat.

'Oh yes I was there because you see I sent the note,' said Rita slowly.

Ada looked puzzled and some saliva was now dribbling down from the corner of her mouth.

'Like you, I also thought Mam was keen on the yank, when in fact she tried to plead with him to marry you or leave you alone. That's the sad thing Aunt Ada. The fact was she loved you and didn't want to see you hurt.'

'You are lying,' Ada stammered.

'No I'm not.' It was me who sent the note to meet him. I wanted to ask him to leave Mam alone but when I arrived there he had already met Mam, so I hid and watched.

Horror etched itself across Ada's chiselled features.

'You saw everything?'

'Yes, I saw Mam and him arguing at the top of the quarry and I saw him fall over the edge.'

Rita still couldn't admit that she'd not actually seen her mam pushing him. She wasn't sure whether what she said next would be true but took a wild guess.

'You were at the bottom of the quarry weren't you?' Rita didn't wait for an answer. 'And you were so jealous you killed him.'

Having said that, Rita suddenly felt drained. She waited for her Aunt Ada to speak, noting her paled colour and glazed-over eyes.

Without warning, Ada got up as if all her remaining strength had joined forces, and before Rita could stop her, she had rushed down the hall and was making for her bedroom. Rita charged after her, her mission in no way finished.

She found her aunt on her hands and knees by her bed, the old army case opened. Rita waited, unsure of what was coming next, but Ada just pulled out the old photo and held it before her; tears edging down her cheeks.

'Yes I killed him; I was at the bottom of the quarry looking up. I watched and saw our Rose put her arms out to him, and then he fell.'

She hugged the photo to her chest, her voice weak and full of great sadness, memories stirring into life.

'He rolled over and over bringing the sand down around him 'til it covered him completely,' she sighed. 'I thought he was dead and ran to the pile digging desperately with my hands until I found him. He was alive and I was delirious with happiness. I thought I'd saved his life.'

A dark shadow crossed her face and she stood up. Rita realised at that moment she was faced with an unbalanced personality that could be dangerous. She edged towards the door. Ada came forward now strengthened with hate.

'He didn't even thank me, he just said he'd had enough of our family and never wanted to see me again.'

Ada's gaze was now vacant and she looked at Rita pleadingly. 'I couldn't let him go, could I? He belonged to just me, so I hit him with an iron bar that lay nearby,' then she went on without showing any emotion, 'he didn't even know he was going to be mine forever as he was walking away.'

'You killed him.' Rita's voice was faint.

'Oh yes, I stopped him leaving me. No one else would have him, he was mine forever.'

She looked down at the photo, tracing her finger across it. 'I'm stronger than you think you see, I dug at the sand with an old shovel and covered him over again,' she giggled. 'But not before I got hold of his tags and emptied his pockets, 'cause those things belong to me and Charlie see.'

'What about your son Charles? Does he know his mother is a murderer who had killed his father?' Rita said it without thinking, then realised she'd made a grave mistake.

Ada let the photo drop and advanced towards her.

'My Charlie knows nothing. I wouldn't let anyone hurt my Charlie. Frank tried once to beat him but I put paid to that quickly enough.'

'Oh God.' Rita remembered Frank's wedding ring and watch. 'You killed him too?' It was with great difficulty as she managed the words.

'Some things have to be proved my girl, and your fancy policeman is not as smart as you think.' She was picking up a brass candlestick holder.

Rita backed out of the room to the top of the stairs, not daring to turn her back on her aunt and wondering how quickly she could descend. Ada's face looked ghastly and she was having difficulty breathing, but she was coming forward with the raised candlestick ready to strike.

Rita's own anger mounted, she felt the lies, the deceit coursing through her, and all because of this person before her.

Her aunt lunged at her, the candlestick dropped and Rita reached out her arm, grabbing at Ada's clothing and pulled, while holding onto the top of the banister to keep herself and Ada from falling. The candlestick went crashing down from one stair to another, followed by a wild scream from Ada. In a flurry of grasping hands and outstretched arms and legs, Ada fell.

Rita stood panting, looking down at the limp and motionless body. She stepped down each stair slowly and very deliberately and gazed at her aunt. Rita didn't need to feel her pulse. Experience told her she was dead, but she did all the same, just because it was part of her training.

She walked away heading for the living room. Pouring herself a glass of whisky, she sat down in Ada's chair, swaying to and fro and humming an old lullaby her mam used to sing to her. Hours passed, the fire burnt down, and the room became chilly, but Rita didn't care. Sitting was very easy, thinking was too hard. Once she got up and switched off the light, needing the darkness to cut off the images around her, the darkness giving comfort.

* * *

Dawn brought its first light as the golden rays played their game of tag around the room. Rita stirred. The fire was out. Gran must have slept in today. Rita got up and started to rekindle the fire 'til she got a good blaze. Let gran rest she thought, and decided to make a cup of tea and toast. Gran always liked that. Said she was such a thoughtful girl.

She glanced down the hallway to see if the postman had been. Nothing, just a pile of clothes at the bottom of the stairs. Aunt Ada must have thrown them down to be washed and Rita turned to cock her head and look back at the stag's head over the door.

'Morning Mr. Stag' she said as she always had.

The kitchen seemed exceptionally tidy, but sometimes there was a burst of energy that produced these results whenever gran's church friends visited. Rita looked puzzled at the tea caddy. It held little square packets of tea instead of the loose stuff.

'Ah well, maybe one of the Americans had given it to Aunt Ada.' She put it into a warmed teapot and poured boiling water over it. She waited a moment or two to let it mash while she cut some bread to make toast. She hunted all over the kitchen for the brass toasting fork with its galleon's head handle then gave up and picked up the carving fork.

Taking the bread and fork into the living room, she knelt down to light the fire. She sat back in her gran's chair feeling peaceful and secure, although she could feel an unusual and irregular beat of her heart within her chest. Listening to the rhythm it was making she slipped into her favourite dream of walking through the park holding young Ernest's hand.

And that's how they found her, a child within a woman's body, cheerful, gentle and happy. She allowed the tall man in uniform to gently lead her away to ride in a big car. One of the other men reminded her of someone.

He had tears in his eyes.

The police found two more people, one lying at the bottom of the stairs. The old lady hadn't died from a fall, but from an overdose of Digoxin and had suffered a massive heart attack.

The second person was a man long buried in the corner of the neglected garden.

The End